KILL THE MESSENGER

A DI FENCHURCH NOVEL 6

ED JAMES

OTHER BOOKS BY ED JAMES

PART I

Sunday, 17th July
Fifteen months ago

Author's note:
This section takes place between books three and four.

1

'WHERE THE HELL ARE THEY?' ABI FENCHURCH SIPPED HER FRUIT TEA AS she caressed her swollen belly. Another impatient check of her watch, then she took another slow sip.

Maroon umbrellas shielded the bright sun. Glass and chrome buildings towered over them. Crowds milled around the revamped markets at Spitalfields, even on a Sunday in the City. A teenage couple snogged each other's faces off over by the small pond, lost in their own little world. A waiter waltzed out of the next-door restaurant, holding two wide plates on his left forearm.

'They'll be here.' Detective Inspector Simon Fenchurch drank tea from a paper cup, barely tasting it. Metallic and nowhere near enough milk. He rasped the fresh stubble on his head. 'Just have a bit of patience.'

'I ran out of patience a long time ago.' Abi took his hand, her skin smooth but cold, even in the summer heat. 'We found her, Simon. Chloe. And now she's...' She tightened her grip, almost hurting him. 'This is the hardest thing I've ever had to do.'

'Sure about that?'

She let go of his hand and went back to stroking her belly, to reassuring the new life growing in there. 'Simon, shut—'

'What a glorious afternoon.' Jeff I'Anson slumped into a seat, the sun catching his glasses, the lenses darkened so they looked like shades. The social worker didn't seem to take any time off — even wore his fraying cream suit today. 'A real pleasure to see you both.'

Fenchurch finished his tea and crumpled the cup.

DCI Howard Savage leaned in behind I'Anson, every inch the Brit abroad, despite being in London — white granddad shirt tucked into belted beige shorts, spider legs of hair crawling all over his pale flesh. Just needed a handkerchief on his head to cover the thin strands combed over. 'Can I get you anything?'

'We're fine.' Abi drummed her painted fingernails on her cup. 'I just want to get on with this.'

'Of course.' I'Anson tucked his briefcase under his chin and pulled out a notebook, then a silver mechanical pencil, clicking it a few times before he set it down. 'Just a coffee, Howard, thanks.'

Savage shoved his hands deep in his pockets. 'I hadn't asked you.'

'Black with one.' I'Anson dropped his briefcase and smiled at Savage. 'I just need a moment.'

'Very well.' Savage poked his tongue in his cheek, then sauntered inside the Pret.

'Now.' I'Anson opened his notebook and trailed the bookmark over the messy table. He scribbled a note to himself. 'Okay, so I'll be brief. I met with Jennifer...' He dropped his pencil on the page. 'I mean, I met with *Chloe* yesterday. Your daughter.' He cleared his throat. 'Well, I won't sugarcoat it. I'm afraid this is going to be a long slog. She's not in a good place, as I'm sure you can imagine. The—'

'I just want to speak to her.' Abi snatched Fenchurch's hand, twisting his fingers into a claw. 'Please.'

'Mrs Fenchurch, I fully understand everything you're going through. Believe me.' I'Anson switched his laser focus to Fenchurch, his grey eyes staring hard, then back to Abi. 'But your daughter is going through the other side of your coin. She doesn't remember you or your husband. Doesn't remember living with you, doesn't remember any of her time with you, before she was... Before she was taken.'

'Before she was abducted.' Fenchurch meshed his fingers round Abi's, as tight as she'd been with him. 'Someone abducted her from outside our home and those scumbags, they—'

'Yes, yes.' I'Anson held up his palms, his fingers and thumbs spread wide like he was deflecting a goal-bound shot. 'I'm not the one you should be angry with, Inspector.'

'The scar...' Fenchurch let go of Abi's fingers and got up from the table, breathing slowly, vaguely aware of people at the other tables staring at him. But he didn't care. He pointed at his temple. 'She has a scar on her head. Right there.' He waved into the café. 'Savage's doctor thought she'd been operated on?'

'That's correct.' I'Anson reached down to get something from his briefcase, but didn't put whatever it was on the table. 'We've had two experts back up that assessment. It's a very experimental procedure, which appears to have wiped your daughter's memories, like she was an old computer you'd left bank details on and—'

'She's not a *computer*.' Fenchurch stuffed his fists in his pockets. *Getting angry isn't going to fix anything. Isn't going to change anything.* He felt his forehead crease. 'You've done the DNA tests, right? She's my daughter.' He sat again and stroked Abi's palm with his thumb. '*Our* daughter. Right?'

'Correct.'

'We just want to speak to her. Surely that's not too much to ask?'

'Well, I'm afraid it is.' I'Anson rubbed his palms together slowly. 'For Chloe — at this moment in time — it's too much.' His gaze crept to their hands. 'I completely understand how you feel. But you're not alone. Okay? You're never alone. I'm here for you. We're going on this journey together.' Steel glinted in his eyes. 'But it's important to prepare ourselves. If we jump in before Chloe's ready, it'll do a lot more harm than good.'

Fenchurch saw his fear reflected in Abi's deep frown, in her pursed lips.

'I'm not doing this to be obstructive, okay?' I'Anson glanced over at the café. 'This is standard procedure and—'

'There's nothing standard about this.' Savage rested the silvery tray on the table and reached over for one of the coffee cups as he took his seat. 'Nothing at all.' He gave a warm smile. 'Simon, Abi, what's happened to your daughter, it'd be *barbaric* if it wasn't so frighteningly Dr Moreau. I wish I could click a switch and she'd remember everything. But she can't.' He tore the lid off his coffee and blew on the surface. 'Jeff here isn't some run-of-the-mill social worker you can just bully, okay? He's a specialist in healing severe trauma in recovered victims of human trafficking. The stories we could tell of the boys and girls we rescued... I'm asking you to place your trust in him, okay?'

The teenage couple left the water feature and strolled past, their hands down the back of each other's baggy jeans.

Fenchurch shifted his focus back to Savage. 'I hear you, Howard. Doesn't mean I have to like it.'

'I don't expect you to like anything.' Savage gave a cheeky wink. 'I wouldn't put anyone in your position. Anyone at all. Not even my worst enemy and, believe me, I have many. What's happened to—'

'*Howard.*' Fenchurch leaned forward, resting his elbows on the metal table. 'It's the seventeenth of July. Eleven years ago to the day. I was washing the bloody dishes upstairs in our flat. One second I saw Chloe playing with a friend. Then Abi and I talked about a bloody garage bill. And then she was gone.' He clenched his jaw, tasting bile. 'Eleven years ago, Howard. And it's one month since we rescued her.

We've got her back, but she won't see us.' He swallowed it down along with his anger. 'Do you know what that's like?' His voice was a croak.

'Of course I don't know what it's like. I can't.' Savage gestured at I'Anson. 'But Jeff is an expert in this process and we will both help you reconnect with Chloe. I understand that it's going to take a lot longer than you expected, but it's a proven process. We just have to have patience. Okay?'

Like we have any choice in the matter.

Like I can just go and see my own bloody daughter and make her see sense.

Like I can just—

Abi gasped, then covered her mouth, her teal nails catching the sun.

Fenchurch glared at I'Anson. 'How long until we can speak to her?'

'Well, it depends on what you mean by speak to her.' I'Anson took a slurp of coffee. 'This week, I plan to broach the subject of reconnection therapy with her.'

Fenchurch looked at his wife, saw some flicker of hope in her eyes, then back at I'Anson. 'That's good, isn't it?'

'Well. Depending on her reaction, it could be six months, could be a year.'

'Six *months*?'

'But it could also be weeks.'

Abi dabbed at her eyes. 'Seems like we don't have any choice but to go along with this. Simon?'

'Agreed.' Fenchurch folded his arms. 'The sooner we get started...'

'Excellent.' I'Anson finished his coffee in one long drink, then dabbed at his mouth with a napkin. 'Like I say, I'll broach the subject of reconnection therapy with... With your daughter.' He closed his briefcase and got up. 'Now. I'll meet with her this evening, so I'm happy to convey any messages to her.'

Abi looked away with a deep sigh. 'Just tell her we love her and we'll wait for her.'

Fenchurch brushed away tears, then nodded.

I'Anson beamed at them. 'Well, I'll be in touch.' He traipsed off, swinging his briefcase.

Savage cradled his coffee in liver-spotted fingers. 'You guys okay with that?'

'I'm very far from okay, Howard.' Fenchurch reached over for Abi's hand again. 'I just wish this was easier. I wish none of this had happened.'

'We all do.' Savage grimaced. 'This is the hardest part of my job.

We're unpicking Chloe's entire psychology and rebuilding her from scratch. It's going to be a long haul, but I know you can last the course. Both of you.' He stood up and sank his coffee. 'Give me a call if you need anything. Both of you.'

Abi was smiling through the pain. 'Okay.'

'Catch you later, Howard.' Fenchurch gave Savage a curt nod, then watched him leave. 'You okay with that?'

'Maybe...' Abi tightened her hands to fists in his grip. 'It just feels like they're dangling hope in front of our faces.' Moisture pooled on her cheeks. 'I can live with hope, but I can't live with what they did to our girl. What she's been through.' She choked up.

Fenchurch smoothed her back. 'It's okay, love.'

'It's not okay!'

She's right.

I want to kill them. The people who pretended to be Chloe's parents, the people who raised her. I want to kill them. The vermin who took her. The vermin who covered it up...

All of them. Until they can't do it again. Until they can't do anything again.

'The number of times I've wanted to bounce their heads off a wall...' Fenchurch took a deep breath. 'But we need to let I'Anson do his job. Then, just maybe, this'll all be fine.'

Abi sipped at her tea, absently staring across the square. 'Why did this happen to us?'

'Blind luck, love. Can't help but—'

Fenchurch's phone blared out The Who's *Won't Get Fooled Again*: a blast of guitar, bass and drums.

'Sorry, I thought this was turned off.' Fenchurch checked the screen.

AL DOCHERTY

He let out a groan. 'It's never good when the boss is ringing me on a Sunday.' He glanced at Abi. 'You mind?'

Abi locked eyes with him. 'It's fine, Simon. Do what needs to be done, okay?'

'I'd rather not.' Fenchurch put the mobile to his ear. 'Boss, what's up?'

'I know what today means, Si, but...' Docherty's Scottish accent hit him like a knife in the back. Wind rattled the microphone at the other end. 'Need you to attend a crime scene.'

2

Fenchurch waited in the right-turn lane for the lights to change. Up ahead, Whitechapel High Street was snarled up, buses and taxis churning out diesel as the nearest cabbie hammered his horn. Like that would achieve anything.

A uniform was positioned in the middle of the street, ignoring the irate driver as he directed traffic.

Fenchurch flashed his lights and waved his warrant card. He got a thumbs up from the uniform and was beckoned through. The cabbie tried to follow but the uniform blocked him, so he got out and started shouting the odds, his words masked by the windscreen glass and the low rumble of the new Mogwai album playing on Fenchurch's car stereo. He pulled up outside the giant Whitechapel sign on the old RBS office building.

A crime scene tent blocked the way through to the City, a number 25 bus parked up alongside. A driver in Transport for London livery slumped on the pavement, talking to a plainclothes DC.

Fenchurch got out and walked over to the tent.

Another car parked behind his, wedging him in. DI Dawn Mulholland flounced onto the pavement like she was getting out of a pumpkin carriage. She dragged her scarf around her neck, her smile turning into a sneer when she saw Fenchurch. 'Simon. Surprised to see you here.'

'Not as surprised as I am to see you.'

'I thought you had a meeting about Chloe?'

Fenchurch swallowed hard. 'One of us could've dealt with this.'

'Well, I have an appointment I can't get out of later on, so—'

'And I don't?' Fenchurch barked out a laugh. 'If you knew—'

'Si, come here.' DCI Alan Docherty grabbed Fenchurch by the coat and led him away. 'Dawn, can you make sure the statements we're taking are tip top? Cheers.' He smiled as he led Fenchurch away, stopping by the almost-derelict jellied eels stand on the corner next to the tent, his skinny arms poking out of a plain black polo shirt, his face even greyer than usual, a few more lines than when he'd left the office on Friday night. 'What's all that about?'

Fenchurch looked back. Mulholland was lost in conversation with a couple of her team. 'Just wondering why we're both here, that's all.'

'Because when I called Dawn, she gave me an earful about her niece's cello recital and—'

'Her *niece*? A cello recital? Jesus Christ. You *know* where I was. Dawn knows.'

'Howard told me.' Docherty grunted out a cough. 'Look, you know I don't trust her, and while Jon Nelson's a good cop, he's still a bit green. I need my best guy on this one, okay?' He clapped Fenchurch's arm. 'Go on, get suited up. You've got a dead body to take in.'

~

Fenchurch snapped on his goggles and took a moment to centre himself. The summer breeze rushed down the street, licking at the crime scene tent.

Docherty tucked his mask and goggles in place, the crime scene suit hanging off him. 'You good?'

'I'm barely adequate.' Fenchurch stabbed the pen at the clipboard and passed it back to the Crime Scene Manager. 'Come on.' He opened the tent and entered the crime scene.

A tall SOCO stood over by the pavement, cataloguing and photographing. Tammy Saunders, judging by the height. 'Mick Clooney's hillwalking in Bosnia, so you've got to contend with me. Sorry.'

'Bosnia?' Docherty shook his head. 'Heard it all now.'

'Rather you than Mick, Tammy.' Fenchurch gave her a wink through his goggles, then took in the locus.

The large tent claimed about ten metres of an entire lane of the road. A pulse of light illuminated three large pizzas scattered across the tarmac, their open boxes lying nearby. The SOCO with the camera knelt down to get a different angle, taking great care in photographing them, like they were the dead body.

Over by a mangled bike wheel, another suited figure obscured whatever the huddle of SOCOs were doing. 'Om pom diddly om pom.'

The chief pathologist, Dr William Pratt, looked up, his wispy beard filling goggles like hair in a plughole. 'Speak of the devil and he shall appear.' The beard twisted into a grin. 'Well, gather round, gather round.'

Fenchurch squeezed past him.

A woman's body lay on the road, all twisted and broken, her lime-and-grey lycra cycling top soaked red near the neck. Fenchurch flinched as he saw the bloody mush that should've been a head, dark blood pooling on the asphalt, dotted with teeth and bone.

Pratt winched himself up to standing with a loud crack. 'The bad news is that we don't have an ID on her.'

Fenchurch's stomach fizzed with fear and hatred and rage. 'What's the good?'

'The good...' Pratt reached into his bag for a pair of metallic tongs. 'Om pom pom.' He picked up a chunk of bone with two teeth still attached, like corn on the cob. 'Well, we know the cause of death.' He gestured over at the tent entrance, flapping in the breeze. 'The poor thing was squashed between a van and a number twenty-five bus.'

Jesus Christ.

Explains the state of the driver.

'Sounds like an accident, William.' Docherty folded his arms, the suit crinkling. 'Why the hell are we here?'

'As a seasoned detective, Alan, you'll have noticed that, while the bus is still here, the van isn't?'

A sly grin showed through Docherty's mask. 'Hit and run?'

'Indeed. A witness says this was deliberate.'

3

FENCHURCH TORE OFF HIS CRIME SCENE SUIT BUT HE KEPT SEEING THE mush where a head should have been. The pool of blood, dotted with teeth and bone. Pratt picking up the shattered jawbone, the teeth still attached. He dumped his suit in the discard pile, sucking in stale diesel fumes and cigarette smoke.

Over at the pavement, DS Jon Nelson clocked Fenchurch. His brown suit was a few shades lighter than his skin, his black hair fuzzing up, long overdue a fresh buzz cut. He gave a sympathetic smile to the bus driver and sauntered over. 'Surprised to see you here, guv.'

'Don't start, Jon.' Fenchurch caught a splash of red on the side of the bus, coating the window and the advert for suntan lotion. A SOCO was photographing it. 'Not in the mood.'

'When are you?' Nelson grinned wide, then frowned. 'Mulholland, right?'

'Right.' Fenchurch waved over at the pavement. 'Saw you talking to the bus driver.'

'Poor guy. People never think about them. Bus drivers, train drivers, lorry drivers. They're the ones who suffer the trauma of someone jumping in front of them to kill themselves.'

'Pratt thinks this wasn't someone jumping in front.'

'Right.' Nelson patted his coat packet. 'You want a word with the driver?'

'Did he see anything?'

'Just felt the impact of the bus crashing against the van.'

Fenchurch did another 360. Definitely no sign of a van. 'So someone squashed her?'

'Looks like it.' Nelson scanned the assembled uniforms. 'We're taking statements from the passengers and pedestrians. Not many of them saw the whole thing. Still a few pedestrians to speak to, but they're all in shock. One witness says it's murder, though. Another cyclist. Calls himself an ogle.'

'A what?'

'O-G-I-L. Old Git In Lycra.'

Fenchurch groaned. 'Show me.'

Nelson led him across the road. The traffic was still heavy, but at least it had started moving and that cabbie had cleared off. He stopped at the shuttered pub front over the road. 'Mr Kelly?'

'Call me David.' A City type, wearing expensive cycling gear that was either skin-tight or dangling free. He shook Fenchurch's hand, firm and tight. 'Pleased to meet you.' Scouse accent, but refined. 'I was telling him I wasn't supposed to even be here.'

'Oh?'

'It's a Sunday. I work up at EBS on Bishopsgate. Got a horrendously expensive IT system going in today and I was supposed to get text updates through the day. Thought it'd be fine to have some time where I wasn't in the sodding office, but no.' Kelly took a deep sigh. 'They made a right mess of it. I was halfway to Brighton.' He gestured at an expensive-looking road bike propped up outside the pub. 'Train to Victoria, then I cycled over. Thought I'd save myself a bit of time, but...' He swallowed. 'As I came round the bend there, I saw this girl pedalling like the hounds of hell were after her. She was being chased by a white van.' The colour drained from his face as he pointed at the bus. 'I was going to follow but...'

'Which way she was cycling?'

Kelly nodded over the road, past the dead pub and the jellied eels stand. 'She was coming down Goulston Street.'

Fenchurch groaned. 'From the City?'

'Relax, guv.' Nelson whispered: 'This is our jurisdiction. Lisa Bridge is verifying the victim's route on CCTV.'

'Good work.' Fenchurch shot a smile at Kelly. 'Did you see her get attacked?'

'Right there.' Kelly stomped across the road and stood at the corner of Goulston Street and Whitechapel High Street, the one-way blocked off by a no-entry sign from this side. He drew his finger down the back street. 'Van clipped her, sent her wobbling, but she stayed upright.' He followed a curved path over the road towards the bus and the tent. 'I mean, she dumped her pizzas and, this van... Jesus. It swerved into her and squashed her flat against the bus.'

'What happened to the van?'

'No idea, sorry. There was a commotion, I didn't see anything. And besides, I was calling 999, you know?' Kelly twisted his face up. 'I mean, I've been chased myself a few times, you know, over the years. Happened so fast.'

'You recognise her?'

'Know her face. Seen her around. I cycle most days. You get to know other cyclists, at least by face.'

'But other than that?'

'No. Sorry.'

~

'WELL, THAT'S WHAT I'M LOOKING AT, TOO.' DC LISA BRIDGE RESTED her laptop on the top of a pool Astra. She brushed her bleached hair over her ear and glanced at Nelson. Then she hit play on the computer. 'Watch.'

A shot of a street filled the laptop screen, across Whitechapel High Street to the shuttered pub. The victim pedalled furiously, a pizza bag bobbing about on her back. A white van trailed after her, but slowed at a gap between two parked trucks. It shot through and swerved round the bend, lurching towards her and clipping her back wheel just like Kelly had said. The cyclist powered on, managing to keep her bike upright. She shrugged off the bag and the pizzas spilled out onto the tarmac.

The van smashed into her, sending her flying across the road. It buckled her bike under its wheels as she slammed against the bus, then dropped to the ground.

The van drove over her skull.

Fenchurch took a few shallow breaths, trying to get himself under control. He stared at the freeze frame of the bus and the van. 'Looks very deliberate to me.' He spotted Kelly on his bike, just by the entrance to Aldgate East tube station. He reached over and scrubbed the footage back to play it again, and scanned the screen.

Kelly's movements matched his story — stopping as the cyclist hit the bus, then calling 999.

'Have you found a good image of her face?'

'Sorry. I've looked, but it's too far away and her helmet obscures it.'

'Figures.' Fenchurch tapped the van. 'Have you traced the plates?'

'It's hired.' Bridge switched to another screen. 'Place out in Lewisham. Got some local uniform paying a visit.'

'Lisa, can you get out there?' Fenchurch gave her an encouraging smile. 'I want my best people on it.'

'I'll try to take that as a compliment, sir.' Bridge nudged him aside. 'Thing is... Just watch this.' She hit play again.

The video wound on, Kelly talking into his mobile as the van drove over the cyclist and her bike. A couple of men in the crowd rushed over to help the stricken cyclist. But the van stopped and the driver hopped out, wearing a motorbike helmet. He crouched down and rummaged around in the victim's jacket. He put something in his own pocket as he stood up, then jumped back in the van and drove off.

'Jesus Christ.' Fenchurch stabbed his finger on the screen. 'Find this guy. Highest priority.'

'Sir.' Bridge packed up her laptop and got in the Astra. The engine roared and she tore off through the crowd.

Nelson watched the car go, sucking on his vape stick. 'So what's our next move?'

'Good question.' Fenchurch took in the scene again, not much different from what he'd just seen on the laptop. Shocked faces standing round, stunned and lost. 'Any ideas?'

'Precious few. The statements will just back up the CCTV. Fingers crossed that Lisa gets somewhere finding the killer.'

A SOCO was bagging and tagging the pizza boxes, while another carefully placed the discarded pizzas into bags.

Fenchurch rushed over and grabbed one. Mario's Pizza. 'This place is just round the corner, isn't it?'

4

Everyone knew Wentworth Street as Petticoat Lane Market, though good luck seeing a sign. A long street lined with brick buildings, shops on the ground floor, three or four floors of flats above. Not many traders left at this time on a Sunday, just an old Arab man bundling shoes back into boxes, muttering to himself. In the distance, the Gherkin poked up above the rough old Sixties buildings, the haves up in their tower, the have-nots down here, buying garish dresses off a rack.

'There it is.' Nelson squeezed past a burly builder type haggling over the price of a pair of dungarees with a trader.

Mario's Pizza lay between a shoe shop and a café that ripped its design ethos from Pret a Manger. Burnt baking smells wafted out onto the street. Bright sunlight cut a long shaft on the gridwork paving.

Fenchurch stopped, sick to the stomach. 'Seen a lot of things, Jon, but that... Jesus Christ.'

'Tell me about it.' Nelson sucked on his vape stick. 'You okay?'

The Arab man shifted another armful of shoeboxes into his shop.

'I'm fine. Docherty's right, though, this does look like a murder.' Fenchurch shut his eyes and caught a flash of the CCTV. 'He's checking she's dead... Nicking her ID...' He opened his eyes again and set off towards the restaurant. A shiny road bike was propped up against the window, not even chained up. 'Come on.' He entered Mario's.

A small family pizza restaurant, busy with Sunday lunch trade, all of the tables full. Chart radio pulsed out of wall-mounted speakers, drowning out the chatter. A female bike courier barged past, the large bag on her back making her look like a snail.

A couple of members of staff chatted over by the salad bar. Young, dark-haired and attractive.

Fenchurch grabbed a passing waiter. 'Need to speak to the owner.'

The guy frowned. 'You want speak to Mario?' His accent was thick. The waiter led them through the restaurant, strutting like he was hitting the dance floor. He leaned in through a door. 'Boss?'

In a filthy back room, a scrawny man perched on an armchair, thick stubble dampening his sharp features, acting out boxing moves, a barrage of swift jabs followed by a hefty upper cut. *Raging Bull* played on the TV screen; Robert De Niro getting the snot punched out of him in the ring. Mario didn't look over at the door. 'What the hell do you want, Sergio?' Thick Cockney accent.

Fenchurch stepped into the room, warrant card out. 'One of your pizza delivery girls is dead.'

That made Mario turn around. 'What are you talking about?' He reached for a remote and paused his film.

'DI Simon Fenchurch.' He showed his warrant card. 'You got a surname, Mario?'

'Esposito.' None of the Latin grace, just spat out in Cockney. 'Now, what's up?'

'Found the body of a girl, had a bag full of your pizzas, left a trail of pepperoni all along Whitechapel High Street.'

'Aw, shit on it!' Mario jumped to his feet and stomped over to the door.

'Oi!' Fenchurch stopped him with a hand to the chest. 'Sir, I need you to—'

'Mate, that pizza oven doesn't work itself.' Mario pushed Fenchurch aside and made to leave again.

Fenchurch held firm. 'Listen to me, sir. This is serious. Someone's murdered your employee. Smacked them between a van and a bus. We don't have an ID. I need your help identifying her.'

Mario took a moment, rasping the salt-and-pepper stubble. 'You know how many delivery drivers I've got? I'd need to see her.'

'She's at a crime scene, then she'll be moved to Lewisham, where our morgue is. You're welcome to wait there.'

Mario set off towards the TV and turned the screen off. 'Mate.' He opened the door and showed a stack of uncooked pizzas sitting by the oven. 'You see how busy I am? Stowed out the bleeding door, I am. Trying to take five minutes to watch a film. I need to redo that order, after I figure out which ones.'

'Mr Esposito, this is a murder. Now, I need to ID this girl, so I can speak to her family and try and find out who killed her.' Fenchurch held his gaze for a few seconds. 'Wasn't you, was it?'

'What, of course not!' Mario huffed out a sigh. 'I've got three girls, and a couple of geezers. They're all on today, all out delivering.'

'They're all out?'

'You don't make this easy.' Mario held up his arms. 'Yes, all three girls are on, all out delivering. Christa was just leaving with a pair of calzones, so it's not her.'

'Then I need you to call the other two.'

'Bloody hell.' Mario slumped in his armchair again and took out his mobile. After a few seconds of fiddling, he put it to his ear. 'Shit on it.' He went over to the kitchen door and barked out some guttural Italian. 'Sergio!'

The waiter came through, masked by noise from the restaurant, a leather-skinned LG to his ear. He replied in Italian. 'Si, si.' More Italian. 'No problemo, Casey, no problemo.' Then he killed the call and nodded at Mario. 'I spoke to Casey.'

Mario sank back against the kitchen wall. 'I can't get hold of Amelia.' He focused on Fenchurch, his red eyes narrowing. 'Amelia Nicholas. Sergio, find the last order and call them, yeah? Tell them their pizza's delayed.'

'Si.' Sergio sloped off with a flourish. He doubled back. 'It was, eh, two orders?'

'Yeah, you're right.' Mario shook his head and made to follow Sergio.

Fenchurch grabbed hold of him. 'Tell me about Amelia.'

'What's there to say?' Mario walked over to a column of photos on the wall, employees reluctantly smiling at the camera. He patted one halfway along. 'This is Amelia. Started a couple of months back.'

'Need a home address for her.'

'I'd need to check.'

'Well, I'm not stopping you.'

'Yeah, my office is up in Hackney. Got a factory. Sell to the supermarkets. I'd have to go up.'

Fenchurch pointed at Nelson. 'DS Nelson will accompany you.'

Mario picked up a heavy coat with another sigh. 'Come on, then.'

Fenchurch got in his way. 'What's the address for her last delivery?'

Mario picked up a notepad and skimmed down it. 'Like Sergio said, she had two deliveries. One for two pizzas, but another came in just as Amelia got back from her previous run. The guy was desperate, so I knocked up his chicken and banana pizza quick smart and sent it out with her.' He held the notepad up to Fenchurch. 'Here are the addresses.'

~

Fenchurch pulled up on a back street not too far from Leman Street station. New-build office blocks loomed nearby, both in modern chrome and older brick. No sign of any flats. He rechecked the photo he'd taken of Mario's order book — certainly looked like the right place.

Nothing ventured...

He headed over, catching the smell of the Thames. A summery racket blared out of the pubs and restaurants of St Katharine Docks over the other side of the building. He found the number at the nearest entrycom system and hit the button.

A loud crackle. 'Down in a sec.' Male voice, gruff.

Fenchurch frowned. *Must think it's his pizza.*

Footsteps thundered down some steps inside and the heavy-duty black door flew open. Another City banker type, sniffing like he was coming down with something. Scruffy jeans with a shirt and jumper combo, shiny black leather shoes. He spun around, twitching. 'Where is it?'

'What?'

'My pizza. I'm starving.'

'Police.' Fenchurch showed his warrant card. 'Need to ask you a few questions.'

'Come on, mate. I'm *starving.*'

'Name?'

'It's Colin. Colin Dunston. My stomach's eating itself.' He was holding an oversized Samsung, staring at it like it could give him his pizza. 'Need to call that Italian git.' He started tapping the screen. 'I'm so hungry, I can hardly *think.*'

'Sir, this is serious.' Fenchurch stepped closer. 'The girl who was delivering your pizza was murdered. Now, I need to know—'

'Chicken and banana, stuffed crust.' Dunston stared at his mobile again. 'Have to order a Domino's now.' He thumbed the screen. 'I'm just back from the gym, called in my order on my way back. Legs day, need my carbs after all that running I did. Three bleeding hours on the treadmill. Bar squats too. Mario said it'd be here.'

'Sir, do you recognise this woman?' Fenchurch showed the photo on his screen. 'Her name is Amelia Nicholas.'

Dunston squinted at it. 'I mean, yeah, she's delivered my pizza a couple of times, you know, but I didn't kill her.' He reached over for a wallet and took out a card. Bulk Gym in silver letters on matt black. 'I was there since ten. Running, weights, sauna. Had a snack, then in the cryotank, then more running. You can check with them, if you want?'

~

FENCHURCH LISTENED TO THE RING TONE AS HE WAITED, BUT HE WASN'T getting around that bus for at least an hour, while a stream of traffic ploughed the other way down Commercial Road. He indicated and pulled in. Then the phone was answered. 'You getting anywhere, Jon?'

'Mario's office is a pigsty, guv.' Nelson's rattling laugh distorted in the speaker. 'But I'll get the address, don't you worry.'

'Can you to get someone out to Bulk Gym in Wapping? Check on the whereabouts of a Colin Dunston.'

'Guv.' Sounded like Nelson was writing. 'I'll get someone out there tout suite.' Click and he was gone.

Fenchurch got out onto Commercial Road, the summer sun burning at his neck, and used the bus to cross. He cut in to Parfett Street and set off down the quiet back street, checking the numbers as he went. There. Loud music came from number thirteen. *At least they're in.* He paced up the path and knocked.

The door clattered open and a stoner stared out, struggling to focus, his pupils filling up most of his eye sockets. Big hipster beard, but the guy would weigh about six stone soaking wet. Lank black hair tied in a man bun. Red velvet Adidas tracksuit like he was in the New York Mafia in the Seventies. 'Yeah?'

'Police.' Fenchurch showed his warrant card. 'Need a word, sir. Start with your name?'

'Adrian. Adrian Hall.'

'Right. And you ordered a pizza, right?'

'Yeah, and it's half an hour late.'

Fenchurch put his ID away and took out his phone, showing the photo of Amelia. 'You know her?'

'Nope.'

Adrian's eyes retracted even further, his pupils giant discs. 'Amelia Nicholas.'

'Never heard of her. Think she's delivered my pizza a couple of times, though.'

'You ever speak to her?'

'Just to tip her.' Adrian dug his knuckles into his eyes. 'What's happened?'

'She was on her way here when—'

'Ade?' Another hipster appeared in the doorway, bulkier like a male model, with a thicker beard and paler skin. 'We getting our pizza or what?'

'What, mate. Scarper. It's the *feds*.' Adrian shifted his focus back to

Fenchurch. 'Mate, I need to feed the five thousand, so if you don't have loaves and fish...'

'Son, I'm murder squad. Amelia was murdered.' Fenchurch stepped inside the doorway. 'Did you—?'

'Woah, woah, you can't come in here without a warrant!'

Fenchurch stepped back outside. 'There something I should be aware of?' He sniffed the dank hair, a sweet smell catching the breeze. 'Is that skunk?'

'No, mate.' Adrian's mate snorted. 'We're roasting our own coffee.'

'Ethiopian beans.' Adrian tried a smile on for size, too big for his pallid face. 'Mate, I don't like cops trampling all over my possessions like you own the bleeding place, know what I mean?'

'The delivery driver, Amelia, was murdered on her way here.'

'Well, mate, I'm truly sorry, but it ain't got nothing to do with me, alright? Now, I'm working tomorrow and I quite like my time off, so unless you're hiding a margarita and a "Death by Meat", you need to get out of my hair.'

Fenchurch stared hard at him. *Guy's just a chancer. A privileged chancer, but a chancer nonetheless.* 'Alright, sunshine, you—'

A rumble in his pocket. He checked the display — Nelson. He gave Adrian a card. 'If the name Amelia Nicholas suddenly means something to you, then give me a bell.'

'Sure thing.' Adrian disappeared behind the closing door.

Fenchurch set off, putting the phone to his ear. 'Jon, what's up?'

'Mario's found Amelia's address.'

5

FENCHURCH TRUNDLED ALONG BRICK LANE, FOLLOWING A SLOW-MOVING taxi that looked like it didn't know where it was going. Still early, but the curry hustlers were out hassling pedestrians. He kept counting the numbers.

There.

Fenchurch yanked the wheel to the right and pulled into a space outside the old brewery. He rolled up the window to stop his car smelling of burnt onions, then stepped out onto the street.

A crowd of lads jogged past, shouting at each other. Whoever they were, it was too early and they were way too old for that kind of nonsense.

Over the road, Nelson sucked on his vape stick, giving a mock salute at Fenchurch's approach. 'That Acting DC was heading round to the gym. Not heard anything back yet.'

'Him? Jon, I want a good person on it.'

'He's good. Trust me.' Nelson toked on his vape stick like he was sharing a spliff with mates. 'How'd you get on with the other delivery?'

'Just a load of hipsters wanting some pizza.'

A thick cloud billowed out of Nelson's nostrils as he tried a door buzzer, marked for the second floor. 'Bit low level for you, wasn't it?'

'Don't like just standing around, Jon. Might be worth getting that Acting DC to run a check on them. If nothing else, they're smoking a shit ton of skunk in there.'

'Practically legal now, guv.' Nelson tried the buzzer again, blowing vape smoke all over the entrycom. 'You okay? You seem distracted.'

'I'm fine.' Fenchurch let out a slow yawn. 'Who am I trying to kid?

We had a meeting with Chloe's social worker. This geezer who works with Howard Savage. Thinks we can get into sessions with her in a month.'

'Right.' Nelson stared back over the road, past Fenchurch.

'I thought you'd be pleased, Jon. Interested at least.'

'Sorry, guv.' Nelson crossed over and set off towards a white van, putting his mobile to his ear. 'Lisa, it's Jon. Give me the plates for that van again.' He paused, briefly making eye contact with Fenchurch. 'Well, get them to hurry up. Just—' He snorted. 'Shit.' He pocketed his phone and pointed at the van. 'Guv, that's it.'

Fenchurch darted over, almost bumping into an arguing couple.

Nelson was round the far side, backing onto the old brewery wall. 'Bloody hell, guv.'

Fenchurch followed him round. Blood spattered the side of the van, covering the suntan lotion advert. His stomach jolted. 'Call Tammy and get her to send a team over here.'

'Guv.' Nelson stuck his phone to his ear again.

Fenchurch started snapping photos of the van. He peered inside the cabin. Something shifted through the front glass.

Fenchurch shot round.

A man lurked on the pavement, looking inside the van.

Fenchurch clocked him immediately.

The mate of Adrian, the hipster who ordered the pizza. The other hipster — furtive eyes and thick beard. He clocked Fenchurch and sprinted off.

'Shit!' Fenchurch chased after him, feet pounding the pavement. A crowd of rugby lads closed around Adrian's mate, blocking Fenchurch's path and view of him. 'Coming through!' He pulled out his warrant card. 'Police!'

'No need to be a cu—'

Fenchurch charged on, scanning the busy street. There — a loping run, like a gazelle in the headlights. Fenchurch barged through a foursome, two couples blagging a deal with a curry hawk.

But the hipster was gone.

Shit.

Fenchurch stopped, spinning round and scanning every single face.

A man loped past on the opposite pavement, jacket collar turned up high, hood covering his hair. But Fenchurch would recognise the stoned eyes anywhere.

He shot across the road.

But the guy saw Fenchurch coming and twisted him in an armbar.

Pain burnt up Fenchurch's arm, shooting up to his elbow. A kick to the right shin and he buckled at the knees, hitting the deck face down.

The hipster let go and sprinted off down the street.

Fenchurch pushed himself up to standing, but he'd lost him again.

Then a scream, back the way, near the van.

Fenchurch shot off into a sprint, running despite the harsh pain in his legs.

Nelson lay on top of the hipster, arms wrapped round him. Must've rugby tackled him.

Fenchurch grabbed the hipster by the wrists, digging his thumbs into the bone. *No chance that little shit's doing that again.* He hauled him up to standing. 'You stupid bastard. Should've ditched that van elsewhere.'

'It's not mine!'

'Bullshit.' Fenchurch bent his arm round his back and walked him towards his car and the van. 'You and your mate Adrian kill that girl, yeah?'

'I ain't done nothing.'

'I don't believe you.' Fenchurch pinned him against his car and started searching him, aware of the crowd of rugby lads watching the drama unfold. He patted the hipster down, finding an old iPhone 4 in the pocket of his drainpipes. 'This yours?'

'No, it's the bloody Queen's.' Hipster barked out a laugh. 'Last great iPhone, that one. Design classic. Plus it fits in my pocket unlike the new ones.'

'Take your word for it.' Fenchurch found a wallet in his back pocket and started going through it.

'I'll save you the bother. My name is Mosé Tronci. And I work at Mario's Pizza.'

6

FENCHURCH STORMED INTO MARIO'S.

Less busy than before, but most of the tables were occupied. A couple argued over by the salad bar, him filling a plate with hard-boiled eggs, her jabbing a finger in his face. A dad chased after a toddler heading for the front door, scooping him up in his arms.

No sign of any staff.

Fenchurch stomped over to the kitchen door and opened it.

Mario was back in the kitchen, wearing full chef gear, sweating as he knelt down to nudge a paddle in to retrieve a pizza from the wood-fired oven. He stopped when he clocked Fenchurch.

'Need a word with you, sir.'

Mario slid the pizza into the top box of a teetering pile and folded the lid. 'There you go, Des. Try not to lose these ones.'

An older guy laughed as he shoved three boxes into a bag. Tall and skinny, the silver stubble on his head catching the light. His tight lycra shirt and cycling shorts didn't exactly hide anything. Arms and legs shaved closer than his face. He lugged the delivery bag on his shoulders and turned to face Fenchurch. A chunky goatee surrounded pink lips, the kind of thick hair Fenchurch could only dream of growing. He frowned at him but didn't say anything.

Fenchurch tried to place the face, but couldn't. *Familiar, though.* 'I know you from somewhere, don't I?'

The cyclist shrugged. 'Must've delivered a cheese toastie or something, mate.'

'I don't live round here. And I'm on this stupid keto diet.'

'I tried that, couldn't stick it.' The cyclist held out a hand. 'Billy Desmond.' He shook Fenchurch's with a tight grip. 'You an 'Ammer?'

'Must be that.' Fenchurch gave him another close look. *So bloody familiar...*

Mario clattered his pizza paddle down on the counter. 'Billy's picking up the delivery slack since I lost Amelia.'

'Talk about drawing the short straw.' Desmond gave Fenchurch a wink, then smiled at Mario. 'Back in about half an hour, yeah?'

'Alright.' Mario watched him go, then shifted his gaze to Fenchurch. 'What now?'

'Need a word with you about a Mosé Tronci. He works here, right?'

'Hell's bells.' Mario scowled as he tore off his apron and hung it up. 'Why are you interested in Mosé? You think he's involved in this murder?'

'Not sure. Maybe.' Fenchurch stayed by the door, leaning against the tatty wallpaper. 'After you kindly passed us her address, we went round, and I found Mosé sniffing round the van that killed her.'

'Shit on it...' Mario slumped down in his chair. 'What the hell?'

'The way I see it, this Mosé character worked here, right? Meaning it's possible he knew where Amelia was going on her delivery.'

Mario looked up. Didn't say anything, though.

'Did he place the order?'

'I don't know, do I?' Mario rasped his callused fingers over the thick stubble on his face. 'This isn't Domino's, mate. I don't have an app. We get a call, we write the order up on the board. I make the pizza.'

'Right.' Fenchurch glanced over at the magnetic strip with ten covers pinned to it. 'Did Mosé know Amelia?'

'Shouldn't you be asking him that?'

'I will, but I want what you know first. And you're telling me now.'

'Come on, mate, I'm backed up here. I need to make ten pizzas in the next fifteen minutes.'

'You answer my question and you get to go back to your oven. What does he do here?'

'The kid works with me in the kitchen, but this is his day off.' Mario squeezed his thumb and forefinger together. 'I was this close to calling him in to help out.' Back to the scratching. 'And now the little bastard's in custody?'

'So Mosé would pass pizzas to Amelia, just like you did there?'

'Well, obviously.' Mario shot Fenchurch a glare. 'I did see them get into an argument a couple of weeks back. No idea what it was about, before you ask.'

'You think he was trying it on with her?'

'I said I've no idea.'

FENCHURCH LOUNGED DOWN THE CORRIDOR IN LEMAN STREET STATION, jacket over his arm. As he neared Docherty's office, the voices got louder, more heated. He stopped outside and listened, keeping an eye on the corridor for watching faces.

'Dawn, I need to know your interview strategy.' Sounded like Docherty was close to losing his rag.

'I just want a shot at him.' The door muffled Mulholland's voice. 'Do you want me to say please? Do you want me to beg?'

'Don't be like that.' Something clunked off the wooden desk, probably a mug. 'It's beneath you.'

'You're entrusting Simon with this investigation?'

'Entrusting? Dawn, it's 2017. Nobody uses words like that any more.'

'Well I do. If Simon goes over the line, this is on you.'

Docherty paused, then something clunked again. 'Thought you had a cello recital to attend?'

'This is more important.'

Here goes nothing...

Fenchurch knocked and entered.

Mulholland craned her neck round.

Fenchurch stepped between them, hovering between Docherty's desk and Mulholland's chair. 'I was just wondering if Mosé was ready for interview, but it seems like you don't need me.' He put his jacket on and made to leave. 'Evening.'

'Si, wait. Dawn was just—' Docherty coughed, hard. Sounded like he'd produced a lung.

Fenchurch clapped him on the back, hard. Then again. 'You okay, boss?'

'I'm fine. Just swallowed a sandwich the wrong bloody way. I don't chew properly.' Docherty took a drink of coffee from his mug. It dribbled down his chin and he rubbed it away.

'Boss, if you want DI Mulholland to run this case, that's fine by me. I've got better places to be.'

'Si, no.' Docherty coughed again, screwing up his face before taking another glug. 'Look, this is your case, Si. You speak to the guy. End of.'

'Sir, I'd appreciate the opportunity to—'

'Wheesht.' Docherty cleared his throat, shooting daggers at Mulholland. 'Dawn, I need you managing the street teams, okay? As it stands, we've barely interviewed half the witnesses. Could be we need to ask this Mosé character about something we don't know about yet, okay? So why don't you see if you can dig that up, aye? Here's a chance to make me and Si look like a pair of arseholes.'

Mulholland stared hard at him for a few seconds, then nodded. 'Sir.' She walked over to the door, her black scarf trailing behind her. 'I don't believe this is the correct approach.'

'Noted. Now, you can attend your niece's recital if you want.'

Mulholland stared hard at him, then left without another word, just the door clicking behind her. Her footsteps clattered down the corridor, muffled through the wood.

Docherty collapsed back into his chair and sipped from his Rangers mug. 'Coffee's bloody cold now.' He nudged the mug away with a slight cough. 'She'll be the death of me, Si, I swear to God. I keep moaning about her to Loftus, but the pair of them go back to Hendon, I think. He's climbed the ladder faster, but I swear she's after my job.'

A bead of sweat trickled down Fenchurch's back. 'Didn't know that.'

'No, didn't think you would. Anyway, Loftus isn't going to do anything about her. Says I need to make it work.' Docherty laughed. 'But I'm sick of her nonsense. All day, every day, I'm stuck with the wicked witch of the west.'

'Like you're stuck with me.'

'Ha, maybe. But she's a worse nightmare than you.'

'Just keep her out of my way, boss.'

'Swear when I die and go to hell, I'll be managing her all day and she'll just be giving me this and that. What I'm trying to—' Docherty lurched forward, coughing hard into his fist. 'Christ.'

Fenchurch kept his distance this time. 'Seriously, boss, are you okay?'

'Not really. This cold's been lingering since March.'

'*March?* It's July. You should go to the doctor.'

'Like I've got time to go to the doctor...' Docherty waved at the door. 'Get in there and interview this prick out before Dawn comes back here, cap in hand.'

∼

'THAT'S IT?' FENCHURCH CRUNCHED BACK IN HIS CHAIR AND SHARED A look with Nelson. The interview room was deadly silent. 'No comment?'

Mosé was sitting opposite, the window behind him. Even with the blinds drawn, the sun blared through, shrouding him in light. 'You heard me. No comment.'

'Let me get this straight.' Fenchurch leaned forward, but his eyes were already hurting from the blinding glow. 'You just happened to be wandering around a van that'd been used to murder someone?'

'Listen.' Mosé yawned into his fist. 'All I've done is go for a walk to fetch some pizza for my mates. That's it.'

'No pizza places up that way, though.'

Mosé yawned again.

'See, it's a bit of a coincidence that you were lurking around that van. And another coincidence that Amelia was on the way to deliver your pizzas when she was killed. Did you order them? Or was it your flatmate?'

More yawning.

Fenchurch pushed his chair back and trudged over to the door. He found a better angle to glare at him without blinding himself. 'You ordered pizzas from the place you work in.' He paused. 'You knew where Amelia would be going, meaning you could murder her with that van.'

Mosé looked over at the door. 'You should let me go.'

'Not gonna happen.' Fenchurch's voice echoed round the room. 'There's no way you're getting out of here, son. You placed that order, then you tailed Amelia in that van and you murdered her.' He left another pause, but Mosé just yawned again. 'When I visited your flat to check on the delivery, that spooked you, didn't it? You went up to her flat, but I don't understand why you parked the van there, though.'

'Let me go.'

Fenchurch took a step closer, but got a flash of light from the window. 'You're not taking this very seriously.'

'Because you've got nothing on me. Just a load of random information.'

'You want to play that game?' Fenchurch laughed. 'Why did you murder her? You worked together, right? Did she knock you back, is that it?'

'Really? That's all you've got?'

Fenchurch gave a shrug. 'Seen much simpler explanations in my time.'

'If you want to put me away, you'll need something stronger than me being near a van. I didn't kill her.'

'Bullshit.' Fenchurch stepped forward again. A flash of sunlight made him blink hard. 'Your housemate didn't want me coming inside your house. Threatened me with needing a warrant.' He leaned in close, using Mosé to block the sun. 'What are you hiding in there? I assume you're not really roasting coffee beans.'

'We are, as it happens. Ade's running a business on the side. You should taste them. Gorgeous.' Mosé gave a smug grin. 'You really need to let me go, mate.'

'Do I? See, if I arrest you, I can get a squad to search your gaff like that.' Fenchurch clicked his fingers, loud and sharp.

'Inspector, you really should've done your homework before you brought me in.'

Cheeky little bastard.

Fenchurch stood up tall. 'Mosé Tronci, I'm arresting you for—'

'I'm an undercover cop.'

Fenchurch stopped dead. 'What?'

'DS Chris Spencer. I work for Howard Savage in the Vice and Trafficking Unit. Do us both a favour and give him a bell, would you?'

7

'THAT LYING, LYING BAST—' DOCHERTY JERKED FORWARD, COUGHING hard again, bracing himself on his office desk. 'Christ on a bike.' He gasped for breath, struggling to keep steady.

Fenchurch stood there, no idea what to do. 'Seriously, are you okay?'

'It's this bastard cold. Or it's hay fever. I'm plagued by it this time of year.'

'Even so, you should get it checked out. I don't want to have to carry you to hospital.'

'Always about you, Si.' Docherty rubbed at his throat. 'Always about you.'

'So, what's our plan of attack with Savage, boss?'

'Once that lying bastard bothers to pitch up, I'm going at him hell for leather.' Docherty coughed again, but it sounded like he'd caught it, whatever it was. 'You believe this boy? Mosé Tronci. Chris Spencer. Whatever his name is.'

'There's a Chris—'

The office door bundled open and Savage paced in, face like thunder. 'Gentlemen.' He still wore his shorts, though he lugged a dark-brown briefcase.

'Sexy legs, Howard.' Docherty flashed a smile, but there was fire behind his eyes. 'You've got a lot of explaining to do.'

'As do you.' Savage gave Fenchurch a tight nod. 'Didn't expect to see you so soon, Simon.'

'Enough chit-chat, Howard.' Docherty cleared his throat again.

'We're running a murder investigation and our suspect numero uno says he's one of your officers.'

'That's quite correct.' Savage walked over to the window, the street outside now in the shade. 'DS Spencer's mother is from Italy, came to study here in the Eighties. Married his father and had young Christian. Given his ethnic background, he's perfect to infiltrate Mario's Pizzas.'

'Howard, you need to prevent your undercover plants making a mess of my cases.'

'You'll make a mess of it all on your lonesome, Alan.' Savage stared out of the window. 'Spencer has been working there for the last eight months. He's earned Mario's trust, but only partially.'

'Care to tell me why he's there?'

Savage turned around slowly and crossed his arms. 'We believe that Mario works for an organisation trafficking Albanians over here, then using them as prostitutes.'

Docherty laughed. 'Are you pulling my plonker?'

'Have you ever known me to jest?'

Fenchurch joined Savage by the window. 'Albanians? Are you serious?'

'Deadly. They've been using pizza delivery as cover for their illicit activities. Mario sends them all over East London on bikes. It's perfect.' Savage walked back over to his briefcase and unclipped the catch. He took out a file and tossed it to Fenchurch. 'Your Amelia Nicholas is really Amelja Nikolla.'

Fenchurch flicked through it. Stills of the now-murdered Albanian national cycling around London. Down by Wapping, Canary Wharf, Mile End, even on Bishopsgate in the City. He found a list of times and dates, with men's names. 'What's this?'

'Prostitution, Simon. Upwards of eighty known clients.'

'Bloody hell.' Fenchurch handed the file to Docherty. 'Your guy's up to his nuts in this, Howard.'

Savage sat and crossed one hairy leg over the other. 'Chris was only doing his job.'

'That include lurking around the van used to kill her?'

Savage straightened up, but didn't say anything.

'You're sure he's not gone rogue, Howard?' Fenchurch tilted his head to the side. 'Maybe decided to take her out?'

'Of course not.' Savage kept his gaze on the floor. 'Christ, Simon, I personally trained him.'

'Like that means anything.'

Savage frowned over at him. 'Let's start with why someone would want to kill her, mm?' His frown deepened. 'It could be the prostitution. It could be another illicit activity, or it could be something else entirely. She could've cut someone up at the lights. This is London — take your pick. Also, it could be the gang who trafficked her here.'

'Howard, I caught your guy red-handed. Are you not listening to me? He was standing by the van used to kill her.'

'That's not exactly red-handed.' Savage made eye contact, the same fury burning in his eyes as in Docherty's. 'Would either of you like to accompany me in debriefing him?'

≈

'BECAUSE I DIDN'T!' SPENCER SHOT TO HIS FEET AND STARTED PACING around the interview room. 'You need to listen to me!'

'If not you, then who?' Fenchurch sat back in his chair and folded his arms. Docherty was over by the door, eyes trained on his watch. Savage sat next to Spencer, like his defence lawyer. 'Who did it, eh? Who killed her? Who squashed her against that bus? Who was driving the van? I've seen the video and it's—'

'I don't know, do I.' Spencer ran a hand through his long hair. 'As per Howard's instructions, I was trying to get to know Amelia. She had the best English of any of the girls. Her and her sister. I was worried about her, it's why I was there.'

'Amelia has a sister?'

'Right. Casey. They share a flat on Brick Lane. When I heard about what happened to Amelia... You told Adrian... I started worrying.'

'Sure you weren't covering your tracks?'

'Of course not.' Spencer sat back down again, gripping his knees with his bony fingers. 'It took me a while to earn their trust. Eight months I've been doing this. But Casey started to trust me. Same with Amelia. She knew more, started slipping me info, little titbits here and there. Stuff about the trafficking operation, about how these guys back home had kidnapped them both and took them by boat from Albania to Italy. There were about twenty of them, she said, but they split them up. Some stayed in Italy. Some went to Germany, some to France, and Amelia and Casey came to the UK.'

'What do you know about these Albanians?'

Spencer looked at Savage, then at Fenchurch. 'You ever come across any Albanians?'

Fenchurch shrugged. 'One or two.'

'Then you haven't.' Spencer laughed, but there was no humour in it. 'You think the Mafia are bad? Please. The Albanians have no lower limit to their depravity. They think nothing of holding a whole village hostage to influence two girls in this country. Talk about the Sword of

Damocles hanging over their heads. I'd call these men animals, but I actually like animals. They're the most-human human beings you can find, exploiting their neighbours for personal gain.'

'Just like listening to one of your chats, Howard.' Docherty sneered at Savage. 'I can see why you hired this boy.'

'Alan, this is serious.' Savage's eyes were half-closed like he was meditating. 'These gangs get away with it by exerting intolerable pressure on the people they bring to this country. The Sword of Damocles, like Christian says. These people aren't seeking a new life. This isn't a Chinese triad operation bringing people over here for a fee, or like the Cartel's activities on the Mexican border with the USA. They don't want to be here, they've been forced into this. And if they resist, their family back home will pay a horrendous price.'

Fenchurch thought it through. He knew next to nothing about the Albanians, other than they were taking over a lot of London's illicit activities. Drugs, prostitution. It all matched, at least on the surface. 'So why are these traffickers still getting away with it?'

'We're on top of this, Simon.' Savage kept his focus on his officer. 'DS Spencer here is but one small cog in the wheel.'

'And how does Mario fit into this?'

'I don't know.' Spencer looked over at Savage, like a child searching for the correct answer. 'I mean, he's as Italian as I am. Born within earshot of Bow bells and all that shit. I don't know how deep he is in this operation. Could be the mastermind, could just be some poor mug forced into it. It's not easy to find out. Designed that way.'

Savage raised himself from his meditation. 'Mario isn't the objective here. Those who transport these people from Albania are. Those who exert the pressure back home. This is a pan-European operation and we're aiming high here.'

'Fine, groovy.' Fenchurch focused on Spencer. 'None of that explains what he was doing next to that van.'

Spencer combed his fingers through his beard in silence. 'Like I told you, it's a coincidence.'

'You expect me to believe that?' Fenchurch started pacing the room. Then he stopped right next to Spencer. 'Because that van was used to kill Amelia. Smacked her into a bus and ran over her skull.' He crouched down next to him. 'I've seen the body, what's left of it. She hasn't got a fucking head.'

Spencer took a halting breath, then covered his mouth with a fist.

'And you having a butcher's at that van, well that doesn't add up for me.'

'I didn't—'

'I spooked you when I turned up at your house, didn't I? Asking questions, like I always do. You knew I'd find answers.' Fenchurch waited until Spencer looked at him. 'Why did you kill her?'

'I didn't.' Spencer shot to his feet and retreated to the corner. 'You turning up at the house... You freaked me out. You were going to blow my cover.'

'Really?' Fenchurch followed him, trying to use his superior size to intimidate him. 'Still doesn't explain why you were sniffing round the van. Or why you knew it'd be up there.'

'I didn't. I found it, just like you did. You pitched up and battered me.'

'Trust me, son, that wasn't me battering you.' Fenchurch took another step closer. 'You expect me to—'

'Listen to me.' Spencer pleaded with Savage. 'I was there because I was worried about Amelja's sister Kejsi. Casey. She works at Mario's. Her life could be at risk too.'

8

'You should've come clean earlier.' Fenchurch glanced over at Spencer in the passenger seat as they trundled down Brick Lane, now in full Sunday evening flow. A pair of drunks staggered up to the front door of an Indian restaurant and even the curry pusher was having none of it. Fenchurch pulled up in almost the exact spot as before and killed the engine. He waited for Spencer to let his seatbelt go. 'I appreciate you need to protect your cover, but seriously, you're not doing yourself any favours here.'

Spencer opened the door and planted a foot on the ground. 'You ever worked undercover?'

'Not for longer than a week.'

'Well, you can't judge me.' Spencer slammed the door and started walking.

Fenchurch got out. A warm breeze blew down Brick Lane, carrying smells of roast meat and caramelised onions. He followed Spencer at a distance, watching his body language. *Not the gait of a man with dark secrets, maybe. But a man trying to hide, a man trying to escape.* His hipster attire blended in with the drinkers outside the pub on the corner, thick woolly beards matching their fisherman's jumpers.

Spencer stared up at the flat. 'There's a light on now.'

'Not so fast.' Fenchurch tugged his sleeve, holding him back. 'Stay where I can see you.'

Spencer muttered something.

'What was that?'

Spencer pointed over at the van. 'You might want to see what forensics you've found on me.'

Tammy was working away inside the van, her masked face pressed up against the open back door.

'Stay here.' Fenchurch jabbed a finger at Spencer then paced over the road. 'Tammy, you—'

She jolted forward, cracking her face off the door, and clambered back. 'Don't do that!'

'Sorry!' Fenchurch held up his hands. 'Force of habit.' He stepped back, trying to let her calm down. 'You getting anything?'

'Just losing a few years off my life, thanks to you.' Tammy jumped out of the van and tugged her mask free. 'Having to do it all myself because of holidays.'

'You know, if this was Mick Clooney, I'd hear no end of excuses.' Fenchurch gave her a warm smile. 'I appreciate you rolling up your sleeves.'

'I can't do that, it'll contaminate the crime scene!'

'I meant—'

She laughed, wagging a finger at him. 'Got you back.'

'Touché.' Fenchurch folded his arms, grinning. Nearby, a lorry was peeping. 'You found anything?'

'Well. There are *some* forensics. Hairs, skin. Could be nothing, could be something. I'm waiting on—Aha.' She shut the back doors and waved at a lorry reversing along the narrow street, the reverse alarm sounding as it went. 'We'll get this van out to Lewisham and give it a proper going over. I'll run the forensics too.'

'I appreciate it.' Fenchurch pointed at Spencer over the road, leaning against the wall, yawning. 'Highest priority is to check against DS Chris Spencer. Works for Howard Savage. Should be on the exclusion database, but he's,' he leaned forward to whisper, 'undercover...'

'Will do.'

'Thanks, Tammy.'

She frowned. 'How's your old man doing?'

'My dad? What's he got to do with anything?'

'No reason.' Tammy blushed. 'Well, other than the work he's been doing with DCI Savage's team. The pair of them would knock on my door every couple of days, asking questions.'

'Curiouser and curiouser.' Fenchurch got out of the way of the lorry driver, who was carrying a thick tow rope over to the van. 'I'll catch you later.' He rejoined Spencer by the flat. 'You want to come up with me?'

'I'm worried she's dead.'

'Any reason?'

'Every reason.'

'Maintain your cover, okay? You're just helping me.'

'Fine.' Spencer kept looking up at the flat as he pressed the buzzer.

The stairwell door clattered open. A young woman stood there, arms folded. Hair soaking wet, like she was fresh out of the shower. 'Hello?' Heavy accent.

'Police.' Fenchurch showed her his warrant card. 'Need a—'

Her face lit up when she spotted Spencer. 'Mosé, what's going on?'

Spencer gave a flat smile. 'Casey, we should do this inside.'

∾

CASEY SAT ON A BATTERED COUCH, HEAD BOWED OVER HER LAP, CRYING hard. She swore in guttural Albanian. The sun shone over the opposite rooftop, a shaft of light crawling over the floor. A lavender scent filled the room, steam lingering in the air.

Spencer reached over and stroked her back. 'You okay?'

Casey looked up. 'Of course I'm not okay.' Anger flared in her eyes, but it slipped away, replaced by more tears, streaking her blotchy skin.

Fenchurch walked over to the window and basked in the fading glow, watching them.

Spencer kept stroking her arm with the intimacy of lovers not friends. And she nestled into him, an instinct now, not a strange sensation.

He's sleeping with her.

Shit.

Fenchurch nodded at Spencer. 'Sir, you can leave.'

Spencer kept stroking her back. 'You're sure?'

'Positive. Thanks for your help.' Fenchurch raised his eyebrows and mouthed, 'Wait outside.'

Spencer grimaced, but did as he was told, taking his time to unkink himself from Casey's embrace. He walked over to the flat door, then caught Fenchurch's glower as he opened it.

'Wait.' Casey was on her feet. 'Stay.'

Spencer looked over at Fenchurch.

'Come back.'

Casey sat again, arms clasped around her shoulders, eyes pleading with Spencer, but he settled in the seat opposite.

Knows he's been rumbled.

'I'm sorry for your loss, Casey.' Fenchurch stayed in the window, waiting for Casey to look over at him. 'But if I'm to find your sister's killers, I need you to answer my questions. You okay to do that?'

She brushed at her eyes, then gave him a steely glare. 'Please.'

'Well, did she have any enemies?'

Casey started shaking her head. And kept on doing it.

'Anyone who'd want to harm her?'

She still shook her head.

'Anyone she'd been in trouble with? Over money, maybe?'

The shaking became less intense.

'Anyone at Mario's? Maybe a colleague.'

The shaking picked up again.

Fenchurch left a pause. 'What about a client?'

She swallowed, but still didn't look up at him.

'Someone who was paying her to sleep with him, maybe? Someone who went a bit far over the line?'

'No!'

'I know what you've been doing. I'm not—'

'No!' She shifted over to sit next to Spencer, snuggling into him. 'You don't know what you're talking about.'

'I'm not judging you, Casey. I know you're being forced to—'

She screamed, burning pain into Fenchurch's ears.

'It doesn't have to be like this, Casey. I'm trying to—'

'I don't know anything.' She waved at the door. 'You should leave.'

Fenchurch rested back against the window frame. 'Casey, I just want to find out why someone would want to kill your sister.'

'Mosé?' She looked round at Spencer, pleading again.

'I don't know, Casey.'

Fenchurch sat on the opposite sofa and leaned forward. 'Casey, I know what you're being forced to do. Selling your bodies. And I know you don't have any choice in it. They took you from your home and they brought you here. I know the control they have over you.'

Casey rocked back, tears flooding her eyes. She stared up at the ceiling, at the pendant light and the peeling wallpaper, as Spencer wrapped an arm around her shoulders. 'It's not all.'

'What?'

Casey's mascara was a smudged mess. 'Mosé, tell him.'

Spencer's eyes widened. 'Tell him what?'

'What else Mario gets us to do. The special bases.'

'What do you mean by that?'

But he lost her to her tears.

Fenchurch thumped a fist off the coffee table, making Spencer start. 'You're sleeping together, aren't you?'

Spencer shook his head. 'You're talking—'

'Shut up. I see the way you touch each other.'

'I'm a very tactile person.'

'Stop lying to me.'

'It's supposed to be a secret. Mario's very funny about his staff fraternising.' Spencer let his head dip. 'Is it obvious?'

Fenchurch settled back in the seat, giving Spencer some space.

'We were very careful. Always left fifteen minutes apart. Sometimes met at my flat, sometimes here.'

'Did Amelia know?'

Spencer coiled his thick beard round his fingers, like he was weaving a rope. 'Casey swore her to secrecy.'

'Is it possible she could've blabbed?'

'Dunno.' Spencer tugged at the sleeves of his jumper. 'Maybe.'

Casey looked up at him, through a wall of tears. 'She wouldn't tell anyone.'

'Casey.' Fenchurch waited for her to make eye contact again. 'What do you mean about the special bases?'

She stared at her lover and gave a slight shake of the head.

Spencer's irises retracted. 'Shit.' Spencer slammed his head back against the headrest. 'I know what you mean.' He made eye contact with Fenchurch. 'I need to show you.'

FENCHURCH PULLED UP IN THE LEWISHAM CAR PARK AND KILLED THE engine. The wind licked at the beech hedge, making it shiver. 'You not going to tell me?'

Spencer sat in the passenger seat of Fenchurch's Mondeo, head bowed, fingers tugging at his unruly hair, sparking out like he was on fire.

'Well, I'll have to tell Savage about what you've been up to, you stupid bastard.' Fenchurch waited for him to jerk round. 'Sleeping with someone when undercover... It's wrong. You're lying to them. And I don't care what you tell yourself to help you sleep at night, it's—'

'It isn't like that.'

'No?'

'We're in love. I—'

'Have you told her you're a cop?'

'Of course not.'

'Then you're a bloody idiot. Now what the hell is going on with these pizzas?'

'Come on, I need to show you.' Spencer got out and led Fenchurch up the steep ramp to the forensics lab.

'If you're wrong about this, you know how bad that'll appear, right?'

Spencer locked eyes with Fenchurch. 'I'm not wrong.'

'I'm serious, son. I've seen undercover cops go bad before. If you think for one second—'

'Get over yourself.' Spencer leaned against the door. 'You need to sign me in. My warrant card's out at Empress State.'

SPENCER WALKED A FEW YARDS AHEAD, HIS BOOTS SQUEAKING OFF THE concourse's rubber tiles.

Over by the forensics lab door, Tammy stared into space, a deep frown clenching her forehead.

Fenchurch stopped short of her. 'You okay, Tammy?'

She grimaced at Spencer, then focused on Fenchurch. 'I was just wondering whether the DNA profiler would run faster if I wasn't in the lab to observe it.'

Fenchurch glanced at Spencer, catching a reflection of his own bafflement.

Spencer waved a hand in front of her face. 'How are you getting on with the pizza boxes?'

'Pizza boxes?' Tammy sucked in her cheeks, then blew out again. 'Preventing my team eating them has been next to impossible. Even though they've been on the ground. Had to call Mick to get approval to order in a few pizzas.'

'Sure he'll have appreciated that in Bosnia.'

'I'm lucky he had phone reception. Why are you so interested, anyway?'

'We need to check them.' Spencer set off.

She blocked Spencer getting through the door. 'My machines are very temperamental and, besides, we have very strong security protocols in place.'

'It's just the pizzas I need to check. Nothing else.'

'Fine. In here.' Tammy slid her card down the reader, still staring at Spencer, and the door thunked open. She entered the busy lab first. 'Who are you, again?'

'He's one of Savage's lot.' Fenchurch scanned the windowless space. No signs of human existence, like the machines had already taken over. Six massive boxes lined the walls. And it smelled of cheese and mushroom toasties. 'I told you back at Brick Lane.'

'Oh, you're the subject of the profile? Interesting.' Tammy lurched over to a machine in the middle of the far wall like the thing was going to bite her. She crouched low and tapped a button. 'I wonder if *your* presence will speed it up or slow it down.'

'Eh? How would—?'

'Trust me, these things have a mind of their own.' Tammy jabbed at the controls. 'Okay, let's tempt fate.' She beckoned Spencer over. 'It's quite safe. It won't bite.' She looked him up and down, grinning. 'Though *I* might.'

Spencer squinted at Fenchurch. 'Should I—?'

'Come here.' Tammy stood up tall, hand on her hip.

Spencer started on over.

The machine pinged.

'Aha.' Tammy beamed wide. 'As I suspected. Your presence ensured a higher degree of quantum entanglement.'

'Are you telling me that—?'

'No, I'm not telling you anything. You saw for yourself.'

'What does the machine—?'

'Clear.' Tammy nodded at the screen. 'Yes, you're perfectly clear.'

'Of what?' Spencer was clearly as bamboozled as Fenchurch.

'Your DNA traces were not in that van.' She looked him up and down again. 'Now, this is where I'd suggest that, if you were indeed present in the van, that you were incredibly careful to clear up after yourself.' She shifted her focus to Fenchurch. 'But there are multiple other samples, so whoever was in that van wasn't at all careful.'

'See?' Spencer looked straight at Fenchurch, teeth clenched. 'I'm innocent.'

Fenchurch joined them by the machine, but the data on the screen meant less than nothing to him.

Tammy clicked her tongue a few times. 'Now, what did you want with these pizza boxes?' She led them across to a workbench in the middle.

'Right.' Spencer grabbed a pair of gloves from the box and pulled them on with a rubber snap. Then he opened the first box. A pizza, covered in sausage rings and hunks of meat, cut into eight almost-equal slices. He took out a wedge and tore it in half, lengthways through the crust.

'What the hell are you doing?' Tammy slapped his hand and snatched the slice off him. She shook her head as she carefully placed it back in the box. 'This is completely unacceptable! Get out!'

Spencer scowled at the pizza like it had just asked him to leave. 'Shit, I swore it would've been...' He dashed past Tammy and opened another box, the pizza's cheese covered in chicken, banana and gravel. 'Here we go.' He tore it in the same way.

Tammy was trying to get at him but he was blocking her. 'What the hell are you—?'

Something fell, hitting the floor with a light thump.

'Stop!' Tammy bent down. 'What the hell?'

At her feet was a plastic bag containing a white powder.

9

'Well, well, well.' Tammy held up the bag, examining the contents closely. 'It's cocaine, I would wager.'

'Tammy, get security here.' As she dashed off, Fenchurch grabbed Spencer's wrist and pushed him to the ground, pressing his cheek against the lino. 'You knew, didn't you?'

'I just bake the pizzas!' Spencer tried to shake him off, but Fenchurch held firm. 'It's Mario! He made the bases.' He wriggled round. 'He always had two sets. I didn't know the system until Casey told us, I swear.'

Fenchurch loosened his grip, letting Spencer go. 'You knew where to look, didn't you?'

'Yeah, because I figured out the system...' Spencer stood up and started dusting himself off. 'If someone ordered a bottle of this Albanian liqueur with their pizza, they'd get Casey or Amelia round for...' He snarled. 'It wasn't on the menu, so you had to know. The girls... They weren't just delivering pizzas, right? They'd sleep with the johns and leave. If someone stopped them, they're just delivering pizzas.'

Fenchurch held up the bag. 'And what about the drugs?'

'Well, this is all slotting into place. I didn't know until you told me that. I wasn't allowed to make any orders with a stuffed crust. Mario would do that, and he'd use one of the special bases.' Spencer took the bag off him. 'Nice, thick plastic case, no dog's going to sniff through that. Might be trained not to eat pizza but... It's genius. Again, if uniform stopped them, it's just a pizza, right?'

The door opened and footsteps pounded towards them, Tammy

trailing after a bulky security guard.

Fenchurch blocked them. 'It's fine. Thanks.'

The guard grunted. 'Sure about that?'

'Sure.' Fenchurch grabbed Spencer by the wrist, yanking it hard enough to make him yelp, and led him over to the exit. 'We're going to see what your master wants to do with you.'

~

'MY WRIST'S BLOODY KILLING ME.' SPENCER WAS IN THE PASSENGER SEAT, stroking his arm. 'You didn't have to—'

'I did.' Fenchurch pulled onto Mile End Road, the long drag that'd take them back to Leman Street, that'd bring Spencer face-to-face with Savage and whatever judgement awaited him. 'There's plenty more where that came from.'

'You're a bully, you know that?'

Fenchurch hit the dashboard dial button again. Not even a ring this time before Docherty bounced the call. 'Bloody hell.'

'Let me try.' Spencer put his phone to his ear. He put it away just as quickly. 'Great.'

'You too?'

'Time was, I could call Savage day or night and he'd pick up. So what do you want to do? Bring Mario in?'

Fenchurch sped up to overtake a trundling Volvo.

Mario's one option, sure.

But I really should run this up the flagpole, as Docherty would say. Get approval from above. Air cover, and all that jazz.

He glanced over at Spencer. 'You honestly think Mario's the mastermind here?'

'I've no idea about that, but I told you about the bases. You saw what he's doing.' Spencer rubbed his wrist again. 'But you know Savage wants the evil criminal mastermind behind this whole thing. Whoever's bringing these girls over from Albania. The whole shooting match. My job was to get close to Mario and his staff. It's been *slow*, sure, but I'm getting there.'

'You've not been slow with Casey.'

Spencer punched his thigh. 'Come on, you need to drop that.'

'Don't you read the papers? There have been so many cases where pricks like you think they can sleep with whoever they want when they're undercover. You're betraying women's trust, Sergeant.'

'I know. But I like Casey. A lot. It feels right.'

'Does it feel right for Chris or for Mosé, though?'

'That's not—'

'No, Sergeant. That's the point. You're Christian Spencer. You're not Mosé Tronci. He doesn't exist. You're betraying Casey.'

Spencer prodded his screen hard, then put his phone to his ear for a few seconds. He tossed it on the floor with a sneer. 'You heard what Savage said, right? These girls were taken from their homes, brought here against their will. Pimped out. But they're smart. God, you should see how sharp they are. They trust Amelia and Casey to go into fat businessmen's homes, right? They can handle themselves, but they also know exactly what they're doing. Casey might know who runs it.'

Fenchurch pulled up at the lights. Ahead was Leman Street, Docherty and Savage. 'If she's half as sharp as you're making out, the second Casey smells a rat — and she will — she'll blow your cover. You're no use to anyone then. And while she's just lost a sister, the rest of her family is still under threat.'

'You got a better idea?'

~

SPENCER HUNG UP WITH A FRESH SIGH. 'SO WHY ARE WE HERE?'

Fenchurch waved up at the flats looming above them. 'This geezer, Colin Dunston, he ordered the chicken and banana pizza, with a stuffed crust. You know what that means.'

In the wing mirror, Nelson shuffled down the street, puffing on his vape stick, and thumped on the back seat. 'Guv, what the hell is he doing here?'

'Just marking time, Jon.' Fenchurch swivelled round. 'Did your guy check Dunston's alibi?'

'He did.' Nelson took a fresh suck on his vape stick. 'But yeah. Hard to tell if he was definitely there or not. The gym said their card machine's broken.' He held up his phone. 'Got a photo of the security log. Dunston signed in, but security's a bit lax. Could've been anyone. No CCTV.' He leaned between the seats. 'What's the plan of attack?'

Fenchurch looked up at the flat, just as a light flicked on. 'Spencer, stay here.' He snatched his mobile. 'I'm taking this.'

Spencer glowered at him. 'Really?'

'Jon, you're with me.' Fenchurch got out and led Nelson down the lane towards the flat. 'What's your take on him?'

'Not spent much time with him, guv.' Nelson thumbed back at the car. 'Undercover can drive the best officer doolally.'

'And the worst?'

'Quite.' Nelson thumbed the entrycom.

'That you, Clive?'

Nelson locked eyes with Fenchurch. 'Yeah, it's me.'

'Up you come!'

Buzz. The door opened with a deep clatter.

Fenchurch set off up the stairs, taking them two at a time. 'Let's play this cool. There's a chance the geezer could've just innocently bought that pizza.'

'Right, but who's buying a chicken and banana pizza?'

Fenchurch stopped by the door, hanging open. 'Sir?'

'Come in!'

Fenchurch gave Nelson a shrug and entered. The hallway was all beige carpet and cream wallpaper, designer furniture and high-tech equipment. David Bowie blasted out of a room — synth stabs and jerky drums. Fenchurch followed the sound into a long room, similar decor as the hall. Wooden kitchen units and wide glass windows overlooking the docks, glowing in the summer evening.

Dunston was crouched over the coffee table, using a rolled-up twenty to snort a long, long line of coke off the glass. He looked up, twitching. 'Ah, shit.'

'—MY OPERATION, HOWARD.' DOCHERTY'S OFFICE DOOR HUNG WIDE open, the sound and fury leaking out into the corridor. 'Why don't you listen to me?'

'Because I've been...' Savage clocked Fenchurch standing in the doorway. 'Simon, I didn't see you there.'

Fenchurch pushed him away and walked over to the window. 'Why weren't you answering your phone?'

'I was driving.' Savage looked over, wild eyed. 'There's this feature—'

'While you two are carving up Africa on a map, I thought you'd want to know that we've made a breakthrough in the case.'

'The drugs?' Docherty grunted. 'Aye, we know.'

Fenchurch leaned against the sill and folded his arms. 'Tammy?'

'Nothing's ever a secret, Si.' Docherty coughed hard into his fist. 'Not in this place.'

A gentle rap on the door. Nelson, frowning at Fenchurch. 'Guv, that's Dunston in custody downstairs. Lawyer on the way.'

'And Spencer?'

'In the canteen, getting a cup of tea.'

'Good work, Jon.'

'The very man.' Docherty got up from his desk and stormed over to close the door, trapping Nelson in with them. 'The name Broadfoot mean anything to you?'

Nelson scanned the room, at Fenchurch, then Docherty. 'I've got a mate of that name, yeah.'

'This mate wouldn't happen to work for the drugs squad, would he?'

Nelson avoided his gaze this time.

'Wouldn't happen to be who you told about our drug lead?' Docherty got in Nelson's face. 'Wouldn't happen to be a DCI who's on his way here to steal my bloody case?'

Nelson pulled away, but just hit his back against the door. 'Sir, I thought—'

'Sergeant, that's not your place to...' Docherty broke off with a cough. 'You couldn't keep your trap shut, could you?'

'I thought he should know.' Nelson flashed him a smile. 'You disagree with that assessment?'

'I don't disagree, *Sergeant*, but it should've been myself or Howard who informed DCI Broadfoot, not the other way round!'

'Boss, I was trying to call you.'

Docherty rounded on Fenchurch, letting Nelson squirm free. 'Aye? But only after you'd told Mr Loose Lips Sink Ships here.'

'You didn't answer your—'

The door shunted open, the wood cracking off Nelson's calf. He grimaced as he got out of the way.

DCI Derek Broadfoot stepped through, hands in suit-trouser pockets. Short, with beady eyes and the sort of tidy scissors-only haircut that made him look like he ran a nightclub. 'Al.' He nodded at Docherty. 'What's done's done, yeah? Jon's just doing what I wish half my officers would. Sharing. We're supposed to be one team in the Met, ain't we?'

Docherty exhaled slowly. 'Derek, this is my parish and I'm the bloody minister.' He prodded his own sternum. 'Me. Not you, and certainly not Howard.'

'Well, my gaffer's just been on with your gaffer. Loftus, yeah?' Broadfoot picked up Docherty's Rangers mug and spun it round his pinky. 'The higher ups are all discussing this case, trying to figure out who's eating the biscuit when they've—'

'Christ, Derek.'

'Too sick, even for you?' Broadfoot laughed. 'Al, if I was a betting man—'

'You are a betting man. Ten grand debt, wasn't it?'

Broadfoot smirked. 'When the fun stops, stop. Yeah? Well, the fun's stopping for you, Al. I'm taking over the case.'

'Aye, bollocks you are.'

Broadfoot waved his phone around. 'Should check your emails, Al.'

'Shite.' Docherty took a seat behind the desk and tapped at his keyboard. 'Ah, shite.' He deflated back in his chair, like all the air had rushed out of him. 'What's wrong with calling people?'

Broadfoot rested the mug on the edge of the table, close enough that it might fall off at any minute. 'So, boys, how we going to play this?'

Savage was tapping at his BlackBerry. 'I must insist that—'

'I don't care about all the people-trafficking shit, Howard. You're welcome to it.' Broadfoot beamed at Docherty, then at Fenchurch. 'Which leaves you pair, eh?'

Docherty pointed at his machine. 'According to this, I'm still running the murder case.' He drummed his fingers on the table. 'Right, Dawn Mulholland's your liaison, Derek. Anything to do with the drugs shite, you speak to her. But I'm keeping the murder investigation.' He shot a pointed look at Nelson. 'It's up to DI Fenchurch and DS Nelson to catch this girl's murderer. As far as I can tell, this drugs thing could be a smokescreen.'

'What? Of course it's not. This is a crucial discovery, Al. You should be proud of yourself. Your team's blown open an unknown drug and whore operation. Smart work.'

'Right.'

Fenchurch's phone blasted out *Sleep Well Tonight* by Gene. He checked the display — unknown number. 'Better take this.' He went out into the corridor to answer it, keeping the door open to see the power play going on inside. 'Hello?'

'Sir?' Lisa Bridge's voice, almost drowned out by traffic noise and light wind.

Fenchurch kept his focus on Broadfoot. 'What's up?'

'Like you asked, I'm digging into the van hire. You know the one that killed Amelia?'

'Right. Is this important? Because—'

'Here's the thing. I came to the hire company but it's shut. I've just spoken to the head office and they've given me the name of the person who hired it.'

'Derek! You can't have it!'

Fenchurch kicked the door shut. 'You going to keep me in suspense all night, Lisa?'

'It was hired by Spencer.'

Fenchurch frowned. 'You mean Mosé Tronci?'

'No, sir. Christian Spencer. The van was hired under his real name.'

10

Spencer staring at his mobile. The locked fridges hummed away, out of phase with the harsh strip lights arranged across the ceiling. Fenchurch stood over him. 'You killed her, didn't you?'

'What?'

'Amelia. You killed her. You hired the van, didn't you?'

Spencer leaned back in the chair and stared up at the ceiling. 'What the hell are you talking about?'

'Son, someone's penetrated your cover and you don't know who?'

'Simon!' Savage stomped across the canteen, fists raised. 'Get away from him!'

'No way.' Fenchurch kept his ground. 'You heard what this clown's been up to. Did you use it to kill her?'

'Simon, back off.'

'No, Howard. Why the hell didn't you hire it under your cover name?'

'We have contacts in the hire company and the paperwork will be amended to Mosé Tronci.'

'Howard, he hired a van used as a murder weapon! Just so happens that it was parked outside her flat! Just so happens that you were trying to get inside it!'

'Simon, let's be clear here.' Savage stepped between them, placing a hand on Fenchurch's chest. 'All DS Spencer has done is hire a van. It's not illegal.'

Spencer stared at his feet. 'I've not hired anything.'

'You sure about that?' Fenchurch passed him a scan of the paperwork. 'Christian Spencer. Your real name. Got yourself in too deep, haven't you? Who did it?'

'Not me!' Spencer pleaded with his boss. 'Howard, I was undercover. I'd use my fake ID, not my own name.'

Fenchurch narrowed his eyes. 'Sergeant, this doesn't look good for you. Not only have you been sleeping with someone when you were undercover, now you're—'

'Fuck off!' Spencer lurched forward and shoved Fenchurch, sending him sprawling over a table. 'You come in here and start shouting the fucking odds at me!' Spit flew and lashed Fenchurch's cheek. 'Do you know what kind of pressure I'm under? Eh?'

Fenchurch kicked out, connecting with Spencer's thigh. He barged him away, buying enough time to stand up.

Spencer jabbed a finger at him. 'You must be a special kind of stupid to think I'd hire a fucking van and kill my bird's sister with it. Is your IQ in single fucking digits?'

Fenchurch laughed at him. 'Special kind of stupid, eh?'

Spencer wasn't seeing any humour in it. His snarl worsened, his face tightening. 'I didn't drive that van and I've no idea who hired it.' He blew out hard. 'I was in the house all day, until you came round. We were... I was... I was smoking dope with Adrian and his mates. All part of my cover.'

'Not grinding coffee?'

'No.'

'Who ordered the pizza?'

'Adrian did.'

'Right.' Fenchurch stood up tall. 'Howard, I need you to keep Spencer in custody until this is sorted out.'

'Simon, that's—'

'Howard!' Fenchurch led Savage away by the arm. 'In case you weren't listening, he was shagging someone while he was undercover. This is a matter for the Directorate of Professional Standards, not us and certainly not you. We need to inform the DPS and they'll take over this investigation. Spencer needs to wait downstairs until they arrive.'

Savage paused, focusing on Spencer. 'Son, this is your chance to open up, okay?'

Spencer just sneered at him.

Savage patted his shoulder. 'Fenchurch is right, Christian. What do you know about this van?'

'I heard Mario talking about a van. He got someone to hire it. But it sounded like he was just going to the cash and carry with it.' Spencer gave him a steely look. 'I found the paperwork and called it in.'

'What?'

'Ran the plates, got a trace on it.' Spencer clawed at his beard. 'Trouble is, that van had been off the radar since just after it left the hire place.' He looked at Fenchurch. 'Just after you left the house, I received a notification. The van had passed a camera and we'd tracked it to Brick Lane. That's why I was there.'

Fenchurch clenched his fists tight. 'Why is this the first we're hearing of it?'

'I...' Spencer let out a sigh. 'You wouldn't have listened.'

'Come on.' Savage helped him to his feet and led him to the door.

Fenchurch watched them go. His pulse was racing, adrenaline fizzing in his veins. *What a pair of clowns. Up to all sorts, the pair of them.*

His mobile blasted out *Love Spreads* by the Stone Roses.

LISA BRIDGE CALLING.

He hit answer and put it to his ear. 'Lisa, you getting anywhere?'

'Sir, I've just hold of the manager of the van hire place. He's coming in to show me the CCTV.'

Fenchurch set off after Spencer and Savage. 'I'll be right there.'

BRIDGE WAS WAITING OUTSIDE TEN MILE CAR HIRE, A SMALL concession by a Tesco petrol station in the arse end of Lewisham. A row of white vans all stamped with the logo sat beside another row of Vauxhall and Toyota saloons. Brick flats as far as the eye could see, all built in the last thirty years.

Fenchurch got out of his car and started walking over.

'Simon!' Footsteps thundered across the car park towards him. Someone grabbed him from behind. 'Stop!'

Fenchurch shook Savage off. 'Is Spencer in custody?'

'That's not the bloody point.'

'Howard, I don't care. This isn't our fight. Let the DPS sort it out. Okay?'

'Simon, I assure you—'

'I said I don't care.' Fenchurch barged past and charged over to Bridge. 'Lisa, where's this manager?'

Bridge pointed at a guy limping towards them. 'Hi, Alec.'

'Got me out of me bleeding bed.' Alec opened the door and limped inside. 'On the early shift tomorrow an' all. You wouldn't believe who wants a bleeding van at five a.m.' The lights flickered on, illuminating a grimy little office. More corporate signage than furniture. 'Having a nice dream I was, but no, you had to drag me out of it, didn't you? Should've turned my bleeding ringer off, but my boss will no doubt choose that exact moment to call me and I'll never hear the bleeding end of it, I swear.' He slumped behind a desk with a deep moan. 'Speaking of the boss, he says he'd sent stuff to you?'

'That's correct. Thing is, we—'

'Wasn't that enough, eh? Couldn't this wait until tomorrow?'

Bridge leaned against the counter and gave a polite smile. 'It's urgent, I'm afraid.'

'Everything's urgent these days.' Alec gestured at the CCTV console behind the front desk. 'Fill your boots, sweetheart. I'm sticking the bleeding kettle on.' He hauled himself up to standing with a deeper moan. 'Get you anything?'

'We're good.'

'Suit yourself. Make the best tea in Lewisham, I do.' Alec trudged off through a door.

'Not the first time I've had the pleasure...' Bridge sat behind the desk and started working the machine. 'He's usually grumpier. And his tea is *disgusting*.'

Savage picked up a leaflet and flicked through it. 'This going to take long?'

'A jiffy.' Bridge clicked the mouse.

The computer screen showed the forecourt outside, dark with grey cones coming down from the street lights. A man limped towards the entrance. Alec. But another man jogged over.

'Could be Spencer, sir.' Bridge was squinting at it. 'But it's really bad quality. And this is the best we can get from it.'

'Well, it matches his story.' Fenchurch leaned back against the wall, listened to the kettle hissing in the other room. 'You not saying anything, Howard?'

Savage just stared at the screen.

'Sir?' Bridge waved in front of Fenchurch's face. 'Watch this.'

The screen filled with more footage, again outside, but an angle showing a white van driving off.

'This was it leaving yesterday morning.' She clicked the mouse and dragged the footage back to an empty forecourt. No sign of Spencer. Just a row of empty vans.

A man carried a bike onto the screen and lugged it over to the van. He dumped the bike in the back, then got in the driver seat. Seconds later, the van drove off.

Savage let out a deep sigh. 'Who the hell is that?'

Bridge switched to another screen and clicked through a list, a second window showing alternate camera angles. 'The quality's not great on that, sir. I'll see—'

'Constable, do you know where the van went next?' Savage was jangling keys in his shorts pocket.

'Just a sec.' Bridge reached below the desk for her police laptop. She opened it on the desk and started clicking at things, way too fast for Fenchurch to keep up with. 'All I have is the van parking outside that flat, not long after Amelia's death. And I can't see the driver getting out.'

'Nothing between those times?'

'Between it leaving here and that murder, it must've been parked somewhere.'

'The incident happened on Whitechapel High Street.' Fenchurch frowned at her. 'You're telling me there's no cameras between here and there?'

'There are, sir, but they're not on the network. I've not had a chance to go through the footage at the office.' She gestured around the room. 'I've been trying to get hold of the information on this hire like you asked.'

'Right.' Fenchurch exhaled slowly. 'Focus on the footage and see if you can get anything out of laughing boy over there.' Tinkling sounds came from the coffee area. 'He might have some trackers or something. Or know how to get better camera angles.'

'I'll see you back at Leman Street, Simon.' Savage marched off towards the entrance.

'Do you mind?' Alec shuffled past, steam billowing up from his tea cup, scum covering the oily surface, and he reclaimed his chair. He cracked his knuckles and snorted. 'Have a peek at this, sweetness.'

Bridge squinted at the machine. 'Who the hell is that?'

Fenchurch got between them. 'Holy shit.'

On the screen, the van driver was frozen in high definition. A chunky goatee and skinhead.

Fenchurch knew the face. *Who is that?*

Then he got it.

It was Billy Desmond, Mario's new pizza delivery guy.

11

FENCHURCH STORMED INTO MARIO'S PIZZA AND HEADED TO THE kitchen.

'Can I help you, sir?'

Fenchurch barged past Sergio and opened the kitchen door.

Mario stood by the oven, whistling to an old Dean Martin tune playing on the radio as he tossed cheese onto pizzas.

'Billy Desmond.' Fenchurch grabbed him by the shoulders and spun him round. 'Where is he?'

'Get away from me!' Mario tried to shake him off, but Fenchurch just tightened his grip. 'Help!'

Fenchurch kicked the door shut in Sergio's face and pressed Mario back against the wall, fists bunching up around his shirt fabric. 'I know what you've been doing here. I know your filthy little game.'

Mario's gaze shifted between the door and Fenchurch. Neither offered any help. 'What are you talking about?'

'Prostitution, drugs, people trafficking.'

'This is bullshit!'

Fenchurch straightened him up and stared right into his eyes. 'You paid Billy Desmond to murder her, didn't you?'

'This is bullshit!'

'You're up to your neck in this.' Fenchurch let his grip slacken off. 'Now you tell where I can find him.' He pulled him close again, close enough to taste his breath. 'Okay?'

Mario nodded.

Fenchurch let him go and he slumped back against the wall. 'Billy Desmond. An address. Now.'

'But...' Mario ran a hand down his face. 'I don't have an address for him.'

Fenchurch hauled him up to standing. 'I don't believe you.'

'Get off me! I don't know it!'

'But he works for you, right?'

'No!'

Fenchurch pushed Mario face first against the wall and pulled his arm back. 'He was here earlier, I saw you giving him a load of pizzas!'

'Shit on it...' Mario slackened off and stopped fighting. 'When Amelia died, I needed someone to deliver my pizzas. What else am I going to do?'

'So you called him in? That means you're close to him, doesn't it?'

'Desmond works—'

The door flapped open. 'Simon!' Mulholland's voice. 'Simon!' She grabbed at Fenchurch, her claws tearing at his arm. 'What the hell are you doing?'

Fenchurch didn't let Mario go, instead yanking his arm further up. Made him squeal. 'Who does Desmond work for?'

The door flapped again and Broadfoot stepped in, eyes wide. 'Christ's sake, let him go!'

Fenchurch twisted Mario's arm another notch. 'Tell me!'

'Loco!' Mario was panting hard. 'He works for Loco.'

Fenchurch let him go and passed him over to Mulholland.

Who the hell are Loco?

Mulholland snapped out her handcuffs. 'Mario Esposito, I'm arresting you for the murder of Amelja Nikolla.' She started cuffing him. 'Anything you say—'

'Dawn, are you sure you—'

Her look shut him up. *Boss's orders.*

Fenchurch stepped back and let her get on with it. He took out his mobile and googled the name. Shiny corporate logo, Wikipedia entry, photos of couriers with happy faces on bikes.

One of those new gig economy delivery companies.

With an address in Aldgate Tower.

FENCHURCH PARKED OUTSIDE ALDGATE TOWER AND CHECKED THE screen grab again, Billy Desmond taking Spencer's hired van.

You were driving that van, probably killed Amelia.

An assassination?

And where the hell do I know you from?

Fenchurch thought back to the earlier meeting in Mario's.

An older guy laughed as he shoved three boxes into a bag. Tall and skinny, the silver stubble on his head catching the light. His tight lycra shirt and cycling shorts didn't exactly hide anything. Arms and legs shaved closer than his face. He lugged the delivery bag on his shoulders and turned to face Fenchurch. A chunky goatee surrounded pink lips, the kind of thick hair Fenchurch could only dream of growing. He frowned at him but didn't say anything.

Cockney, old East End. He's not Albanian, unless they're taking on old lags. Could be anyone.

Fenchurch got out into thin drizzle. *Bloody hell. London summers ain't what they used to be.* A wide rainbow arced in the sky, way out west. *Always where the gold is.*

A car pulled up over the road and flashed its lights. Savage got out, now wearing dark grey trousers instead of shorts. 'Inspector.' He set off towards Aldgate Tower without another word.

Fenchurch rushed to catch up with him. 'You still in a huff with me?'

'Of course I am.' Savage stopped by the entrance. 'I gather that we've arrested Mario against my better judgement.' He looked up at the tower with a grunt. 'You'd better hope that DI Mulholland can get a tune out of him.'

'What she does best, Howard. What she does best.' Fenchurch gave him a smile. 'We need to plough this path, okay? There's a lot of runway left and the plane's not even taken off.'

'You really need to work on your metaphors.' Savage entered first.

An unwelcoming tunnel led over to a spangly security desk. A young woman tilted her head to the side. 'Can I help you, sirs?'

'Detective Chief Inspector Savage.' He showed his warrant card. 'Need to speak to someone in charge of Loco.'

'You're in luck, sir. They're working a Sunday.'

A humourless smile flashed across Savage's face. 'So, which floor?'

'Oh, they're part of Travis.'

'Fantastic...' Savage groaned as he set off towards the lift. 'London's favourite ride-hailing app is still trading?'

'You'd be surprised what people put up with, Howard.'

'Employing murderers?'

'Yeah but it's cheap.'

The doors shut and the lift whirred up, then opened at the next floor. Someone had pressed all the buttons and, try as he might, Fenchurch couldn't get them to cancel. So they stopped at every single floor. He kept trying.

'You seem a bit tetchy, Simon. Worse than usual.'

Fenchurch looked over at Savage, eyes narrow.

'It's about Chloe, isn't it? I know what you're going through and, despite your actions, I'm with you every step of the way.' Savage patted him on the back. 'You're going through the worst... Just the worst...'

'She won't even speak to us, Howard. Won't recognise who we are. You saw what it was like with I'Anson. She's giving us messages through some social worker, won't even meet us.'

The doors opened to another empty floor, bright and smelling of cleaning products. Not Travis's floor. Again.

'I understand. It must be horrific.' Savage hit the door close button and the lift complied. 'And I wouldn't wish it on anyone. At all. Okay? But, you need to compartmentalise this, okay? I know you can do it, because you've done it for the last eleven years. You heard Jeff — just a few more months.'

Always a few more months.

Every time we climb to the top of the hill, there's another ridge behind it. Every bloody time. It just never ends.

But maybe he's right. Maybe I'Anson can work miracles. Maybe we can get Chloe back into our lives. Just speaking to her without her pushing us away would be like climbing Everest.

Another empty floor. Another press of the door close button.

'But what if it just goes on and on? What if she moves to America? Or Australia?'

'Knowing you, you'd just follow her, wouldn't you?'

Fenchurch laughed. Couldn't help himself. 'Probably.'

'You want me to lead here?' Savage's forehead was creased with concern. 'I know you have previous with this operation.'

'It led to us finding her, Howard. That case. Bloody hell...' Fenchurch took a deep breath and stood up tall. 'I'll lead. It's still a murder, okay? Still our case.' The lift pinged and opened onto their floor. Fenchurch strolled over to reception like he owned the place. 'Is Pavel Udzinski about?'

The security guard was stuffed into a brown uniform, his bulky arms spilling out of the short sleeves like burst sausages. 'One second.' He reached for a phone and put it to his ear, then hit a button.

Fenchurch scanned the area again. Not much different from his previous visits, just a little bit more lived-in, more human, more spoiled. Past the security barrier on the left, the floor was filled with office drones, even on a Sunday. Smelled of pine air freshener and fresh espresso. Floor-to-ceiling windows at the far end looked out onto Tower Bridge, the middle section raised to let a boat through. The rainbow looked like it deposited its pot of gold either on the London Eye, the giant Ferris wheel spinning slowly over the Thames, or on the Walkie-Talkie, the accidentally car-melting skyscraper.

The guard put the handset down with a grunt and nodded to his left.

'You again.' Pavel Udzinski paced across the carpet tiles, his mirror shades catching the low strip lights, showing miniature versions of Fenchurch and Savage in the lenses. His dark hair was cut short and messed up, either deliberately or through constant stress. He'd lost his goatee, but his sideburns had stretched down to his solid jawline. 'Remember our deal? I only speak with DCI Bell?'

'Well, he's on holiday, I'm afraid.' Fenchurch rested on the edge of his desk, acting all casual. 'But I need to ask you about—'

'As per our agreement with the Mayor of London's office, the official liaison between Travis and law enforcement is via DCI Jason Bell and his team. If there's an *incident* involving one of our *co-signs*, then we need to—'

'This isn't about Travis.'

'What?' Pavel's face twisted tight. 'Then get out of—'

'It's about Loco. Your bike courier business.'

Pavel peered round at Savage. 'What about it?'

'One of your cyclists is chief suspect in a case.'

Pavel's mouth hung open. 'Then I *definitely* need a warrant. We've no agreement for the Loco business.'

'Or we're in virgin territory.' Fenchurch folded his arms. 'So I need you to—'

'No, Inspector. I won't be bullied like last time. I need you to speak to DCI Bell or, like I said, someone in his team who can—'

'Can you imagine what it must feel like to be squashed between two vehicles until your ribs crack, then to be run over so that your skull caves in?'

Pavel slumped back against the security desk.

'That's how Amelia Nicholas died.' Fenchurch stepped forward. 'She'd been chased by a van, one of your—'

'Okay.' Pavel tore off his shades. 'I will help, but we need to formalise this, okay?'

～

'HERE WE GO.' PAVEL SAT AT HIS MACHINE IN THE BUSY OFFICE SPACE AND rested his shades on the desk. Two giant monitors mounted above a fancy laptop, giving a third screen filled with emails. He typed at the laptop keyboard and the screens burst into life, inscrutable data tables and graphs. 'Who are you after?'

'Billy Desmond.' Fenchurch wheeled a chair over, but Savage stayed standing, acting like he'd rather be elsewhere. Fenchurch pulled out his notebook and opened it on the desk. 'I need to confirm his whereabouts around half one this afternoon.'

Pavel glanced round. 'We track our riders by GPS.'

'Using their phones?'

'On the bikes. We have chips on each one. They don't know, but it's for our protection in cases like this.'

Fenchurch raised his eyebrows at Savage. 'Is that legal?'

'It's in their contract.' Pavel leaned forward, typing on this laptop. 'If they don't want us tracking them, they don't have to work for us.' He hit a key and tapped at the left-hand screen, filled with a spreadsheet. 'Okay, I have him on Brick Lane at half past one.'

'That's where the van was.' Fenchurch shuffled forward in the chair, getting closer. 'And before?'

Pavel hit a few keys, then the right-hand screen filled with a map of East London. A red dot appeared over Lewisham, then turned into a red line speeding through the East End, down to Whitechapel High Street, then up to Brick Lane.

Fenchurch stood up, grinning. *Got you, you bastard.* 'Can you export this data?'

Pavel gave a reluctant nod. 'I can...'

'Please.' Fenchurch passed him a business card. 'Send it to this address.'

'I still have it from last time...'

Fenchurch put the card in his pocket. 'Okay, so where is he now?'

'Two seconds.' Pavel typed then scuttled his mouse, leaving it lying on its back. 'His tracker's off.'

'What?' Fenchurch sat with a thump. The chair skidded back a few inches. 'Does he think we're on to him?'

'No, no, no.' Pavel tapped the laptop screen. 'The trackers switch off when the rider is off duty. The bikes are partly theirs, but we install the chips and keep them topped up as part of the weekly service. Oil the chains, check the brakes, replace the transmitter's battery. We don't track them when they're off duty.'

Frightening.

But not getting us anywhere.

Fenchurch ran a hand over his mouth, thinking through the options. *Doesn't feel like there's much else.* 'Okay, last question — I need Desmond's address.'

'Of course.' More typing. 'Hmm.'

'What does that mean?'

'It's... Billy Desmond isn't his full name, though.' Pavel waved at the screen. 'It's William Desmond Webster.'

Fenchurch felt acid bubbling in his gut. 'What did you say?'

12

Fenchurch started pacing the room. 'Jesus Christ.'

Desmond Webster?

How the hell did I not recognise him?

Fenchurch searched for the name on his mobile. The screen filled with news stories of Desmond Webster back in the day.

Photos of him arriving at the court in a stretched suit. Greasy, lank hair, heavily overweight. A drawing of him getting sent down in the Old Bailey. An interview with his victim's parents, looking crestfallen outside their Essex bungalow.

He thought back to seeing Billy Desmond in Mario's Pizza. Tall, thin. Shaved head, thick goatee.

Easy mistake to make.

Webster's lost a ton of weight, shaved his long hair. Guy even looks younger. All that cycling, on top of fitness he gained in the prison gym.

But the psychopathic bastard just acted like I was someone he didn't know. Pretended it was because we're both Hammers fans.

Savage came over to Fenchurch and spoke low: 'Simon, do you know him?'

'You should too, Howard.' Fenchurch showed his phone. 'William Desmond Webster. Worked for the late, great Flick Knife.'

'He worked for Blunden?' The blood seemed to drain from Savage's face. 'You're positive?'

'One hundred percent.' Fenchurch looked him straight in the eye. 'When Flick Knife ran the East End, Webster was one of his assassins. Step out of line or stop paying and he'd shoot you. Tap, tap, tap. Mouth, heart, brain. And he's out, walking the streets again. Cycling them.' He stared at the monster's face on the screen. 'My old man put him away. One of his last big cases. Webster did a ten stretch for murdering a prostitute. I'd heard he got out last year, but...' He swallowed hard. 'Don't get my old man started on it. Guy was an assassin, but he couldn't get anything to stick. Then all he needed was a good lawyer, good behaviour, overcrowded prisons. You name it, he's back out.'

Savage perched on the edge of the desk. 'Ten years for murder is hardly paying any debt.'

Pavel frowned at them. 'He's an ex-prisoner?'

'Thought an operation like yours would love guys like him. They've paid their debt to society and all that, but nobody else will employ them.' Fenchurch focused hard on Pavel. 'I need that extract of his movements now. Okay?'

'Very well.' Pavel turned back to his machine and clattered the keyboard, muttering to himself.

Fenchurch spotted Bridge coming through the office, flanked by the bulky security guard. 'Over here.'

She rested her laptop on the desk and held out a friendly hand to Pavel. 'DC Lisa Bridge.'

Pavel shook it. 'Pleasure.' He focused on his computer again, his shades back on.

'Have you made any progress, Lisa?'

'Sort of.' She opened her laptop. 'It's not easy, though. Should have a team of six people on this.'

'You're as good as at least five, you know that.'

Bridge rubbed at her eyes. 'The Met will have to pay for me to get my eyesight fixed, I swear.' She scowled at Pavel. 'Are you looking at my legs?'

'What? No!' Blushing, Pavel pulled up a map on the left-hand screen, a red-dashed route cutting from east to west. 'Mr Webster cycled out to Lewisham, but it seems the bike was driven to Hackney.' He clicked the screen and zoomed in on a satellite map. 'Looks like garages to me.'

'Lisa, can you work with Pavel here and check if Webster was driving? Cross-reference it against street cameras, see if there's any images.'

'A lot of opportunities to swap drivers from Lewisham to Hackney.'

'Exactly.' Fenchurch focused on Pavel. 'Now, you're going to give me Webster's home address?'

'I'll need to check—'

'No. You're giving me it now.'

'I can't. Legally. I need to check with—'

'Fine. Lisa, get someone in DCI Bell's team over here.'

'Sir.'

Fenchurch stared hard at him. 'Can you call me the second Webster's tracker thing turns back on?'

Pavel thought about it. 'That I can do.'

'The *very* second. You hear me?'

FENCHURCH DOUBLE-PARKED ON A QUIET STREET IN LIMEHOUSE. YEARS ago, kids would've been out playing on a night like this. Including him. Tonight, it was just parked cars and two old women sharing gossip under a streetlight, the lamp not yet glowing. He left his hazards on and got out to cross the narrow pavement to thump on his old man's front door.

And he waited.

Nothing.

He put his ear to the door — quiet as the grave. No sign of Dad inside, no sign of anybody.

Where the bloody hell is the old sod?

He took out his mobile and checked the location again.

Says he's right here.

Wouldn't be the first time he'd left his phone at home, would it?

Even after what happened last month... I told him to keep it on him at all times. And did he listen?

Could be lying on his couch, a bottle of single malt in his belly.

Another thump, then he crouched down to bellow through the letterbox: 'Dad!'

'Here, what's going on?' Footsteps came from behind. Fenchurch's dad wandered along the street, weaving slightly. He grabbed the lamppost and scowled. 'Simon?'

'*Dad.*' Fenchurch charged over to meet him. 'I told you to keep your bloody phone on you at all times!'

'The battery was dead and I was just meeting Bert for a swift half.' Dad hiccupped. He swallowed something down then rubbed a hand over his thick moustache. 'Thought you'd know to find me in the Queen's Head.'

'I bought you that so I could make sure you...' Fenchurch got a whiff of second-hand alcohol. 'Christ, you smell like a brewery.'

'Those in glass houses...' Dad aimed his keys in the general direction of the door. Then dropped them. 'Bloody hell.' He went down in stages to pick them up, but managed to get the key in the lock at the second go. 'You want a nice cup of tea?'

'More like a very strong coffee for you.'

'An Irish one.' Dad bellowed a laugh as he led Fenchurch inside.

The flat was a mess. A square of four holes in the wall, right through the plaster. Torn-off wallpaper in two corners.

'You really need to get this place fixed up.' Fenchurch paced over to the sink and picked up the kettle, his hand shaking. 'You know I'm happy to help.'

'I told you, I'll get a bloke in to do it.' Dad collapsed into Mum's old favourite armchair, the side fabric ripped open. 'Been really busy, you know how it is.'

Fenchurch stuck the kettle on and jammed the spoon into the jar of instant coffee. It was all glued to the bottom, so he had to dig around to liberate enough for a cup. Three spoonfuls should do it. 'You got any milk?'

'Take it black, like my women.'

Fenchurch stopped pouring hot water in. 'Dad, that's not funny.'

'Sorry.' Dad pinched his nose. 'So what have I done now?' He took his coffee and blew on it. 'You okay, son?'

Fenchurch sat opposite. *Could do with a cup of tea but no milk...* 'Did you know?'

'It's one of those, is it?' Dad took a sip and grimaced. 'Simon, you've always got something going on that someone didn't know about and should've done, or they knew about it and shouldn't have. What is it this time?'

'Desmond Webster.'

'That prick.'

'Tell me. Everything. Now.'

'You got a few months?' Dad cupped his hands round the mug. 'Heard old Webster was a good boy inside. So good that he only served ten for that murder.' He took an angry sip. 'I remember going ballistic at my gaffer at the time. We *knew* he killed at least twenty people. Off the top of my head, I can still list ten victims that had his name all over them. But we couldn't get him for any of them. Compromise was we did him for murdering Diane Slocum, this prostitute who Flick Knife was running. She'd nicked some money from him, so that was it for her. But he'd been careless. We thought he'd be off the streets for good, but ten years...' He pushed his empty mug away. 'Number of people we had to put in witness protection just to get that to stick, it'd make your eyes water, Simon, I swear.'

'I need to speak to him.'

'What's he done?'

'Can't tell you that. You know that.' Fenchurch smoothed down the arm of the chair. Could still remember his mother sitting there. Still smelled of her, even after all these years. 'I've checked for his address, but it's like he doesn't exist.'

'Right, so you want me to call his parole officer?' Dad reached over to a pile of letters on the kitchen table and rummaged around. He pulled out a file and started rifling through it.

'What the hell?' Fenchurch snatched it off him. 'Have you nicked police files?'

'Don't be daft.' Dad took it back off him and put it at the top of the pile. 'I'm an old cop, son, so I keep files on stuff.' He sifted through and seemed to find what he was searching for. 'Here we go.' He tossed it to Fenchurch. 'Eddie Morris rang me up a while back. Webster's parole officer. Told me Webster was getting out and he'd caught him as a client. Only ten years, for murdering a hooker.' He shook his head and took another sip of coffee. 'Asked me if I minded doing some digging into his client for him. A regular PI...'

'What did you find, Dad?'

'Not much. I tracked down a few of those old geezers he worked with. Me and Bert met up with them, had a couple of beers, asked them about Desmond Webster...' He burped. 'You know when you've done something and you regret it but you keep telling yourself it never happened? Then you can't even remember it. Well, I swear, these guys... They lie to themselves every day of their lives and they believe it.'

'I know what you're saying, Dad. Any idea where he is?'

'Want me to speak to his PO?'

'That'd be a start. Known associates, home address, that kind of thing.'

'I'll give him a bell. He'll answer to me all hours.' Dad hauled himself to his feet and waddled over to the kettle. As it came to the boil again, he yawned wide. 'You think this is related to Chloe?'

'What?' Fenchurch frowned. 'Dad, I'm talking about Desmond Webster.'

'Ah, shit.' Dad poured more instant coffee into his mug. 'Forget I said anything.'

Fenchurch shot over. 'What are you hiding from me?'

Dad looked up from his steaming cup, his expression full of grief and shame. He eyed the door like he wanted to run, then the window like he was going to dive through it.

'Dad, what is it?'

He sucked in a deep, deep breath. 'Webster took Chloe from outside your flat.'

13

FENCHURCH LEANED AGAINST THE SINK, HIS WHOLE BODY SHAKING. 'What did you say?'

Dad shut his eyes. 'Desmond Webster. He's the one who kidnapped Chloe. Stuck her in the back of his cab. Passed her on to someone, and they passed her on, and someone heard the call over the police radio and... He was the one.'

'You knew?'

Dad just nodded.

'But we caught them. All of them.'

'No, son. You found the guy who Webster passed her on to. Howard found the woman who pretended to be her mother. But you never found the guy who took her. You didn't find Webster.'

'You knew?' Fenchurch clenched his jaw, almost biting his tongue. 'You *KNEW*?'

'That's why I put him away, son. It's how me and Bert knew all about the Machine — about what that lot were up to. That was the start of it all. But we could never get him for anything. Until I did. But he still just... He just kept quiet. Just sat there, laughing at me. He knew I knew.'

'How did you find out?'

'Word on the street, son. Desmond liked a drink. Geezer was usually very tight-lipped, but one time his shame got the better of him. And he started talking about this girl he'd kidnapped in Islington. Just a one-time thing. But one of my sources told me. Couldn't back it up, but all the times and dates fitted.' He rubbed at his chin. 'I thought I'd taken him off the street, son. I thought he'd paid the price, not for what he did, but... But no. *Ten years.*'

Fenchurch tried to process it. And failed. He started again, but it hit him in the gut. 'Why didn't you tell me?'

'What good would it have done?'

'He took Chloe, Dad. He. Took. Chloe.'

'I know, but I'll ask you again, what good would telling you have done?' Dad raised his bushy eyebrows. 'I'm asking you that honestly, son. Webster was inside, he was away. Someone might've slotted him in there.'

'We could've found Chloe sooner.'

'Really? Because I was on that case and Desmond still had all the cards, and he kept them close to his chest. And if he spoke, if he told us what happened, he would've got out, wouldn't he? There's no way someone like that's giving anything up without a deal. I decided that a life sentence for him was enough penance.'

'It wasn't life.'

'I know that. But think of the lives I saved with him being off the streets, eh? Think of that.'

'Dad, this was ten years ago. He could've led us to Chloe.'

'And maybe he'd have just shut up and sat there, laughing. Or maybe he'd have talked and you'd still be none the wiser. You know what these people are like, Simon. He'd have had ways of warning them.'

'Jesus Christ, Dad, he's killed again.'

Dad set the mug aside. 'This is why you're here?'

Rage simmered in the pit of Fenchurch's stomach, sending spasms up his legs and down his arms.

I could kick off, start throwing shit around.

But what would that achieve?

Nothing.

I'd be no further forward. I need to find Webster. Need to bring him down for Amelia's death.

Need to make him pay for taking my daughter.

I need to find him. Then I'll kill him with my bare hands.

'Dad, you need to make this right.' Fenchurch stood up tall and folded his arms. 'You need to help me find him. Start with an address.'

FENCHURCH POWERED DOWN THE MILE END STREET, HIS FEET CLIPPING the pavement. 'What's going on back at base, Jon?'

'Guv, hold up.' Nelson was struggling to keep up, toking on his vape stick. 'Load of *Game of Thrones* bullshit, guv. Wish I'd never called Broadfoot.'

'You shouldn't have.' Fenchurch stopped in the street and checked again. *Right address.* A rundown little end terrace house, two-up, two-down. Ex-council, and not well cared for. 'Follow my lead, Jon.'

Nelson blocked his path. 'Guv, you okay?'

'I'm fine.'

'You don't seem it.'

'Just follow my lead in here, okay?' Fenchurch knocked on the wood. The white paint had half flaked off.

Chart pop played on a speaker somewhere inside. Footsteps got louder, along with someone singing out of tune. The door opened and a young woman peered out. Early twenties, maybe late teens. Bottle-blonde hair tugged back in a ponytail. Baggy tracksuit bottoms and a crop top showing way too much flesh. 'What?'

Could be a trophy wife, could be his daughter.

Either way, Fenchurch smiled at her. 'Is Desmond in?'

'He ain't.' She hugged the door frame, keeping the crack as narrow as possible.

'Know when he'll be back?'

She shrugged. 'He's out on his bike. Could be any time. Last week, he cycled out to Southend. *Miles,* that is. He's mental.' She laughed, her mouth hanging open.

Laughing is good. Means she trusts me.

'You his partner?'

'Hardly.' A genuine laugh this time, no teen snark. 'I'm his daughter.' She held out a hand. 'Holly.'

'Simon.' Fenchurch shook it. 'Didn't know he had a daughter.'

'Neither did he.' Holly winked. 'You want to come in and wait? Get you a cup of tea or something?'

'Nah, we need to shoot, Holly. But if you could give your old man a bell, that'd really help us out.'

'I'll let him know.'

'It's kind of urgent.'

'Sure. How about I call him?' Holly disappeared inside.

'Guv, this isn't right.' Nelson had his mobile out. 'You're playing her.'

'Stay here, then.' Fenchurch followed Holly inside, leaving Nelson on the front step. The house was even grottier inside. Stank of stale chips and cat piss, though there was no sign of the little buggers. He stepped into a large living room, a row of battered kitchen units taking up one wall. Stairs led up, washing hanging over the banister. A monster TV blared out some YouTube channel, a young woman talking to the camera as she applied makeup. The smoked-glass coffee table was covered in powders and lotions.

Holly muted the telly and put the phone to her ear. 'He's not answering.'

'Tell you, he used to be a right bugger for not answering. Could never get hold of him.'

'Never knew him back then. Grew up without a dad, you know?'

'Must've been hard.'

'You get used to it.' Holly slumped down on a sofa, resting her feet on the small patch of coffee table not covered in makeup. 'Mum and her sisters used to say how she never knew my father, that he was just some bloke she met in a club. A one-night thing. But she knew him. Course she did.' Her grimace was cut off with a gasp. 'Daft old cow died of cancer few years ago. She was lying there in a bed.' She pointed at the window. 'Dying at home with *dignity*, thin as a skeleton... And she told me who my father was. Went out with him for a year, that cow did. Never even told him she was pregnant.' She leaned forward, arms folded across her chest. 'I tracked him down, found him in prison. Didn't put me off, you know? That's my old man. All I've got left. I was only sixteen when...' She let out a sigh. 'When Mum died. And I wanted to meet him. My old man. My father. So I went in and met him.' She smiled, broad, seeming genuine. 'And we got on like a house on fire. He's a good bloke. I know he did wrong, with... that bird all those years ago. He said it was a mistake, said he's trying to turn a corner.'

'I heard. Mutual acquaintance said he's a bike courier now. That true?'

'Like I say, can't get him off the thing. Tell you, it's been good having him around. Not easy raising my little girl on my own.'

Fenchurch covered his shock with a laugh. 'He's a grandfather?'

'I know. He's not even that old, is he?' She tugged at her ponytail, draping it over her left shoulder. 'He's been a lifesaver. Looked after Sandy a few weeks ago, let me catch up with some old mates. Been *ages* since I did that. Good to let me hair down.' She pushed her ponytail away.

'Always was a kind soul when he put his mind to it.'

'He's been great. And having some money's been great too. I mean, things were tight. New start for him. For both of us.' She looked over at Fenchurch again. 'I'm taking Sandy to see her old man next week. Kirk's in Belmarsh.'

Repeating her mother's life. Christ...

Fenchurch got to his feet and wandered around. 'It's important we speak to Des. Holly, back in the day, your old man would disappear for a bit every so often. Go on a bender, end up in some casino out west, or in some drinking den south of the river.'

'He's a changed man. Doesn't even touch it these days.'

'It wasn't the drink that was the problem.' Fenchurch tapped his left nostril. 'He used to call it bugle.'

'He ain't touching that shit any more. Cleaned up inside.' She folded her arms and eyed him differently, like she suspected him of something, just not sure what yet. 'How did you know him again?'

Fenchurch reached into his pocket for his warrant card.

A baby started crying in another room.

'Sorry, I'll be right back.' Holly stood up and left him.

Fenchurch kept his warrant card in his pocket.

I need to find him, and soon. He could be headed to France or Morocco or anywhere.

Below the wall-mounted TV, a row of framed photos lay in a wiggly row on the mantelpiece. One in the middle had Webster, post-prison physique, sitting in a café with Holly, resting a blonde baby in a pink jumpsuit on his lap and grinning like he hadn't murdered at least twenty people.

If he was going to run, he wouldn't leave these two behind.

Holly came back down, carrying the baby from the photo. She'd grown, but still wore the pink suit. 'You still here?'

'Really need to speak to him, Holly. That's all.'

'He in trouble?' She sneered at him. 'You're Old Bill, aren't you?'

Fenchurch showed his warrant card. 'Just want a—'

'Well you can fuck off! Get out!'

'I'm worried for him.'

She hugged Sandy tight. 'What?'

'Some people are after him. People from his old life. I need to speak to him.'

'I told you the truth. Wish you'd done the same with me.' She kissed Sandy's head. 'This about the money?'

Fenchurch frowned. 'I've heard about that, yeah.'

'Shit.' She perched on the edge of the sofa, rocking Sandy. 'He said we could go on a holiday to Spain. He went to Santa Ponsa with my mum, few months before I was born. Wanted to take me and Sandy back there.'

'Where did he get the money from?'

'He said it was some old mates of his.' Holly stared at her daughter. 'Quite a lot of money, half up front. What's he done?'

'It could be that this money comes from some old mates who are less than good people. Or it could be those mates heard about his windfall and want a piece of it. I just want to help your old man. He ever mentioned any names?'

'Never.' Her right eye twitched. Maybe fear, maybe nerves. 'Find him for me.'

FENCHURCH SHUT THE GARDEN GATE AND SET OFF DOWN THE ROAD towards his car. 'What does money half up front sound like to you?'

'Could be a hit.' Nelson walked alongside, thinking it through for a few seconds. 'Then again, lots of people have gone freelance these days. Could be anything. Half up front doesn't mean it's for shooting someone.'

'With Webster's history, though?' Fenchurch unlocked his car. 'He's not exactly writing for the *New Statesman*, is he? A leopard never changes his spots.'

'It could be a book advance. True crime shit.'

'You think?'

'No. You think it was for Amelia, don't you?'

'Need to check into it.' Fenchurch stared back at the house, saw the silhouette of Holly holding Sandy through the blinds. 'Holly seems like a good kid. Messed up, like a lot of them.' His gut churned again. 'I worry about girls in her situation. Her baby's father's inside, God knows what for. They never seem to realise that the handsome geezer they let into their knickers is a total scumbag. Wish I could get rid of men, sometimes.'

'Assuming we're both still around, it'd make our roles a hell of a lot easier.' Nelson laughed. 'Can't even think what it must be like for her. For them.'

Fenchurch waved at the gentrified streets around them. 'These areas are coming up, but not for people like Holly, and not for her daughter. The council will shunt them out into Essex at the first opportunity. Knock this lot down and sell it to some bankers or management consultants fresh out of Oxbridge. How's that helping the people of London?'

Nelson raised his eyebrows. 'You don't sound like a policeman, guv.'

'The worse this bloody city gets, the more angry I get. Used to be anyone could buy a flat round here. Saw the other day you need to be on a hundred grand a year to buy a little shithole in Hackney. Can you imagine it?'

'And you're sitting on a nice little investment in the Isle of Dogs...'

'Yeah, and no bugger's buying it.'

'Sure it's not you wants to shunt out to Essex?'

'Not Essex, no, but... Abi's talked about Kent, maybe. I dunno. We can't even think about it until this shit with Chloe's sorted out. And the baby on the way...'

'A wise move. Speaking of which, what now?'

Fenchurch unlocked the car and opened the door. 'We could head back to Leman Street, maybe. Brief Docherty.'

'You'd rather lose a bollock than do that.'

'Maybe.' Fenchurch stared into the middle distance. The night breeze picked up the faint pop melody from Holly's house.

'What's happened?' Nelson was sucking on his vape stick again. 'You look like you're going to kill someone.'

Fenchurch stared at the ground. A puddle had formed on the pavement, from the earlier downpour. No pots of gold out this way.

'You were with your old man, weren't you?'

Fenchurch looked up at Nelson.

But his phone blasted out. Sex Pistols, *Pretty Vacant*.

DAD

'Just a sec, Jon.' Fenchurch put it to his ear. 'Dad?'

'Simon, I've just spoken to Eddie Morris, Webster's parole officer.'

'And?'

'Had a little chinwag, you know how it is. Says Webster's doing well. Been out a year, not slipped once. Never even put a line on at the bookies. Had another PI on it too, not just me. Got himself a decent enough job at Loco, cycling around and delivering pizzas or something. Lot of his guys do that. Lets them get back on their feet, see a bit of the city rather than the insides of a choice boozer.' A sigh rasped the speaker. 'Said Webster had turned a corner. His baby mother died when he was inside and he changed his life around. Got fit, discovered fasting and meditation and all that Buddhist shit.'

'All very good, Dad.' Fenchurch leaned back against his car. 'He give you any idea where he could be?'

'Not really, sorry. There's a Tibetan meditation centre up the Holloway Road.'

'Dad, this isn't the time for—' Another rumble in his hand. Fenchurch checked the display. Unknown number. 'Sorry, Dad, I need to take this. Thanks. And call me back if you get anything else.' He ended the call and took the other one. 'Hello?'

'Hello, it's Pavel from Loco. I've got Webster's location.'

14

FENCHURCH SHIFTED DOWN AND TOOK A HARD RIGHT, POWERING DOWN the narrow street, desperately searching the road for cyclists. 'Where is he?'

Nelson sat in the passenger seat, grabbing hold of anything as he was thrown around. 'There!'

The Royal London Hospital loomed over them — the giant blue mosaic tiles glowing in the fading light. The side road was blocked off with bollards, a lone cyclist powering through.

Webster, standing on his pedals to look back at them.

And they couldn't follow him.

Then he was gone, lost to the night.

Fenchurch stuck the car in reverse and whizzed back the way they'd come, swerving to avoid a smoker in a wheelchair.

'Just a sec.' Nelson reached over and pressed buttons on the stereo. 'Hello?'

'Hello?' Pavel's voice burst out of the dashboard speakers.

Fenchurch revved the engine as he thundered back towards Whitechapel Road. 'Get me an update on Webster's location, now!'

Pavel tapped away in the background, his keyboard sounds clicking loud. 'I really need to head home, but—'

'I'm not in the bloody mood for this!' Fenchurch swung round the corner, then hit sixty as he overtook a pair of buses. 'Where is he?'

'Okay, okay. He's heading east along Mile End Road.'

Fenchurch swerved left into the bus lane and powered past a Range Rover. 'Can't see him.'

'He's heading north on... Don't know how to say it? Cephas?'

'Got it. Cephas Avenue.' Fenchurch hit the brakes and tugged the wheel left, hurtling over the wrong side of the road. Managed to avoid hitting anything.

No sign of Webster, but his house was halfway along the street.

Fenchurch screeched to a halt and tumbled out, hitting the tarmac running.

Lights on downstairs, music bleeding through the windows. Holly stood there, her lips moving in sync with the song.

A squad car pulled up across the street and Bridge jumped out, a couple of male DCs following.

Fenchurch waited on the pavement, heart racing, scanning the street for any signs of Webster. Nothing.

Bridge joined them. 'You see him?'

'Not yet.'

Bridge pointed at the house. 'There's a squad car in place in the street behind.'

'Good.' Fenchurch nodded at the male DCs. 'Okay, you two, stay here. Jon, sit in the car in case he scarpers.'

'Guv.' Nelson jogged back to the idling Mondeo.

'Lisa, you're with me.' Fenchurch waited, blood thudding in his ears, watching until Nelson got behind the wheel. 'Okay, let's do this.' He led Bridge up to the door and knocked. 'I promised you I'd get you away from the CCTV.'

'Gee, thanks.' Bridge rolled her eyes. 'I'm kidding. This is good.'

Another knock.

The door opened and Holly glowered at them, rocking the baby in her arms. 'What now?'

'Holly, where is he?'

'Get out!'

Fenchurch stepped inside, blocking her slaps with his forearm, keeping her at arm's reach. 'I know he's here.'

'Get out!' Holly slapped his face, like hitting water from the top diving board. 'Get out of here!'

Bridge grabbed Holly's wrist and took the baby in one fluid movement.

Fenchurch charged through the house. The large kitchen-living room was still a bomb site.

Two doors.

The first was a small bathroom, empty, but the cistern filling up.

The second was a utility room, empty, with a washing machine rolling its drum round. A big cupboard dominated the space, big enough to hide a man, even Webster.

Fenchurch snapped out his baton and poked it open.

An ironing board fell out, clattering off the lino.

Fenchurch stomped back through. Holly was now sitting on the sofa, cradling the baby.

Bridge stood over her, blocking any attempt at an exit. She held an Airwave radio in her hand. 'DS Nelson says there's no sign of him outside, sir.'

'You can't do this!' Holly hugged her daughter tight. 'He's not here!'

'I like to see things with my own eyes.' Fenchurch took the stairs two at a time.

Three doors.

The first was a bathroom. He flicked the shower curtain aside — Webster wasn't lying in the bath.

Back in the hallway, he tried the next door. A bedroom, filled with a super-king, just a narrow path separating it from the wall. IKEA chests filled the opposite wall.

Nowhere to hide, except...

Fenchurch dropped down onto all fours and checked underneath the bed. Not there, either. He jumped back up to standing and went back out into the hall.

The third door hid a smaller bedroom, barely furnished. An exercise bike rested by the window, cold and dry, no tell-tale signs of sweat or anything. The bed was solid, made out of shipping pallets. No space underneath, either.

Fenchurch sifted through the crap on his bedside table: bills and Post-It notes and so on. Nothing to indicate where Webster might be. He stormed out and skipped down the stairs.

Holly held Sandy at arm's reach, the baby screaming at her mother. 'You've woke her up, you pig bastards.'

Fenchurch stood over her. 'Where's your old man, Holly?'

'He's not here.'

'I can see that. Where is he?'

'I don't know. He says it's best if I don't.'

Fenchurch crouched in front of her, making eye contact. 'Holly, we've got reasonable suspicion that your old man murdered someone, okay? Before we put him away, ten years ago, he worked for a nasty piece of work. He was an assassin. He murdered people in cold blood.' He let it settle in but it didn't seem like she was even listening, let alone caring. 'Now, this job he was doing for some old mates, just so happened to be around the same time he hired a van that was used to squash a girl against a bus. Doesn't take too smart a person to figure out what that work actually was, does it?'

Holly slumped back in the sofa.

Bridge took the baby off her again, without a fight this time.

'This is your chance to help us, okay? Your father's killed someone. I don't know who he's working for, but he's probably doing it for you and Sandy.'

Holly flinched.

'I'm not saying you're involved, Holly, but your old man killed a girl. She was about the same age as you.'

Still nothing.

'Only, this girl and her sister were taken from their homes in Albania. Forced to work as prostitutes, forced into dealing drugs to people. If they so much as looked at their boss funny, their family back home would be slaughtered. But your old man killed her. He smashed her between a van and a bus, Holly. There's nothing left of her head.'

Holly gasped. She stared at her daughter, then back at Fenchurch. 'What do you want from me?'

'Your old man—'

Something clattered outside. Bins knocked over.

Fenchurch shot over to the kitchen window.

Webster was lugging his bike along the path.

The man who took my daughter.

Right there.

Right fucking there.

Fenchurch ran over to the door. 'Lisa, stay here!' He piled outside and paced down the side of the house, trying to keep quiet.

But Webster was getting on his bike, lifting his left leg over the crossbar, then down onto the pavement. He hit the pedal and wobbled off.

Fenchurch swiped with his baton. Caught clean air.

Webster raced off down the street, knees pounding away, in and out of streetlights. Then he hopped down onto the road and sped up.

Fenchurch tried to run faster, but he was chasing a man on a bike. *Maybe I can throw my baton?*

Behind, a car engine revved and Fenchurch dived out of the way, sprawling over the bonnet of a Fiesta. He looked at the road as his Mondeo clattered into Webster, sending him flying across the tarmac.

Fenchurch darted off, catching up with the car just as Nelson got out.

Webster hauled himself up to standing and took one look at his discarded bike, then sprinted away from them. He was holding his shoulder.

Fenchurch sprinted off after him, all his rage building up in his head.

You fucking animal.

You took my daughter. You ruined my life. Stole years. Made someone else raise her.

His feet thumped the road, every step jolting up his spine.

And she doesn't speak to us. The sweetest girl in the world, twisted into a young woman who hates her parents.

All because you took her, you craven fuck!

He closed on Webster, metres away, then centimetres.

You worked for the worst people alive. Took a child from her life, from her parents, from her world.

For money.

Fenchurch launched himself into the air and smacked into Webster's shoulder. A scream tore out into the night air. Loud, like a trapped animal.

Fenchurch lay on Webster, then got up first. He kicked Webster in the face, he pushed his shoulder against the kerb.

Another scream.

Then Fenchurch grabbed Webster's lycra shirt, panting, breathing hard, and got in his face: 'You fucking animal. You took my daughter!' He gripped Webster's ears and bounced his skull off the pavement with a sickening crunch.

15

FENCHURCH WAITED IN THE CORRIDOR, SIPPING MACHINE TEA FROM A beige plastic cup, his hand shaking.

Face-to-face with a monster, the vermin who took our girl. The animal who deserved to die.

But he's finally in a cell, being checked over by the duty doctor.

Did I go over the line there?

No. Nowhere near. Webster deserves to die, deserves to swing for what he did to us. For what he's done to countless others, as well.

He got off lightly here.

Fenchurch's phone throbbed in his trouser pocket. He took another shaking sip of tea as he checked the display. Missed calls and unread texts from Abi stacked up on the screen. He hit dial. The ring tone drilled against his skull.

'We're sorry but the person you're calling is unavailable.'

Fenchurch exhaled slowly. Took another sip, spilling a dribble onto the carpet tiles.

'Please leave a message after the tone.'

'Abi, it's Simon. Sorry, I just saw your messages. Give me a call.' Fenchurch put the phone away and took his tea into the Obs Suite.

Broadfoot rested against the wall in the far corner, narrowing his eyes at Fenchurch.

Fenchurch took a seat in front of the giant display, split in quarters to show different angles of the interview.

Mulholland filled the two left-hand panels. Arms folded, feet crossed at the ankles, sitting next to DS Uzma Ashkani. 'Mr Esposito, you're going away for a long time.'

In the top right side, Mario sat next to a male lawyer, scratching at his stubble. He looked like he'd been taken from the trenches, shell-shocked and brutalised. He didn't respond to Mulholland, didn't even acknowledge that she'd said anything.

Mulholland smoothed out a sheet of paper on the table. 'We finished searching your restaurant. Three kilos of cocaine under the sink. Not very well hidden. I assume there's more?'

Still nothing, just Mario giving his thousand-yard stare. Could be practised, like he'd been trained by someone senior in the people-trafficking operation. Could also be that *he* was that someone, sitting at the top of an empire, brutalising the innocent and the guilty alike. Or it could be that he was one of those innocents, coerced into drug-running and prostitution.

'My team is searching your factory in Hackney.' Mulholland stared up from the sheet of paper, wetting her lips. She gave him a few seconds. 'What will they find?'

Again, nothing.

Fenchurch looked into the corner. 'She's getting nowhere, right?'

'That how it seems.' Broadfoot stayed focused on his phone, staring at the glowing screen in the dim room. 'Doesn't really matter, though. We've got him on countless drug charges. We've picked up five of his couriers, all Albanian nationals. Just awaiting lawyers, then we can get in and about them. And that factory in Hackney is a treasure trove, I swear. I just know there's a ton of drugs there.'

'Feel it in your water, right?'

Broadfoot gave Fenchurch a withering look. But the draw of the mobile pulled him back, his thumbs tapping away at whatever was going on elsewhere that was much more important than the interview unfolding on the screen.

Fenchurch waved at the display, not that Broadfoot noticed. 'Doesn't seem like Mario's folding.'

'He doesn't need to, Inspector. We have way more than enough evidence to convict him.'

'Has Dawn asked about the people-trafficking?'

'That's Howard Savage's purview. He's getting my sloppy seconds.' Broadfoot sniggered, looking over at the door. 'Heard you caught Desmond Webster?'

'Just waiting on his lawyer.' Fenchurch checked his phone, still no word. 'You know him?'

Broadfoot gave a curt nod. 'I was on the case that put him away. A DC at the time, wet behind the ears and all that. Me and Dawn Mulholland were partners.'

'So you go back?'

'Oh yeah. I know her.' Broadfoot locked his gaze on Fenchurch's and held it for a good few seconds. 'Never put your trust in her.'

'I don't.'

Broadfoot's steely expression softened to a tight smile. 'Good.'

Fenchurch folded his arms, trying to reflect the smile. 'Any chance you can give me a couple of minutes with Mario?'

Broadfoot was back at his phone, frowning at some piece of news from elsewhere. 'Why?'

'Like you say, I've got Webster, but I've also got a shitload of questions. He's killed this girl, that's pretty obvious, but I want to know who he's doing it for.'

Broadfoot thumbed the phone again. 'You don't think he's the big bad wolf?'

'No, I don't. But I think he knows who is.'

Broadfoot stretched out like a dog getting up from its bed. 'Come on, then.' He traipsed out into the corridor with a yawn.

Fenchurch followed, catching up as Broadfoot knocked on the door.

The door creaked open and Mulholland peered out into the corridor, settling a glare on Fenchurch, then on Broadfoot. 'Sir?'

'Need a word, Dawn.' Broadfoot stepped away from the door and beckoned her out. He gestured for Fenchurch to go in.

Mulholland stood her ground, arms wide. 'Sir, this is *my* interview.'

'And Si's just keeping your seat warm, that's all. Come on.'

Mulholland folded her arms. Still didn't get out of the way. 'Do I have a choice?'

'Let him make an arse of it, Dawn.' Broadfoot winked at her. 'Thanks.'

She grudgingly shifted to the side, finally letting Fenchurch push past into the interview room.

Ashkani glanced round at the door, then did a double take, eyebrows raised. Her black hair was pulled back in a tight ponytail, but her forehead creased enough to slacken it off. She leaned into the microphone. 'DI Simon Fenchurch has entered the room.'

Fenchurch stayed standing, resting his weight on the chair next to Ashkani. He stared at Mario, gave his lawyer a broad smile. 'Good news. Webster's in custody.'

Mario slumped back in his chair. He didn't give any eye contact.

Fenchurch rounded the table and towered over him. 'We know he killed Amelia.' That got his attention, but Mario broke off eye contact quickly. 'The only thing missing is who Webster's working for. Was it you?'

Mario just sat there, his jaw clamped shut.

'See, I don't think it was you. The way I see it, there's someone pulling your strings. Same with Webster.' Fenchurch left a long pause. 'I just want to help, Mr Esposito. Just want to find out who's been terrorising you. And I want to take them down.'

Still nothing.

'You should know how this works. If you're not as deep in this as you seem to be, you can help us and we can help you. You could get out with no time served. Maybe even get a new identity. Maybe even get a medal.' Fenchurch waited for eye contact. 'All depends on what you give us. I need your help. I need you to put your cards on the table.'

Muscles along Mario's jaw pulsed in a chaotic rhythm. His nostrils twitched. 'Like it's that easy.'

'So you know?'

A tight shake of the head.

Because you don't know or because you don't want to say?

Or because you can't?

Fenchurch took his seat next to Ashkani and gripped the table edge. 'I sympathise with you. I've been working these streets a long time. I've worked murders for years, but what gets to me every time is all the shit that causes murders. A slight domestic turns into two dead bodies? Bread and butter to me. I'll catch them. But I have to mop up when gang shit spills out into the real world. When innocent people are snuffed out by evil scumbags like Flick Knife.'

Mario blinked, hard and fast, matched by his breathing. 'Frank bloody Blunden...'

'You knew him then?'

Mario ran his tongue over his lips.

'How well?'

Mario looked away.

'Come on, mate. You're in deep, deep trouble here. We found a ton of drugs in that restaurant. You know how much we'll find up at your factory. It's in your best interests to spill. Now, what was Blunden making you do?'

'You think it's that easy?' Mario stared into space, still shaking his head. 'I can't.'

Mario's lawyer was similarly unmoved.

Fenchurch whispered to Ashkani: 'Is the lawyer legal aid?'

'Top of the duty list, yeah.'

'Definitely not bent?'

'As far as I know.'

Fenchurch gave her a nod. 'Confession's good for the soul.'

Mario slouched back with a gasp. 'This isn't who I am. Okay? I've been running a pizza restaurant for twenty years. I deal with drunks. I deal with rugby teams smashing the place up. And I fix it up, all the bleeding time. And I start again. Every time, for ten years.'

'But...?'

Mario rubbed his forehead, but he let out a sigh. 'Ten years ago, these men came in, they said they worked for Flick Knife. And I... I knew the name. Heard all about him. They tell me how it's going to be. At first it was protection money. You know, pay them a few hundred quid a week and my windows are fine. Skip a payment and they're smashed in.' He snarled. 'I told them I'm not paying. The next Sunday afternoon, my restaurant's busy, full of people. And they smashed my windows in. Of course, they made it seem innocent. A kid on a Lambretta crashing into it. And I saw this man hanging around oppo-site. The one who'd been in.' He shut his eyes. 'And I started paying.'

'Thanks for that.' Fenchurch waited for Mario to open his eyes, then gave a generous smile. 'I know how hard that must be to admit.'

Mario sucked in a hollow breath. 'Thank you.'

Fenchurch did some calculations in his head. *Flick Knife died a month ago, but Spencer had been working there, what, ten months? Meaning there was smoke before whatever fire was currently burning his soul.*

'It wasn't just protection money, was it?'

'What?'

'You were doing other things for him?'

'Blunden, he... He told me to put drugs in my pizzas, told me to... I told him where to go, next thing I know there's a fire in my kitchen. I put it out, but... I thought about talking to you lot.'

'Why didn't you?'

'Didn't get a chance.' Mario scratched at his stubble. 'Blunden paid me a visit himself. Wearing this snakeskin suit, he was. And he got me... dealing drugs for him. I had no choice. He threatened my family and I knew he'd follow through on a threat. Five years I'd been doing that.'

'You could still have come forward.'

'Like you'd protect me.' Mario covered his face with his hands. 'When Blunden died... I thought I'd be free. I thought that was it. But the very next day, another man comes in. Said he's running things now.'

Fenchurch felt his pulse jolt. 'Who was it?'

'I don't know his name.' Mario flared his nostrils. 'I didn't see him again, this geezer. But he knew exactly what I'd been doing for Blunden and he offered me a way out. I just had to work for him, keep doing what we'd been doing, but...' He rasped at his stubble. 'I had to do a few other things. He called them favours. These girls and boys, his people, I had to employ them as delivery cyclists for my pizzas. But I knew what they were delivering. And I had no choice.'

'This guy ever come back?'

'I never saw him again. After that, he sent people. Every Monday, nine o'clock. The same people, nasty people.' Mario laughed, but it seemed nervous rather than humorous. 'Delivery, you know? A few bags of flour, but you know what was really in it. And I had to give him money.'

Fenchurch let him wallow in his own filth for a bit, let him realise how deep he was into this. 'You could've come to us. At any time. You could've been honest with us. You could've told us what was going on. You'd get a reduced sentence in exchange for knowledge.' He left another pause. 'And we could've saved Amelia's life.'

Mario jerked forward, elbows clunking the table. His body rocked.

'You've still got a chance, Mario. Who was it?'

'I can't tell you.' Mario still hid behind his hands, his voice thick with tears. 'He's threatened my family.'

Fenchurch stared hard at him until he made eye contact. 'Just a name.'

The door opened. Fenchurch craned his neck round and saw Broadfoot stood there, eyebrows raised.

Time's up...

Fenchurch joined him in the corridor.

'You're getting nowhere, Fenchurch.'

'That's what you took from that? We know he's been threatened. Twice now. Five more minutes and he—'

'No chance.' Broadfoot patted him on the arm. 'You did really well to get him to admit to that.' He gave a snide look to the side.

Mulholland lurked in the Obs Suite doorway, watching the screens, but clearly listening to their exchange.

Broadfoot cracked his knuckles. 'Much as it pains me to admit it, you've done much better than we've managed so far, but I don't think Mario knows anything more. Either way, I'm taking over. Let's see if I can't get the truth out of him.' He slouched off into the interview room.

Fenchurch stared at the closing door. 'You okay, Dawn?'

'What do you think?' She shut the Obs Suite door.

I should follow her in, talk to her. Be the big man, rise above it all. But I can't.

He caught Tammy wandering down the corridor, a distant look on her face like she'd just found out she was in a parallel universe. 'You okay?'

'Mm? Oh, yes. Yes, I'm fine.' She focused on him, like she was back on this side of the quantum divide. 'Very fine. It's just that... Well, I've found an anomaly on the forensics.'

'Oh?'

'There are sufficient DNA traces in the van to suggest that Webster was in the van.'

'That's good. Thanks.'

'But he was also accompanied by a Terence Oldham.'

Fenchurch frowned. Meant nothing to him. 'You any idea who this geezer might be?'

'Your father might know.'

'Come again?'

'Well, he arrested him twenty-five years ago.'

Fenchurch exhaled slowly. 'Okay, thanks for that.' He watched her walk off.

Terry Oldham. Who the hell was he?

The door to interview room four clunked open and Savage barrelled out, staring at his BlackBerry. He looked up and scowled. 'Simon.'

Fenchurch looked in and saw Spencer sitting there before the door closed. 'You getting anywhere with Spencer?'

Savage evaded his gaze. 'A final briefing. It's with the DPS now.'

'Right place for it.'

'Well, yes. But now it's done, I'm free to prosecute Mario for this people-trafficking.'

'Good luck grabbing that from Broadfoot's cold, dead hands.'

'I have ways and means.' Savage snorted. 'What's of greater import right now is that, now Flick Knife has left this mortal coil, there's a new broom. Someone with a new MO. A much darker one.'

'Mario was talking about him.'

'I know. I watched your performance in there.' Savage thumbed at the Obs Suite. 'Bravo.'

Fenchurch's neck burned.

Savage set off towards the door to room six. 'Mr Webster's lawyer has arrived.'

16

DESMOND WEBSTER OCCUPIED THE INTERVIEW ROOM LIKE HE OWNED the place. Been inside one more than enough. Probably even this very room a few times. His head bandage softened the hard man image slightly, virgin white fabric wrapped around the back of his skull like a footballer who'd just had a nasty head knock.

Dalton Unwin sat next to him, his tailored suit straining as he reached down for a black leather notebook. He took his time to unfold it on the table, then gave Fenchurch a weary look. 'You're lucky nobody saw what you did to my client.' Spoken in a rich, plummy Oxbridge tone.

'It was a standard arrest.' Fenchurch smiled at Webster. 'Glad to know you're not concussed. Means I can interview you now rather than next Tuesday or whatever.' He leaned across the table. 'Let's start with where you were yesterday at five o'clock.'

'At home.'

'Really?' Fenchurch placed a pile of photos in front of Webster. 'You didn't drive this van?'

'Nice looking fella, but it ain't me.'

'Really? Where were you?'

'Someone tell you I was there?'

Fenchurch tapped the photo again. 'This is you.'

'You'll need better proof than that, mate.'

'We've tracked your movements to the van hire place in Lewisham.' Fenchurch pointed at the photos again. 'You were driving that van.'

Webster leaned back in his chair. 'I know I've been inside and missed a good few years, but when did driving a van become a crime?'

'Amelia Nicholas.'

'No idea who you're talking about.'

'No?' Fenchurch laid out photos of the crime scene, of Amelia's dead body.

Webster didn't even flinch. Just sat there, still as a monk in deep meditation.

'Amelia was one of seven Albanian nationals who'd been taken from their homes and brought here. The men who did it forced them to work delivering pizzas for Mario's.'

'Not just driving vans.' A smile crawled over Webster's face. 'Delivering pizzas is a crime now, is it? Well, I'm guilty as charged.'

'Here's what happened. You collected that van.' Fenchurch tapped the first CCTV still. 'Then you squashed Amelia between that van and a bus, maybe to make it seem like an accident. Maybe not.'

'Mate, the van's nothing to do with me.'

'Your DNA is in it.'

'Oh yeah? Just mine?'

'You drove it from the van hire company to the crime scene.'

'Did I?' Webster glanced at Unwin, then back at Fenchurch with a cough. He tore the photo from Unwin's grip. 'You want to know about this van? Mario hired it for me.'

'Mario?'

'That's what I said.' Webster rolled his eyes like a snarky teenager. 'His van was knackered and he needed someone to go to the cash and carry. I just had to pick it up for him. A favour, you know? So I cycled out to Lewisham, dumped my bike in the back and drove it to his shop. Presumed he'd do a trip and drop it off himself.'

'Where'd you take it?'

'Look, I needed to take a mate shopping. Terry Oldham, you've probably heard of him?'

The DNA trace. Shit.

'Continue.'

'Tegsy's missus died when I was inside. Can't take care of himself. Pathetic, really, but a mate's a mate. Anyway, I ain't got a car of my own, so I took old Tegsy up to the Tesco in Hackney, not far from his gaff, but you know, he's not the fittest these days. And I told him about home delivery but he ain't got a computer and I've no idea what I'm doing with one half the time. Holly does all that shit for us. So I took Tegsy shopping, then dropped him off with his stuff, made him a cup of tea, helped him put it all away. Tell you, his flat was a state. Had to empty his fridge before I filled it, know what I'm saying? Then I got back outside, and the van had been nicked.'

Bullshit.

Absolute bullshit.

'Can I see the police report?'

'Not got round to it yet. Sorry. Speak to Tegsy, he'll back it up.'

'You should've reported it.'

'Thing is, some copper prick's intent on breaking my skull, isn't he?'

'Who did you kill Amelia for?'

'I ain't killed nobody.' Webster held up a hand. 'I've served my time for that crime.'

'Someone forced Amelia and her sister into the sex trade, forced them to deal drugs.'

'Take it you've spoken to Mario Esposito, yeah?'

'You think he's involved?'

'I know what's going on here. Mario got me in because that bird got squashed, like you say. He called up Loco and I helped out. But that's barely ten percent of the story.'

'What's that supposed to mean?'

'Mate, you think someone's forcing Mario to run these girls as prostitutes?' Webster grinned wide. 'That what he told you?' He laughed. 'Classic.' He straightened his expression. 'I know your type, Fenchurch, you're always hunting for some big bad. In this case, it's him. That geezer's up to his nuts in this.'

'You got any evidence?'

'Mate, he's the one getting these girls to deliver blow jobs. He's the one shoving drugs in his pizzas.'

'How did you know about that?'

'Forget about me, mate. It's him. Mario. He's running this whole operation.'

'How do you know that?'

'Because he paid a tithe to Flick Knife.'

'A tithe, eh?' Fenchurch leaned back and folded his arms. 'Surprised you know what one is.'

'A tenth. It's for protection against the nastier elements in our broken society.'

'Flick Knife's dead. That mean he stopped paying?'

Webster gave a shrug. 'How should I know?'

'You and Flick Knife go back a ways, right?'

'Went to school with his nephew.'

'Way I hear it, the day after old Flick Knife died, some geezer comes into Mario's pizza shop and takes over this tithe business. You know who that might be?'

'Mate, I'm just a bike courier. I work for Loco, a legit business.'

'One who's just out of prison after a ten-stretch for murder.'

Webster scratched at his goatee. 'Look, mate, I really don't know anything and that's the truth.'

'Pretty soon, you'll be back in prison. You'll not get ten years this time. Life with no parole, I suspect.'

Webster stopped scratching. 'I ain't done nothing.'

'I reckon at least twenty years inside. You soldiered through ten, knowing you'd get out. You had the extra motivation of getting out to spend time with your grandkid. Young Sandy.'

'You...' Webster clenched his fists, his forehead knotted. He let out a deep breath and shook his head.

'When you did time before, you didn't know about Holly, did you? Your daughter. And you sure as hell didn't know about Sandy. She'll be in her twenties by the time you get out next. She'll probably have had her own kid.'

Webster pointed a finger at Fenchurch. 'Listen to me, sunshine. It was Mario. Everything. It was all him. And I'm saying nothing more.'

'Why did you kill Amelia?'

Unwin sneered as he whispered in Webster's ear.

Webster waved him off. 'No comment.'

Unwin folded his arms, a broad grin on his face.

Webster ran his tongue over his rotten teeth. 'You ain't got nothing on me.'

'You drove a van into a woman, killing her. You stole her personal effects.'

'You spoken to anyone else who worked for Mario? Like young Mosé?'

Savage broke off his trance to get up and start pacing the room. 'What did you say?'

Webster followed his path, clearly enjoying pressing the buttons. 'Mario told me that kid paid for the van. I just picked it up and someone nicked it.'

Savage stood over Webster, reaching past to show the crime scene photo. 'Who was driving when this happened?'

'You tell me.' Webster took the photo and let it drift to the table top. 'That Mosé kid seems to be Mario's mate.'

'I think it was you.' Savage spoke in a harsh whisper, just loud enough for Fenchurch to hear. 'Who are you working for?'

'Loco.'

Savage glared at him. 'Come on. Tell me who you're really working for.'

'I'm a nice guy so I'm trying to help you here. I'm still in touch with some of my old crew and they've been talking to me about some new people moving in on the East End. People taking over Flick Knife's playground. These geezers make Flick Knife look like a saint. They're the ones you want to speak to. They took over Mario's protection racket. They forced him to do what he did, whoring out these boys and girls. Mario told them he wanted out. They weren't happy. Maybe they planted Mosé there, working for Mario? Young kid, but he's on the radar of these old lags, you know. Naughty boy.'

'What is this Mosé's surname?'

'Something Italian.' Webster grinned at Savage. 'But he's a good Christian.'

Savage couldn't look at him. 'Did these people think that Mario would talk?'

'Maybe. Look, these girls, they see them as evidence, don't they? Makes sense that these people would hire someone to bump off Amelia.' Webster gave a look that chilled Fenchurch's bones. 'I'm not involved, if you're wondering.'

The door burst open and Mulholland strolled in.

Fenchurch leaned forward. 'DI Mulholland has entered the room.'

She crouched between the seats and whispered into Fenchurch's ear: 'Press him on Mosé.'

Broadfoot was standing in the doorway, hands in pockets. He gave Fenchurch a nod.

Bloody hell...

Savage stared into space, jangling coins in his pocket like he was wondering if the guy he'd been defending had gone bad.

Webster eyed up Mulholland like she was a lump of sirloin behind a butcher's counter. He gave her a flirty grin. 'You've aged well, Dawn.'

She just stood there, eyes wide.

'Oh come on, don't you remember me?'

Mulholland's eyes widened.

'We're done here.' Unwin shot to his feet, struggling to fasten his briefcase. 'My client will say no more on the matter.'

'Right.' Fenchurch leaned over to the microphone. 'Interview terminated at,' he checked his watch, 'ten forty-three p.m.'

Webster yawned, staring at the shut door. 'I know her.' He licked his lips. 'Young DC Dawn Mulholland. What a lovely piece of skirt she was. Interviewed me, but it was more like making love, I tell you.'

'But she won. She put you away.' Fenchurch clenched his fists. 'You were lucky to spend ten years inside for what you did.'

'Oh, Inspector. I'm talking about a different case.' Webster laughed. 'Few months before. She thought I'd kidnapped this young girl from outside a flat in Islington.'

Fenchurch tightened his fists. 'What did you say?'

Unwin seized Webster's arm. 'Desmond, I suggest you stop talking.'

'I was there, though.' Webster brushed a hand across his head, ignoring his lawyer. 'Little girl. Beautiful thing she was. Like my Holly. Blonde hair. Wearing an England shirt.'

Fenchurch's pulse was like drums in his head.

'*Desmond.*'

'Your mate there, Dawn? Sexy little thing. She'd heard I'd been in the area, and she interviewed me. I mean, I thought that was it for me. Game over, they'd fit me up for it. But Dawn Mulholland...' Webster shut his eyes. 'She let me go, didn't she?' He reopened them, focusing on Fenchurch with fire. 'I gave some alibi, but I know she didn't even check it because it didn't hold water.'

Fenchurch stepped forward, ready to punch him. Ready to smash his skull off the table, harder this time, not stopping until it was like what he did to Amelia.

Webster folded his arms across his chest and spoke in a harsh whisper: 'Dawn Mulholland could've rescued your little girl. But she didn't.'

All this time, when everyone else was concerned about Chloe or my hunt for her, Mulholland was always sticking the knife in, trying to get a reaction.

And I've got this burning hatred of her, eating away at my gut. Every time I hear her voice, see her snarling face, even spot her bloody scarf on her chair in our office...

It just eats away at me. And I could never put my finger on why.

And now I know.

Now I know.

'Desmond!' Unwin grabbed him by the shoulders.

Webster shut him down with a look.

The door flew open and Docherty burst in to the room. 'Who the hell do you think you are?'

'Oh, you know who I am.' Webster rocked back on his chair and stared up at the ceiling. 'Chloe was such a sweet girl.' Back down at Docherty. 'Chloe Fenchurch.'

'You piece of shite!' Docherty raced over and shoved Webster, sending his chair back, cracking his head against the wall.

Webster screamed, primal and loud.

Unwin stood there, mouth open.

Docherty grabbed Webster's wrist and twisted it, bending him over, face first.

Fenchurch jerked into action, tearing over to break them apart.

But Docherty tugged Webster's arm, hard. 'You filthy piece of shit.'

Something snapped, and Webster screamed. The terror of the East End lay there, face white, squealing.

17

FENCHURCH SLIPPED INTO HIS OFFICE AND STOPPED DEAD.

His father was sitting at Mulholland's desk, glasses on, squinting at the screen. 'Simon.' Then he went back to whatever he was working on.

'Dad.' Fenchurch sat at his desk and logged in. Muscle memory kicked in and, for the millionth time, he pulled up the case file for Chloe's disappearance.

For the first time, he found exactly what he was searching for:

WILLIAM DESMOND WEBSTER, INTERVIEWED BY DC DAWN MULHOLLAND. TWENTIETH JULY 2005.

Jesus Christ.

Fenchurch sifted through the image-capture of the old file and found the scan of the action log, the list of to-do items captured from the interview:

FOLLOW UP ON D. WEBSTER ALIBI — AT CINEMA WITH M. EDWARDS AND S. INGLIS.

ACTION OWNER: DC D. MULHOLLAND

DATE: 20/07/2005

DUE: 21/07/2005

A cold sweat ran down Fenchurch's spine. There it was, in black and white. Handwritten on a pro forma.

Mulholland's... What? Ineptitude? Incompetence? Maliciousness?

Fenchurch logged in to two separate PNC windows and searched for Marcus Edwards and Susan Inglis.

Shit.

Both arrested three weeks ago as part of the crackdown on the organisation which took Chloe.

Arresting officer DCI H. Savage.

Fenchurch's mouth was dry. He logged into HOLMES and found the original case's action log. The whole thing was archived off, so he had to log in to the backup server. *There.* Action 94, raised by Mulholland:

STATUS: CLOSED

REASON: NO LONGER A VALID SUSPECT

Mulholland let that son of a bitch go.

The scumbag who kidnapped my daughter.

He sat back and looked over to Dad hammering at Mulholland's keyboard. 'Come here.'

Dad seemed to take an age of man to creak his way over. 'What's up?' He stood there, massaging his back.

Fenchurch pointed at the PNC screen.

Dad squinted at it. 'Ah.'

Fenchurch crunched back in the chair and let the breath slip out of his lungs. 'You knew. Of course you bloody knew.'

'Simon...' Dad rested on the filing cabinet and tore off his glasses. 'You need to stop this. Mulholland's done nothing wrong. She's just an arrogant arsehole. And you treat her like your worst enemy.'

'This action.' Fenchurch tapped the screen. 'We had him, Dad. *Webster*. Right in our clutches and... And *she* let him go. Didn't even follow up on the alibi. What else is it other than evil?'

'Incompetence?' Dad glowered at the screen. 'She was just a *DC*, Simon. So she spoke to someone. Big deal.'

'She spoke to *Webster*, Dad. He was a cabbie who was in that neck of the woods. Got lost. That was their MO. He was on a back street in Hoxton. He wasn't picking anyone up at the time in question, he was dropping Chloe off to... to... Dawn let him go. If she'd asked the right questions, pinned him down, checked his alibis, his story would've fallen apart. He panicked and gave the names of two co-conspirators, knew his alibi was shit. We would've found her, Dad. Eleven bloody years ago.'

'Simon, you blaming Dawn isn't going to get you back all them years.'

Fenchurch stared hard at him. '*She* messed this up. Things could've been different.'

'Simon, I knew the SIO on Chloe's case and he told Dawn to focus on the door-to-doors. There's a million people you could blame. Christ, I put Webster away not long after.' Dad scowled at his son. 'If you want to blame someone, blame me.'

Fenchurch didn't have a response.

'I'm not to blame for this, Simon. Just like Dawn Mulholland isn't. You've spent eleven bloody years going through the "if onlys". If only you'd never let her out of your sight. If only you'd been on the case. It just never ends. It never ends. The important thing is we've got her back, son.'

'No. I need to make Dawn Mulholland pay for her slip up.'

'You think Dawn screwed it up deliberately, don't you? She didn't know you then.'

He's right. But...

If I go to Docherty with this, what's he going to do? Just excuse it? He's got enough fires to put out for himself.

What if I go to Mulholland with it? She'll just deny it even happened, or somehow turn the tables so that I'm the bad guy. Same as it ever was.

But if I do nothing, it'll just eat away at me. Nibble away at my soul like the rest of it.

Is Dad right, though? Would everything have stayed the same?

Webster's old-school. He would've always taken a fall for Flick Knife and the rest of that organisation. And it would've been some jump to go from him lying about his whereabouts to convicting him of Chloe's abduction and of rescuing her.

But giving a false alibi... It would've opened the door.

Maybe they would've searched his car. Found her hair on the back seat, maybe. Skin cells. Fingerprints. Anything. Match that DNA to her profile and suddenly the whole case changes.

A prime suspect, someone implicated in a child abduction. Trace his movements, maybe get lucky. Find Connolly, find the others and—

Fenchurch caught himself. *And here it is, eating at my soul.* 'I need to do something with this.'

FENCHURCH STOPPED OUTSIDE DOCHERTY'S OFFICE AND NUDGED THE door open.

Broadfoot stood by the whiteboard, jabbing a finger in Docherty's face. 'You almost snapped his arm clean off, you stupid arsehole.'

'Take that finger away from me or I will snap *it* clean off and shove it in your lug hole. Not that there's anything between your ears to stop it coming out of the other side.'

Broadfoot stepped back with a laugh. 'You always were a complete c—' He clocked Fenchurch. 'I'll be in touch.' He adjusted his suit jacket and left them to it.

Docherty watched him go, like he was going to tear off after him and snap his bones as well.

Fenchurch slumped in a chair and just felt everything deflate. 'I'm happy to take the rap for it, boss, if you want me to. The number of times—'

'Jesus Christ.' Docherty punched his whiteboard, making it spin round a couple of times. 'Of course I don't! I'm wearing my big boy pants for once. Christ on a bike.' He checked his watch. 'Julian Loftus has called me over to the Yard. Midnight on a Sunday night and I've got a meeting.'

'You did assault a suspect.'

'Aye, funny.'

'The offer's there, boss. I would've done it, but you beat me to it.'

'I appreciate it, Si. That prick really got to me. All the shite you've been through... You, Abi, Chloe, your old man. And that arsehole took her. And he acted like it was nothing.'

'I've checked, boss. Dawn interviewed him when he came up as a suspect. She had an action to follow up on an alibi. Never did. Meaning he got off with it. Meaning she let the man who kidnapped my daughter go free. A few months later, he murdered someone.'

Docherty collapsed into his office chair with a groan.

'Webster took her from outside my bloody house.' Fenchurch tasted tears at the back of his throat. 'We could've found Chloe eleven years ago.'

'I'm sorry, Si.' Docherty stared into space. 'This is a bloody disaster. We had him. Now he'll get away with it, won't he? Ah, shite.'

'We can still make a case here. Who's the prosecutor?'

Docherty checked a notepad and scowled. 'Neale Blackhurst.'

'He's good, boss. We can still make this work.'

'Not so sure.' Docherty stared up at the ceiling for a few seconds. 'I've got an idea. We could stick a couple of irons in the fire here. We'll prosecute him for murdering that lassie, but we can also do him for what he did to your family.'

FENCHURCH PACED AROUND THE LEMAN STREET CANTEEN, THE PLACE empty but smelling of raw onions, mobile to his ear. Just ringing and ringing and ringing and—

'There you are.' Dad staggered in and collapsed onto a chair. 'Mulholland kicked me out of your office.'

Fenchurch caught a fresh whiff of stale booze from him. 'Are you sure you're sober?'

'Sober as a judge.'

'Most of the ones I know are borderline alcoholics.' Fenchurch folded his arms to check his watch. *Where the hell is he?*

'You need to relax, Simon.' A cough turned into a hiccup. 'Oh, Christ on the cross.'

'How much did you have?'

'Enough. Reminds me of when you was sixteen, seventeen. Me and your mother, God rest her soul, we'd wait for you to trundle in on a Saturday evening. Half four, one time. And you'd vomited everywhere. All over the bathroom. Even covered that little table your mother kept the phone on. You woke your sister too, put her in a right grump. I was due on shift at seven in the bleeding morning, so you can imagine how popular you were.'

Fenchurch checked his watch again. 'Is there a point to this?'

'Just saying that the tables are turned.'

The door opened and Savage waltzed through. 'Just in here. Yes.'

Jeff I'Anson came in next, the social worker's glasses still dark despite it being close to midnight. He stopped and smiled back out at the corridor. 'It's fine, come on.'

Chloe entered the room, her eyes shifting around. She avoided eye contact with Fenchurch, barely looked at her grandfather.

Fenchurch couldn't help but smile. 'It's good to see you.'

Chloe skulked by the counter, arms clasped round her shoulders, her focus trained on the door.

I'Anson sat between her and Fenchurch. 'Jennifer has agreed to come along to assist you with the investigation. But...'

'I don't want him here.' Chloe didn't even look at Fenchurch.

I want to grab hold of you and shake you until you remember who the bloody hell you are. Who gave birth to you. Who raised you. Who taught you to ride a bike.

Who let those animals kidnap you.

Who hunted for you for years, let his marriage fall apart, all while you were in bloody Dorset, thinking some of those animals were your parents.

'It's fine.' Fenchurch walked over to the door. 'I'll give you whatever space you need.'

Dad made to follow.

'He can stay.' Chloe gave Dad another look.

'I...' Fenchurch let out a deep breath. 'I'll be in my office.'

FENCHURCH STARED INTO HIS TEA MUG, THEN LOOKED OVER AT ABI, surrounded by all the crap in his office. Box files and paperwork, nothing meaningful, just delayed busy work. He gripped her hand tight. 'Wouldn't even give me the time of day.'

'Oh, Simon.' Abi let go and sucked in a deep breath. 'I'Anson said it'll take time. We just have to trust the process. Maybe in a couple of months we'll be in therapy sessions with her. That's what I'm clinging to. That hope.'

'Hope is a bastard.' Fenchurch clunked the mug off the desk. 'Feels like it's killed me a few times over.'

The office door opened and Dad sauntered in, all spritely.

Abi got up. 'Well?'

'Hiya, Abi. You look well.'

'I look like a whale, Ian.' Abi held her belly. 'Are you getting anywhere?'

'You need to give her time.' Dad sipped a machine coffee. 'Okay?'

'Okay?' Abi stormed over to him. 'What the hell do you think we're doing? We're giving her all the time and space she needs. Whatever it takes, I just need my daughter back. Is it going to happen?'

'I don't know.' Dad was still hiccupping. 'I really don't know. I mean, she wanted me to stay. That's progress, right?'

'I'll take your word for it.' Fenchurch slumped back in his chair. 'Have you got anything out of her?'

'No idea. I needed to go to the toilet, so I left.'

'Christ, Dad, she's our only—'

'Keep your wig on. Howard has ways and means. And that I'Anson fella, he's good, him. I worked with him a while back. Decent bloke. Gets results. Bit of a smug arsehole, but then aren't we all?' Dad laughed at his own joke. 'Here, hang on.' He winked at Fenchurch. 'I'm Ian and you're my son. He's I'Anson.'

'Great.'

The door creaked open and Savage slipped in, silent.

Dad waved a hand in front of his face. 'Howard?'

Savage looked up at them, like he was surprised they were even there. 'Oh.' He took Mulholland's chair. 'Well, Chloe... Jennifer... Chloe... well, she says she recognises Webster.'

That bastard.

Jesus Christ. Five minutes in a room with him. Five bloody minutes and I'll sort that prick out. He'll be praying that I just break his arms.

Hope glittered in Abi's eyes. 'That's good, right?'

'She says he visited her parents a couple of times.'

Dad puffed out his cheeks. 'Christ on a bike.'

'Would've been not long before you prosecuted him, Ian.' Savage gave Dad a dark look. 'We can add this to the case against him, I suppose. Your daughter won't need to testify given what's... Well.'

Fenchurch grabbed Abi's hand and held it tight. 'Whatever it takes, we'll be there for her.'

'I know.'

I'Anson barged through the door, swinging his briefcase. 'Well...' He cleared his throat. 'Good news, I suppose. Chloe has agreed to enter counselling with you.'

The good starting to outweigh the bad...

Fenchurch folded his arms. 'Why? Ten minutes ago, she didn't even want me in the room.'

'Well, the presence of your father there was crucial. And she... She had a flashback of sorts. She remembers you. And you, Mrs Fenchurch.'

Abi screwed her face tight. 'Jesus Christ.' She let Fenchurch hold her.

'Listen, I've got a friend at Southwark University, name of Paddy Mackintosh.' I'Anson rested his briefcase on Mulholland's desk and rummaged around inside. 'He's got a lot of experience of these sorts of things. Done a lot of work with Howard over the years.' He passed Fenchurch a business card. 'Anyway, I'll be in touch with dates and times and so on. Have a good night.'

'Thanks, Jeff.' Savage showed him out of the office.

Fenchurch held Abi tight.

And there he is, that bastard called Hope, entering the room, needling me, pricking my sides.

PART II

Tuesday, 3rd October
Fifteen months later

18

ABI HIT THE BRAKES AND FENCHURCH LURCHED FORWARD, THE SEATBELT digging into his chest. He twisted round to check the back. Baby Al was cooing away to himself in the baby seat. He let out a breath of relief.

Abi was grimacing at the road ahead. 'London traffic...'

'Never changes.' Fenchurch sat back against the headrest. The Old Bailey towered ahead of them — the eight tall pillars guarded by a row of uniformed officers in acid yellow. *God knows who they think's appearing in court today...* Another glance at Abi. 'You sure you don't mind, love?'

'I'm fine. I know this is high priority.' She looked at her son on the back seat, who was giggling at something only he could see. 'Besides, a day out with my little angel, just the two of us is...' She exhaled. 'It'll be hell, but it's what I've dreamed of for over a year. Can't believe he's *home*. After all that...'

'Never rains but it pours.' Fenchurch caught her smile. 'Wish I could be with you, love. But I've had this date in court for ages. If it was anyone else, I'd defer it.'

'I know. Give 'em hell.' Abi reached over and pecked him on the cheek. 'Remember we're taking Al for his check-up at five.'

'I'll be there with bells on.' Fenchurch returned the kiss and got out into driving wind, harsh rain lashing at his face. And it felt like it was only going to get worse. He waved Abi off and set off towards the court.

A crowd swelled around the entrance. Fenchurch clocked a couple of familiar faces in the uniform contingent, old City police lads from

Snow Hill or thereabouts. He charged through the crowd towards them, warrant card ready.

Spit lashed his cheek.

He rubbed at it with the back of his hand and scanned the crowd.

A young woman stood inches away, her peroxide hair fanning out like an Eighties model's. Her face was twisted into a scowl, worsening as Fenchurch grabbed her by the arm. Holly shrugged him off and stormed off towards the court entrance.

You'd think I was the bad guy here...

Fenchurch followed her up the steps, but lost her by the time he walked through the hulking great doors. Typical City opulence inside. A golden glow came from the ceiling, ornate and hand-carved with some medieval folk tale played out in masonic etchings. Right in the middle of the room was a square inside a circle. No doubt some ancient power focused on that spot.

Right in the middle, DI Jon Nelson sucked on a Pret coffee and sneered at his surroundings. 'Guv.'

'I'm not your guvnor, Jon.' Fenchurch gave a broad grin. 'Not any more.'

'Right, sure.' Nelson returned the smile with interest, then took a sip of coffee. 'What're you doing here?'

'Giving evidence against Webster. You?'

Nelson tilted his coffee. 'Trying to energise myself. Finally letting our old mate Younis have his day in court.'

Been a while since I heard that name. Lose track of all the cases, all the villains we drag in. And he's a worse one than most. His quasi-legal camgirl empire is still running, as is his very illegal drug and prostitution one. And if it wasn't him, it'd be someone else doing it.

Fenchurch stared at Nelson's cup, wishing he had one. 'Be good to get that scumbag off the street'

'Well, we're not there yet. He pleaded not guilty.' Nelson finished his coffee and stuffed it in the bin. 'What's the latest with Webster, then?'

'Just here to give my statement.'

'Right.' Nelson kept glancing away.

'What's up, Jon? You're looking very shifty. And you're asking me about Webster. Why?'

Nelson ran a hand down his face. 'It's nothing.'

Fenchurch still felt the spit on his cheek. *But it wasn't that. It was something else.*

Oh.

There.

The reason for the heavy police presence outside. Dimitri Younis, wearing a sharp suit that fitted perfectly. He swivelled round, his snarling mouth hanging open. The row of rings on his brows was gone — no doubt a risk in prison — but his eyes were still full of menace.

Younis blew a kiss and gave a knowing wink. 'Hiya, Fenchy, my love. I thought you'd be here to see my case, but it must be hard to watch, especially given your feelings for me.'

'Come on, sunshine.' A pair of burly court officers led him away, their bulk only partially hidden by their regalia.

Younis still managed to wink at Fenchurch. 'See you soon, my love.'

Fenchurch watched him go. 'He gets worse, doesn't he?'

Nelson smirked. 'Definitely got a soft spot for you.'

Fenchurch laughed. A cold sweat trickled down his back. 'I'll ask you again, why are you so interested in the Webster case?'

Nelson's gaze was locked on the path Younis took as he weaved out of the court building. 'It's maybe nothing, but we've been through Younis's financial records. We found a payment that came from Mario's Pizza.'

'You serious?' Fenchurch waited for a nod, still didn't get Nelson's attention. 'Protection money?'

'That's what we're thinking. He ran a lot of scams like that. Still does.'

'Keep me posted on—'

Fenchurch's phone thrummed in his pocket and he checked the display. A text from Loftus:

I'M DOWNSTAIRS.

Fenchurch patted Nelson on the arm. 'Keep me posted, Jon. And I'll catch you later.'

DOWNSTAIRS WAS LESS ORNATE — MORE LIKE THE TROPHY ROOM IN A provincial bowling club. Still had the whiff of money, but at least it wasn't shoved in your face quite so much.

'Ah, Inspector.' Detective Superintendent Julian Loftus sat on a bench, scratching his bald head. His full uniform fit his athletic frame like a tailored suit, not even stretching as he reached forward to sip tea from a fancy tray, replenishing his cup from a silver teapot. 'Good to see you.' He poured milk from a silver jug and it ran out. 'Bother.' His gleaming forehead creased with effort. 'I swear, this place is going to the *dogs*.'

Fenchurch spotted a court usher down a side corridor and waved until he got his attention. 'Excuse me? Can we get some more milk, please?'

The usher looked down his nose at him. 'Very well.' He buggered off back down his corridor.

Fenchurch took a seat on the long bench next to Loftus. 'Been here a while?'

'I have. They've changed up the order. You're on next.'

'Right.' Fenchurch poured himself a cup. Strong enough, at least, but now he too was praying for milk.

Loftus focused on his tea, seeming amused by it or like he wasn't telling Fenchurch something. 'I gather your friend Younis pleaded not guilty?'

'Par for the course, sir.'

'Indeed. But still. It's a concern.' Loftus gave a fresh frown. 'He's not going to get off, is he?'

'Not sure, sir. Jon's team are good. If anyone can get him, it's them.'

'Well, I shall cross every one of my extremities.' Loftus caressed his furrowed brow. 'The weight of it all…' Anger flashed in his eyes. 'It gets to you, you know? At least, it does to me. This last year has been a nightmare. A genuine *annus horribilis.*' Another twitch of rage. 'I, uh, I visited Dawn Mulholland this morning.'

Mulholland barged past Fenchurch into the room. Something splashed all over her face. She screamed. Sounded like the gates of hell had opened. Acid hitting flesh. Screeching. Squealing.

Fenchurch took a shallow breath and covered his mouth. 'And how was she?'

'Early days. The, uh, the specialist is going to see her later today. They're hopeful of some sort of recovery.'

Fenchurch just sat there, his own acid burning in his gut.

Loftus clapped Fenchurch's arm, gently. 'Like I say, Inspector, an *annus horribilis.*'

'Doesn't even come close to describing it.' Fenchurch started pacing the small area, a flash of guilt churning in his belly.

I wouldn't wish what happened to her on my worst enemy. And for so long, I thought she was.

We're both police officers. Supposed to put people away, not play games with each other. Whatever she did back in the past, I can't blame her. She was only a DC at the time. It wouldn't have made the slightest difference — not in the end.

'How's your boy? Al, isn't it?'

'Right. Al. He's fine, sir. Good, actually. We, uh, took him home, sir. Yesterday.'

'That's fantastic news. *Fantastic.*'

Fenchurch smiled, struggling to keep it under control, to stop it taking over. *Sod it.* He let go. 'It is fantastic. I don't know—'

'Sirs.' The usher put a fresh milk jug on the tray. Wouldn't even do Fenchurch's cup, let alone both of theirs.

Loftus poured milk into his. 'Excuse me, but when will we—'

'Sir.' The usher gave a withering look. 'I'm afraid I don't control time. I merely ensure you're here when requested, and present in court when needed.' He tilted his head back. 'That and fetching milk, it would seem.'

Loftus lifted his cup, but held it in front of him. 'I just want to know when we'll be called to give evidence.'

'You'll be called when you are called, sir. I extend the judge's profound and deepest apologies.' The usher traipsed off, shaking his head.

Loftus sipped his tea. 'Your news sounds very promising.'

'Thank you, sir. It'll be good... It is good. Getting Al home, sir. Finally, after all that shit. A hole in the heart...' Fenchurch poured the rest of the milk into his cup and drank his tea. Tasted very good, like from a tea room in a posh hotel. 'I worry when things are good, though. But then, they've been shit for so long I must be due a break. Swear I must've smashed a mirror eleven years ago and someone upstairs forgot to stop sending me bad luck after seven.'

'Well, I gave you some good luck.'

'What?'

'Do I have to spell everything out? The offer of a DCI position? When I offered you it, Inspector, you didn't respond. That was a few weeks ago.'

Fenchurch leaned back on the bench with a creak. 'My wife called, sir. Had to dash off to hospital.'

'Ah yes. Yes.' Loftus drank his tea, but kept his focus on Fenchurch. 'Well?'

Fenchurch poured a second cup for himself, even though he didn't have any more milk.

Do I want it?

Eleven years as a DI now. I used to be going places, then the drawbridge went up and I was stuck. But now this plonker's letting it back down and sending me out. Do I want to go there?

Where I am now, I get to do good. I'm effective, even if I need air cover from time to time. If I take this position, I'll be the one having to provide that cover.

I'll be stuck behind my desk.

Behind Docherty's old desk.

A stinging pain hit his gut.

But we have a new baby. A chance to take a step back, focus others on the job, on getting the worst vermin off our streets. Less stress, more time with Abi, with Chloe, with Al. A chance to be a present dad for a kid.

He looked Loftus in the eye. 'I'll take it.'

'Excellent.'

'But only Acting.' Fenchurch raised his finger. 'And only to honour Al Docherty's memory. I want to see if being a DCI is for me.'

'Of course.' Loftus reached into his pocket and stared at his ringing mobile, the exact same old telephone sound half the world had. 'Well, I'll get on with the paperwork as soon as we're done here.' He put it to his ear. 'Neale? Yes, in court just now. Where are you?'

'Inspector?' The court usher barrelled in. 'It's your time in the sun.'

Fenchurch made to stand. 'See you on the other side, sir.'

Neale Blackhurst, the lead prosecutor. He'd taken Fenchurch through everything in the case, prepared and rehearsed so many times that lies almost became true. One single narrative emerged, a logical thread from the words in the witnesses' mouths through to the jury's guilty verdict.

That was the plan at least.

When the rubber hit the road, it was all about improvisation. Tiny little tweaks to the plan, adjustments here, new angles there. The narrative stayed the same, but the logic could change. Like a long chain, sometimes you needed to unhook the weakest links and attach another couple of links. Sometimes you just took it out and tossed it away.

But sometimes someone ripped the chain clean out of your hands.

'Simon.' Loftus cupped his hand around the microphone. 'That's Neale Blackhurst informing me that Terry Oldham has just walked into Bethnal Green nick and told the desk sergeant that he murdered Amelia Nicholas.'

'Oldham?' It hit Fenchurch in the gut. 'He's Webster's mate. He… Webster gave him a lift to Tesco.'

'And now he's claiming that he murdered Amelia.'

'That's bollocks. We interviewed him.'

Loftus shook his head. 'Get to the bottom of this. Now.'

19

Fenchurch inched through the bollarded chicane and found a space next to the park, opposite the row of silver-and-orange squad cars outside the brick police station. Down the one-way street, a fire engine trundled out onto Roman Road, whooping out a holler of siren as he got out of his car. He checked his mobile as he stepped across the street.

Nothing from Loftus — no doubt reassessing strategy still.

He entered the police station and walked over to the grimy front desk, a poor match for the recently refurbished exterior.

'There you are.' Sally McGovern, Blackhurst's number two, sat in a leather chair in the waiting area. She smiled as she got up. Bright red hair, cropped to a severe fringe. Her ears pointed out at different angles. 'So you're here to mop up the mess?'

'Something like that.' Fenchurch offered her a hand, but she didn't take it. So he put it in his pocket. 'Where's the fire, then?'

'Upstairs.' She set off towards the staircase. 'A DS Ashkani is interviewing.'

Fenchurch stopped at the bottom. 'She's one of my bloody officers...'

~

Fenchurch found them in the bowels of Bethnal Green station. The Observation Suite here was high spec, full of brand-new monitors and furniture.

Fenchurch focused on the screen. DS Ashkani and DC Bridge were in the interview room, opposite Terry Oldham and — wonder of wonders — Dalton Unwin. 'He sure gets around, doesn't he?'

'Unwin? Wish he didn't.' McGovern sat back and glanced over at Fenchurch, turning the volume down a few notches. 'So how high is the platform we're going to be suspended from?'

'Usual one, I'm afraid. More likely to break our necks and live.'

She laughed.

'How's it going?'

'Just getting started, but...' She groaned. 'How did we not know?'

'Because it's bollocks.' Fenchurch gripped the arms of the chair. 'We interviewed him, backed it all up with evidence and now he's taking one for the team. He'll go down for it, meaning we get our result, while he gets...' He gestured at the screen. 'Come on, it's obvious what's going on here. He's been paid off. Old git like him, it's the only way he can be useful.'

'You're *sure* Webster killed her?'

'I'd stake Loftus's life on it.'

She laughed again, then turned the volume back up.

'My client was there. He's admitted it.'

Ashkani was nodding along. 'Trouble is, we get a lot of cases like this, where someone takes the rap for something. Usually means money or a favour.'

'My client is helping you here, you should give him some respect.'

'He's taking a hit for a mate.' Ashkani clicked her tongue. 'What is it? Money? Debts? Pay your family off?'

Oldham laughed at her. His grey hair was swept back over his head, though more white than black. The sort of red face that was hard-earned from a lifetime of fry-ups from his local caff, whiskies from the local offy. But his eyes... Like tiny lumps of coal recessed into a snowman's skull.

'Or have you got cancer and you're just taking one for a mate?'

'I ain't got nothing, love.'

'So, you took this van from Mr Webster, correct?'

'That's what I said.' Oldham's gaze got even colder. 'You not listening, or something?'

'I'm listening.' Ashkani paused. 'You're acquainted with Mr Webster?'

A glimmer of amusement flashed in those dark eyes. 'We go way back, me and Des. He's a good kid.'

'Why don't you tell us what happened after you took the van?'

'Well, I drove off, didn't I? Me and Des went shopping. Took it all back to mine, loaded up me fridge. Then I drove it round to a lock-up in Hackney and told Des it'd been nicked. Next day, I went back and well. This girl was cycling, big load of pizzas in a bag on her back. I followed her along a stretch, tried to clip her, but she didn't go down. She was pedalling so fast, I swear it was like she was on a bleeding motorbike. But I smashed her into a bus.'

Ashkani glanced over at the nearest camera, then leaned forward, tapping her thumb on the wood. The only sign of movement in there. 'So you were driving the van?'

'That's right.'

'And you killed Amelia Nicholas?'

'That's right, love.'

'And how did you know she'd be there?'

'I called the place she worked in. Said I'd ordered a pizza from that shop, knowing she'd deliver it. Then I followed her.'

'Why did you kill her?'

'Because I'd got into an altercation with her on the road, didn't I? She cut me up, called me an old bastard.'

'That's it?'

'I killed that girl. End of.'

'We interviewed you last year, why didn't you tell us then?'

'Because Des told me not to. That he'd take one for me. I'm too bloody old. But he's been inside for, what, fifteen months now, doing time for me. I can't handle the guilt.'

'We need some evidence.'

Unwin pushed a piece of paper across the desk. 'David Kelly provided this. He was there, he saw my client.'

Fenchurch frowned at McGovern. 'Where do I know that name?'

She looked through her paperwork. 'He was the cyclist who witnessed the death.'

'Shit. And he saw Oldham?'

She nodded. 'This is a disaster for you.'

Onscreen, Ashkani tossed the page on the desk. 'We spoke to Mr Kelly and he didn't mention Mr Oldham.'

'Well, he did to my company. You should've done your job properly.'

'Bugger this.' Fenchurch got up and stormed through to the interview room. He gave Ashkani the cut-throat gesture.

She leaned forward. 'Interview terminated at fifteen oh seven.'

Fenchurch whispered in her ear: 'Get hold of this clown, tear it apart.'

'Sergeant?' Unwin waved at her. 'Hello.' He smiled. 'Mr Kelly's waiting in reception to give a statement.'

'Right.' Ashkani left the room, phone to her ear before she'd even opened the door.

Fenchurch nodded at Bridge, then the exit. Gave her a few seconds to leave. Then he took the seat opposite Oldham. 'Let's have a little chat off the record, yeah?'

'I killed that girl.' Oldham glanced at Unwin. 'Not the first. Probably my last, mind.'

'You're a serial killer?'

'Not like that. I don't wear their skins as suits, nothing like that. Just keeping order on the streets.'

'Because someone called you an old bastard?'

'In my day, it paid to respect your elders. Girl like her, foreigner too, coming here and calling me that.'

'This is all bollocks. I know you've been paid to take the rap. Who was it?'

'Fuck off, you arsehole.'

'Taking care of your family, was it?'

'Fuck off.'

'You're a charmer.' Fenchurch smiled. 'You take the rap for this and they take care of your family when you're inside, yeah?'

'You need to do your homework, son. My boy lives in Australia with his wife. Me daughter's in Dubai, working for that airline. Neither of them need my help.'

'So it's debts, then?'

Oldham looked at Unwin.

'Nailed.' Fenchurch laughed. 'Gambling or drug?'

'Inspector, I suggest you speak to the witness we have provided, then we can commence prosecuting my client. I assure you that he will put in a guilty plea and we can be done with this whole charade. My client has lived with the guilt of a lie for the last fifteen months.'

Fenchurch took a long hard look at Oldham. 'You're making a big mistake.'

While Fenchurch couldn't really recall speaking to him, David Kelly clearly could remember Fenchurch.

'Inspector.' Kelly rose to his feet and held out a hand, like they were meeting to discuss a mortgage or a promotion. He wore a navy pinstripe suit, white shirt and a light-salmon tie. His thinning hair had miraculously regrown in the fifteen months since the crime scene in Aldgate, though he had tell-tale red marks around the scalp. 'How you doing?'

Fenchurch left his hand hanging and took a seat.

Ashkani leaned forward. 'DI Fenchurch has entered the room.' She widened her eyes at him. 'Sir?'

Fenchurch smiled at her, then gave Kelly a frosty look. 'So I gather you've suddenly remembered some new information?'

'That's correct.' His soft Scouse tones exuded confidence. 'I saw this article in the *Standard*. Saw the guy who's in the dock for it and... it wasn't him.'

'We spoke to you, sir. Took a statement. You said you didn't see the attacker.'

'Well, that's not quite what I said.'

'It's what you signed.'

'Well, that was remiss of me.' Kelly smoothed down his tie. 'I told your colleague here that I saw an older man. The guy you've got in court for it is about twenty years too young.'

'You decided to contact a criminal defence lawyer instead of coming in to us?'

'That's right. I...' Kelly carefully refixed his slight quiff. Probably cost a DI's salary to install and six months to bed it. 'I needed legal advice, so I thought, you know, kill two birds with one stone.'

'You spoke to Dalton Unwin about this?'

'Right. I went to his office and... Look, could you just sit there while an innocent man faced trial?'

'No. But I'd make sure I told the police who I *did* see.'

'I saw Terence Oldham.'

'Excuse me.' Fenchurch gave him a policeman's stare, the kind that'd make the toughest Saturday night hardman wilt. Kelly just took it. 'You know his name?'

Kelly pointed at Ashkani. 'Your colleague here took me through this VIPER thing.'

Ashkani nodded. 'He picked out Oldham.'

Fenchurch bit down on his lip. 'What did you see him do?'

'Like I told you ages back, I saw someone,' he swallowed hard, 'smash a cyclist into a bus. They drove over them. Then they got out and nicked their wallet.'

'And you saw Mr Oldham?'

'Swear on my life.'

'Has anyone put you up to this?'

'What? Of course not. This is my conscience speaking.'

Fenchurch let out a slow breath as he stared at the camera. Shirley McGovern would be watching this, would probably have already called her boss to break the news. He pushed his chair back and got up. 'Okay, Sergeant, please finish taking Mr Kelly's statement.'

'I know you don't believe me, but I saw what I saw. It'll go with me to the grave.'

'Just make sure that grave isn't filled in early.'

20

Loftus was in one of the top-floor offices of Bethnal Green station, now long since emptied. Just a local policing hub, all the strategic units in nearby Leman Street or back in the Yard. He fidgeted with his cigarettes, the box unmarked except for unheeded health warnings, as he talked on the phone, then snapped the lid shut. 'Neale, Broadfoot and Savage are still investigating Webster from their respective angles. Okay, me too. Catch you later.' He killed the call and started patting himself down, fingers twitching. 'I need a cigarette.' He walked over and wrestled with a patio door, holding it open for Fenchurch to step out onto the balcony. He shut the door behind them and clicked a lighter, JFL embossed in the side. 'Gave up ten years ago.' He took a deep suck and held the smoke in his lungs. 'But this last year...'

Fenchurch stepped further from the door to get upwind of Loftus. 'Sir, did you get my message?'

'I did.' Loftus looked round at him, then away again, letting the smoke out in a slow puff, his eyes closing in almost-orgasmic pleasure as he watched the cigarette burn. 'Maybe I should get a vape stick like your mate, Jon Nelson. Though that'll no doubt prove to be just as bad as this.' He took another long drag, holding the smoke in his lungs, and stared over the rooftops towards the City. He let the mist out slowly, eyeing Fenchurch again. 'What's your take?'

'Someone's pulling in favours. Getting Terry Oldham to take the rap for this. But getting David Kelly to change his statement.'

'You believe him?'

'I don't believe anyone, sir. It is what it is.'

'I get that.' Loftus waved out into the wind, then leaned back against the wall, arms folded. 'You don't believe Oldham, then?'

'No, I don't. I was with McGovern and her and Blackhurst will drive a bus through us. Let me make it right, sir.'

'How?'

Slash Unwin's tyres. Cut his brakes.

Follow Webster home. Stab him in his sleep. Get him drunk, set fire to the house.

'I'll get a team together and rebuild the case against Webster.'

Loftus exhaled smoke through his nostrils. 'You still think it's him?'

'I know it's him. Let me dig into his story. Give me DS Reed and a couple of officers. She's good.'

Loftus took another drag. 'Good, yes. Great, though?'

'I trust her with my life, sir. God knows she's saved it enough times.'

'What about Uzma Ashkani?'

Fenchurch almost laughed. He caught himself just in time. 'Uzma's one of Dawn Mulholland's officers, sir. I don't know her well enough to give a frank assessment.'

'Inspector, I've lost a DCI and a DI in the last few months. I don't have time to step down to this level.'

'I'm stepping up.'

Loftus tapped off some ash. 'Okay, I'll file the paperwork this evening, but we'll still be down two DIs.'

'You should ask for Jon Nelson back.'

'I should, should I?' Loftus squared up to him, the cigarette perched between his lips, smoke wafting all over Fenchurch. 'No, Jon Nelson's doing fine away from your clutches. Broadfoot speaks highly of him.'

'Let me reopen the investigation, reinterview the witnesses. Shake things down.'

The door thundered open and Blackhurst charged through, his knuckles white from clutching his briefcase. Neale Blackhurst noticed Fenchurch and gave a baleful look long enough for Fenchurch to have a proper taste before staring at Loftus's cigarette, jaw clenched. 'You got one for me?'

Cigarette clamped between his lips, Loftus held out the packet and his lighter.

Blackhurst took a long drag and the smoke from the cigarette coiled over towards Fenchurch. No escaping it. 'Which of you pair dropped the clanger here?'

Fenchurch joined them, his mouth dry. 'This is on both of us.'

'Really? Because I've just had a word with Sally and I fail to see how we can de-fuck this.'

'Neale, this is on you as much as us. You were to—'

'I went over your evidence, Julian.' Blackhurst rested against the stone walls, leaning over as he blew out smoke, hitting Fenchurch in the face. 'We've dropped the case against Webster and we're prosecuting Oldham for her murder.'

'Webster killed her. The forensics were solid. He was in the van.'

'All we could prove was that Webster was in the van *at some point*. His story has always said that. And wasn't Terry Oldham in it, as well?'

'We... Yes. Webster said he was, told us he took him to the shops.'

'You checked it?'

'The till receipt is on file.' Fenchurch stared at Blackhurst. 'Then they conjure him as a confessor.'

Loftus took a long drag on his cigarette, staring at something far down below. 'What do you want to do?'

'Well, while Mr Blackhurst here prosecutes the wrong man for Amelia's murder, I want to progress Webster.'

'The wrong man...' Blackhurst got between them, dropping his bulging briefcase on the flagstones. 'You've made a right arse of this, Fenchurch.'

Loftus stared hard at Blackhurst. 'I treat this as a failure in the CPS as much as in the Met.'

'Julian, Julian, Julian... This one's definitely on you.' Blackhurst glared at Fenchurch. 'You should've been more thorough with the forensics.'

'We had everything tight, Neale.' Loftus fumbled his cigarettes out of his pocket, dropping them on the scarred flagstones. He crouched to retrieve them. 'This is all of our mess.'

'I'll see you around.' Blackhurst left them to it, taking two goes to push through the heavy door.

Fenchurch crouched to help with the last couple of cigarettes. 'Whoever's behind this has created a perfect storm, sir. I don't know how they've done it, but they've paid off Oldham to take the hit for this. Neale's got a collar for a murder, meaning Blackhurst's going to be happy.'

'You honestly think it was Webster?'

Fenchurch could only nod.

'Okay.' Loftus lit another cigarette. 'First thing tomorrow, take DS Reed and DS Ashkani, plus their teams. Ashkani is to shadow you. I'll brief her to make sure she knows. I need to know that everything's above board. Since we lost Alan Docherty, you've not had the same air cover. You've been much more focused. Most of all, though, you've been more controlled.' He smiled as he stamped out his cigarette against the bin. 'Make sure Webster stops terrorising this city.'

'I'll put him away, sir. Mark my words.'

21

Fenchurch slumped behind the wheel, low enough to get a good look at the Old Bailey's back door.

Dalton Unwin stood there in a loose suit, next to his client Desmond Webster. He'd bulked up in the year or so inside, shaved his head even closer.

Holly burst into tears, rushing forward to grab her old man in an embrace.

Humour in Webster's eyes. He even winked as his daughter treated him like they'd just masterminded an improbable cup final victory.

Maybe not so improbable.

Unwin's office will be calling round coach firms looking for someone to do an open-top bus tour of the East End for them. Announce the reign of terror is back.

Bloody hell.

Fenchurch slid the window down to listen, but couldn't hear anything. Nothing like them owning up to getting Oldham to take the rap.

I should go and—

And what?

What the hell would I do?

That arsehole got off, because Terry Oldham took a hit for him.

Jesus. The man who took my daughter. The man who put us through this whole thing. Back out on the street.

I need to get him for this.

Unwin led Webster across the road towards the Magpie and Stump, simultaneously the safest and most dangerous pub in London.

Half-filled with cops and journos, the other half with lags and mates of lags.

Fenchurch reached into the glovebox and found the small locked case. He opened it and eased out the knife, still in its sheath.

But instead of going in, Webster opened a waiting black cab's door and let Holly in first, then got in the back beside her.

Unwin stood on the pavement, watching the cab disappear towards Holborn Viaduct.

Fenchurch gave them a count of twenty before driving off.

Two cars ahead, the taxi trundled up to the lights, indicating left.

Fenchurch took it slow, shifting gears early to let the engine slow the car. He glanced in the left-hand wing mirror, checking for any oncoming vehicles likely to try anything. Nothing.

The lights shifted to green and the taxi set off with a belch of fumes. Dirty old cab, not one of those new electric ones. Old-school, just like the passenger. The left indicator pulsed.

The car between them started up and Fenchurch followed slowly.

A Porsche Cayenne powered past Fenchurch on the inside, hurtling round the bend. Webster's taxi stopped, the horn blaring. Not that the Porsche paid any heed.

Fenchurch flashed for the cab to go, then flicked the indicator and followed it into the left-turn lane. Just as the lights turned red.

He sat there, listening to that last Tycho album, the bass throbbing. He snapped off the stereo and set off. No sign of the taxi.

Bloody hell.

Fenchurch sped up, catching the Porsche at another junction.

Where the hell is Webster's cab?

He lives round here. At least, his daughter does.

Fenchurch mapped out the route in his head, and took a right.

There.

The idling taxi pulled up onto the kerb and the driver stepped out, his hazards dancing in the fading light. He opened the back door, his lips twisted into a whistle.

Desmond Webster got out, rummaging through his pockets.

Fenchurch parked a few car lengths away, on the opposite side from Webster's home. Engine off, seatbelt released, door cracked.

Ready.

Waiting.

He reached into his coat pocket and felt the blade, sharp through the sheath.

Perfect.

Bought twelve years ago, for the man who took my daughter. And now he's here.

Webster sifted through his change, saying something that made the driver bellow with laughter. Always one for the cheeky banter. The driver took the money and got back in, the hazards giving way to a left indicator.

Now.

Fenchurch put his foot on the pavement and put the knife away. He left his door ajar and set off, his soft-soled shoes sucking in the sound of his approach, eating up the distance between him and his prey. He reached into his pocket and grabbed the knife handle, unsheathing it so he was ready.

The taxi engine started up, pumping a fresh cloud of dirty diesel into the air. The engine swallowed up the rest of the sound.

Fenchurch slowed as he approached, ducking behind the next car, a gleaming Fiesta.

Holly's heels clicked as she walked round the back of the cab.

Fenchurch peeked out again.

The taxi drove off. Webster was over at the door, pressing the wrong key into the lock. 'I'd kill for a gin and tonic. Nice slice of lemon, too.' He tried another key. 'Settle for some tonic water, though. You got any in?'

'Dad...' Holly snatched the keys off him and dropped them herself, the cymbal crash rattling Fenchurch's head.

'Sorry.' Webster bent over for the keys.

Now.

Do it now.

Race over there, stick the knife in Webster's neck. Stab, stab, stab, stab. Quick, fast, as many as it needs. Puncture his lungs, let him drown in his own blood.

Any defence lawyer I could hire would tear Holly's story apart in seconds.

No witnesses on the other side of the road. Even if I'm missing any, there are enough parked cars to block the view of the most ardent curtain-twitcher.

Do it.

Do it now.

Kill him.

Webster reached over to open the door and beckoned his daughter inside.

A skinny man in a tracksuit stood in the doorway, peering out, his lank and greasy hair like it was slicked with whale blubber. His drawn face brightened at the sight of Holly. 'Whassup?' He reached over for a kiss, but Holly darted past him.

'Evening, Kirk.' Webster stopped by the porch, hand held out. 'Lovely to see you outside, son.'

'Pleasure's all mine.' Tracksuit shook Webster's hand, his lips twitching, thinking something over.

Webster grabbed him into a hug, clapping his back in an age-old power move.

A child's scream jerked him from his reverie.

Webster led inside and Kirk followed. The door slammed, the sound echoing round the quiet street.

Fenchurch crouched, watching. Thinking.

Too late.

Way too late.

Missed my chance.

He glanced back at his car on the opposite side, hazards blinking in the harsh evening light.

Plan B — a good old-fashioned stakeout.

Maybe that's the trick, beat Webster at his own game. Buy some tonic and some lemons. Dress up in lycra, head up the short garden path and knock on the door. Present from some old friends. Then bang, stab him in the chest. Make him see what's coming. Let him know who's done it.

But make sure I kill him.

Then I'm gone, into the car, and off.

Done.

Fenchurch crossed the road, hands in his pockets, whistling.

The house door opened again and Webster came out, mobile to his ear. 'It'd be my pleasure, mate. Thank you for keeping hold of it so long. Be good to reacquaint myself with it.'

Fenchurch crouched by his car, cupping a hand around his ear.

What the hell?

His gun?

Headlights washed the street as the taxi returned with a fresh cloud of fumes. Webster flagged it down and slid in the back.

WEBSTER'S TAXI PASSED LEMAN STREET STATION, BUT DIDN'T STOP, instead trundling past and crossing the lights. It stopped outside Aldgate Tower.

Loco.

Fenchurch parked, killed the lights and wound down his window. Traffic noise, some lads shouting at the football pitches a few streets away, the rumble of a passing train heading out to the Essex coast. Nothing else.

'Hopefully not, mate.' Webster paid the driver. 'Should be okay to get back myself.' He watched the cab drive off.

The tower door slid open and Pavel wheeled a gleaming racer bike out onto the street. A car whooshed past, masking what he said.

Webster knelt on the pavement, stroking his bike like it was a family pet.

Another car passed, slower, blocking their voices. Hard to read what they were saying.

'—didn't kill anyone.' Webster winked at Pavel. 'They framed me.'

Pavel patted Webster on the arm. 'I'll see you tomorrow, okay?'

'Cheers, mate.' Webster hopped on his bike and sat there, nodding his head. Then he bumped down onto the road and cycled off.

Fenchurch started the car and the engine woke up with a growl. He rolled up the windows and tailed Webster at a distance.

His phone rang, blasting out 'Thank You' by Led Zep. Abi. The dashboard clock read 4:58.

Shit. Al's hospital appointment.

He pulled in at the kerb, reached into his pocket and answered the call. 'Sorry, love, running a bit late. Be there in five.'

22

FENCHURCH'S FOOTSTEPS WERE LOUDER IN THE BUSTLING HOSPITAL, squeaking on the lino as he traced the yellow line to the ward. He checked his watch. Ten past.

Abi's going to kill me.

He yanked open the door and bumped into someone.

'Jesus!' She scowled. Chloe Fenchurch, his daughter. A smile filled her face. 'Dad!' She grabbed him in a tight hug.

Fenchurch let himself be wrapped up in it.

Every time, it's a fresh reminder that she's back in our life. Living under our roof again. Owning her real name, not the one those monsters gave her. The one we gave her. The one on her birth certificate.

'Jeez, Dad.' Chloe broke off the hug. 'You okay?'

'I'm fine.' Fenchurch caught his breath. 'You?'

'I'm good. My little brother's doing well today.' She pointed into the room behind her. 'Us Fenchurches are made of hard stuff.'

'The hardest.'

'The doc wanted a word with Mum, so I'm going to get coffee.'

Fenchurch's gut lurched. 'What about?'

'Wouldn't tell me. Do you want anything?'

'I'm good. Isn't it too late for a coffee?'

'Never too late.'

'Just like your grandfather.'

'Not just him.' She pecked his cheek and powered off, just like her mother. Never enough time in the day.

Fenchurch watched her go. *So hard to believe it's actually her. A grown woman, at least physically. Still needs to grow up mentally and emotionally, but... It feels like a dream, like a hallucination. Like being in some alien's virtual reality game and they're pushing my emotions to the limits.*

Fenchurch took a sharp breath and entered the room.

Abi sat in the corner, arms tight around her torso, legs crossed. She glared at Fenchurch.

For being late? Or something else?

Mr Stephenson was behind the desk, bouncing Baby Al on his knee. He wore a grey suit, the fabric matching his hair. 'Well...'

Fenchurch sat next to Abi and tried to take her hand. She yanked it away. He rubbed her arm to apologise, but her expression stopped him. So he leaned forward. 'What's going on?'

Stephenson was still focused on Baby Al. 'Your wife was telling me how well he's been sleeping.'

'Like a baby. And not a screaming one.'

'Indeed.' Stephenson didn't laugh, just twisted his head to examine Al that little bit closer. 'And how would you say he's been settling in?'

Fenchurch glanced at Abi. Hard to read her expression, other than annoyance. He took Abi's hand and this time she let him. 'I can't believe he's home with us after all this time. I was up three times in the night to check he was actually there and that I hadn't dreamt it.'

'That's a common occurrence.' Stephenson passed Al to Fenchurch. Abi reached over to take him. 'Well. I like what I see. He's doing really well.' He smiled at Fenchurch. Actually smiled. 'As far as I can tell, there are no issues with young Alistair.'

'Alan.'

'Yes, of course. Another six months of checks here, starting with weekly for a month. Then fortnightly for two, switching to once a month, and then he'll be under your GP's care. I'll still want to keep an eye on him every year until he's eighteen, but I don't foresee any issues.'

Fenchurch looked over at his wife, cuddling the baby tight. 'He's clear?'

'Absolutely.'

Abi grabbed Fenchurch's hand. 'That's fantastic.'

≈

FENCHURCH CLIMBED THE STAIRS TOWARDS THEIR FLAT. AT THE TOP, A tell-tale Quentin letter placed carefully on the doormat. He bent over to collect it, opening it as he got up again. An invoice for their share of a bill for fixing the common chimney.

Not that we can use it for a proper fire.

Fenchurch opened the flat door and went in. Dark, voices in the living room. He hung up his coat and tried to listen.

Abi was in the living room doorway. 'Simon. What's up?'

'Well, you just ran off at the hospital.'

'You were late.'

'I...' Fenchurch tugged off his clip-on tie and dumped it on the sideboard. 'Been a shit day, love.' He saw Chloe behind Abi in the living room, playing with Baby Al. 'A really shit one.'

'You want to talk about it?'

'Wouldn't mind.' Fenchurch let out a long sigh. 'Why did you leave me, though?'

'Because your daughter left her keys at home this morning. That's all.'

'Wonder where she gets that from?'

'This isn't the time, Simon.' Abi grinned though, despite herself. 'Now, do you want to talk about your day?'

'JESUS...' ABI SAT THERE, THINKING, THE KITCHEN SILENT AROUND THEM, electronic music bleeding through from the living room. 'He's free?'

'Afraid so, love.' Fenchurch walked over to the doorway and looked at Chloe in the other room, lost in a world that only contained her tiny brother. 'I wish he'd paid for what he's done to us. I know he's not the ringleader, but he's the one who...' He waved at the kitchen window, at the sink he stood at all those years. 'Webster drove up, lured Chloe and bundled her into the car and did God knows what... He's the one who took her. And he's out. He's free.'

'What does Loftus say?'

'He's fuming.'

'That's it?'

'He says we can reopen the case against Webster if I find enough evidence. But they're going to prosecute this guy who took the fall. The look of him, he won't survive a year in prison.'

'Meanwhile, he's free to kidnap other children?'

'I don't think he'll be doing that, love.'

She gave a fiery glare. 'You told me he was some sort of assassin?'

'That's right.'

'So he'll be killing people?'

Fenchurch could only shrug.

In the living room, Chloe was dancing Al on her lap. She spotted Fenchurch and smiled, making Baby Al wave at them.

Abi waved back at her children, but the fire stayed in her voice. 'This'll be all over the papers, won't it?'

'Probably.'

'She's making good progress and… This could derail her.'

Fenchurch scratched his head. 'I'll tell her in the morning.' He took off his jacket, the knife in the pocket hitting his hip. 'Tonight, I almost…'

'Almost what?'

'Had a pizza.'

Abi laughed. 'Carbs won't kill you.'

'Feels like it sometimes.' Fenchurch leaned over and gave her a kiss. 'I'll tell her tomorrow, okay?'

'Okay.'

Fenchurch walked through to the living room and took Al from his daughter. 'Who's for a pizza?'

Chloe joined him, standing. 'Even with your diet, Dad?'

DAY 2

Wednesday, 4th October

23

'—MING UP NEXT IS A REAL STONE-COLD CLASSIC FROM OCEAN COLOUR Scene.'

Fenchurch reached over and turned off the kitchen radio just as the jerky guitar riff kicked in. 'That's quite enough of that.'

'I like that song.' Abi was bottle-feeding Baby Al at the head of the table, still piled with empty pizza boxes.

'It's not a song, it's...' Fenchurch went back to stirring the porridge. Just about done. He took it off the heat and got three bowls out of the cupboard. 'Never mind.'

Chloe padded through, staring at her phone, and sat at the far end of the table, brushing a hand through her hair.

Abi frowned at her. 'What's up, love?'

Chloe scowled at her mother, then her father, then poured a cup of tea from the pot.

'Chloe?' Abi pulled the bottle away from Al, then sniffed. 'He needs changing.' She raised her eyebrows, first at Fenchurch, then at Chloe. 'Fine, I'll do it.'

Fenchurch tried to stop her. 'Love, I'll do it.'

'You've got work, haven't you?'

'You say that like it's a bad thing.'

'It is. You're supposed to be off this week. Like I am. You know how hard it was for me to get that time off.' Abi got up, jiggling Baby Al as she kissed Fenchurch on the cheek, hugging him tight. 'It's fine.' She left them to it, singing a lullaby as she went.

Fenchurch took two bowls of porridge over to the table, putting the smaller one to Chloe. 'Here's my carbs for the day.' He burped. 'God, that pizza's repeating on me something rotten.'

'Gross, Dad.' Chloe stayed focused on her phone.

'What's up?'

Chloe slathered her porridge in maple syrup and rested her spoon on the edge of the bowl. 'When were you going to tell me about Desmond Webster?'

Fenchurch put his bowl to the side. 'Listen, I—'

'The guy who took me *is out on the street*?' Chloe clenched her fists. 'You should've told me.' She brushed her long hair to the side, revealing the long scar above her ear. 'You didn't think I should know about him getting released yesterday?' She dropped her spoon onto the table. 'He's *out*, Dad! Out there, somewhere. Why didn't you tell me?'

'I—'

'You said he'd be going away!' Chloe waved her mobile around. 'The case collapsed! What happened?'

'I'm going to get him, love. One way or another.'

'Is this what you and Mum were talking about last night? Through here? Thinking I wouldn't know something was going on?'

'Partly. I will catch him.'

'Listen to me.' Chloe drilled her gaze into him. 'I'm sick of secrets and lies, and you guys hiding things from me. Okay? I'm sick fed up of being this weak girl in your eyes.'

'You're not—'

'Dad, I get that you want to protect me. But I need to stand on my own two feet. If I can't trust you, then—'

'You can trust us.'

'How? You didn't tell me!'

'Chloe, I...' Fenchurch blew on his tea, making the surface ripple. 'I wanted to make sure you slept well last night.'

'But he's out there!'

'And he'll come nowhere near you.' Fenchurch dipped his spoon into his porridge bowl. 'I want to protect you. Always have, always will. But I don't want to smother you.' He reached over, offering her his hand. 'But I will do everything in my power to bring Webster to justice. For what he did to you, to your mother and me, and for whatever else he's done. I want him off the streets. Everything I do is to protect you, okay? I'm sorry if it's overbearing — if it's stifling — but I can't help it.'

She took his hand. 'Thanks.' She took a spoonful of porridge and blew on it. 'Are you confident you'll get him?'

'Your auntie Kay and I will do everything we can to take him down.'

'At least she won't make an arse of it.' Chloe ate the porridge, her teeth clanking off the spoon.

'Thanks for the vote of confidence.' Fenchurch took a mouthful. 'You need a lift to university?'

'Mum's driving me.'

'What about tonight? Need a lift home.'

'Thanks but no. I'm going to go for a drink with a couple of the girls I work with.'

'That sounds good.'

'It is, Dad.'

≈

'So where does that leave us?' Fenchurch sipped tea from the paper cup. His office was cold, like the heating was still on the summer setting. 'Kay?'

DS Kay Reed sat opposite, fiddling with her short ponytail, just about long enough again to tie up. 'Well.' She rifled through her notebook. 'I didn't work the original case, so I've got a fresh pair of eyes on it. I started on the file first thing. As far as I can tell, we've got precious few leads.'

DS Uzma Ashkani perched on her chair with perfect poise, like she was doing yoga. She smiled, betraying how much she liked herself. 'That's not exactly what he wanted to hear, Kay.'

'Sorry, but it's the truth.' Reed leaned back with a sigh. 'I'm not sure where else we can look.'

Ashkani snorted a laugh. 'There's a whole raft of—'

The door creaked open and the mail lad slipped in — skinny and tall. Most days, he had a quip about West Ham, either results or fixtures or possible transfers. Nothing today, just a letter. 'Alright, mate?'

'Cheers.' Fenchurch took it off him and waited for the door to shut before opening it.

Bloody hell, that was quick.

The Acting DCI position, a contract in black and white. A slight salary bump, enough for a week away.

God knows we need one.

'What's that?' Ashkani was frowning at him.

Fenchurch stuffed the letter in his drawer. 'Both of you should be aware that I'm now Acting DCI.'

'Congrats.' Reed gave him a wink.

'Well done.' Ashkani's smile was cold. 'So, will there be an Acting DI?'

Always the same with her...

'I'll discuss that with Superintendent Loftus.' Fenchurch finished his tea and chucked the cup in the recycling bin. 'Until then, you two are front and centre on this case, okay?'

'And what is that case? Going after a man who was cleared yesterday?' Ashkani rolled her eyes. 'I was in that interview, Simon. Neale has another suspect for this, one who's confessed. With a witness backing up his story.'

'You believe Oldham?'

'You don't?'

'I could list a million reasons why I don't think Oldham killed Amelia.'

'I've got three reasons that he did. A confession, another statement, and the forensics.'

Reed tossed her notebook onto the desk and sneered at her. 'It's always the—'

'*Kay.*' Fenchurch shot Reed a warning, got her to back off. He focused on Ashkani, trying to keep his expression neutral. 'Uzma, Loftus wants us to validate the story. Okay?'

'It feels very much like you're going after the man you believe kidnapped your daughter.'

Fenchurch lost any neutrality in his expression. 'Kay, I need you to go through all of the existing evidence against Webster. Every single item, check there's nothing we've missed. And go through everything we've got on Oldham. Historical shit, plus his recent movements.'

Reed grabbed her notebook and stabbed her pen against the page as she wrote. 'Okay...' She looked over at Ashkani, then at Fenchurch. 'And what are you two going to do?'

'Someone's got to break the news to Amelia's sister.'

FENCHURCH TRIED THE BUZZER AND WAITED. BRICK LANE BUSTLED around them. Two Asian men lugged bags full of shopping down the street, kicking a door to a curry house to be let in. In the other direction, a gaggle of hipsters hung around outside a bagel shop, sipping coffees from small cups.

Ashkani was watching the street as well. 'She definitely still lives here?'

'According to Howard Savage, yes.'

'Do we need to clear the air?' She locked her gaze on him, her irises almost black. 'I know we've not seen eye to eye over the years, so I want to make sure we're on the same page on this case.'

Fenchurch caught a whiff of cooking pastrami, the heady meat smell mixing with the spices. 'Why would you think that?'

'It stands to reason, doesn't it? I worked for DI Mulholland. And you... Well.'

Fenchurch tried the buzzer again. 'I still don't see why that's a problem.'

'You didn't get on with her.'

'She ever tell you why?'

'You were being unreasonable.'

'*I* was?' Fenchurch tried the other buzzer, marked for a flat on the first floor. 'That's interesting.' He shook his head. 'I just need you to act professionally. Back in my office, you—'

'Hello?' A male voice rasped out of the speakers.

'Police, sir. Need access to the stairwell.'

'How do I know you're cops?'

Fenchurch caught a snide expression on Ashkani's face. 'I can read out my warrant number, if you want. Or you could come down and see it for yourself.'

Silence.

'Oh, bloody hell.' Fenchurch hit the buzzer again. Nothing.

Feet thundered down the stairs and the door opened wide. An old-school pervert — thick specs, spots, greasy hair, Gola tracksuit — gurned into the light. 'Let me see it, then.'

'What?'

'Your warrant card.'

'Right.' Fenchurch held it up. 'Happy now?'

Pervo stared at it, running his fingers across it like he was checking a twenty-quid note was counterfeit. 'Well, this appears to be in order.' He scanned it again. 'Or it's a very, very good fake.'

Ashkani frowned at him. 'How would you know?'

'Walter Baker.' His lips twitched as he held out his hand for her to shake. 'I work at Lewisham.' He gripped Fenchurch's, tighter than it looked like he could manage. 'I manage the security system for the whole force, plus the City lot. Very possible that I printed that warrant card off personally. Course it's not just that, it's all manner of security. Doors, access to cells, you name it.' He wagged a finger at both of them. 'I've seen your faces out in Lewisham, haven't I?'

Fenchurch nodded, keen to keep him going. 'I'm there all the time.'

'Leman Street, eh? Not been in that nick for ages. Due an overhaul next summer, unless I'm very much mistaken.' Baker's face twisted tight. 'Hang on, you don't know an Ian Fenchurch, do you?'

'My old man.'

'Good lord. How's—'

'We just need access to your neighbour's flat, sir. Be out of your hair in a jiffy.'

'By all means.' Baker stepped back. 'What's she done now?'

'What do you mean?'

Baker glanced up the stairs. 'Well, she's always in and out. All day long. Makes me suspicious, you know?'

'She's a bike courier, sir.'

'Oh, I see. Well, that explains it.' Baker didn't seem satisfied with that. 'But she must've done something, yeah?' His shifty gaze switched between Fenchurch and Ashkani. 'Why else would two of Julian Loftus's finest officers be here?'

'That's confidential, I'm afraid.' Fenchurch set off up the stairs to the second floor flat. 'Sure you can understand that, right?'

'Course I do.' Baker followed up as far as the first floor. 'My mother and father bought one in 1981 for a pittance, and now it's—'

Fenchurch cleared the second-floor landing. The flat door was hanging open. He snapped out his baton. 'Stay here, sir.'

Ashkani inched towards the door, slowly, baton out, eyebrows raised.

Fenchurch matched her pace step for step, creeping through the hallway, catching a whiff of stale coffee.

Ashkani froze in the living room doorway. 'Oh my God.'

Casey lay on the couch. A gunshot dotted her forehead. Another through her mouth. Blood stained her T-shirt red over a hole where her heart should have been.

All the signs of a Desmond Webster hit.

24

Tammy crouched low as she dusted round the body. Her mask covered her face, but not her irritation as Fenchurch ghosted past.

Casey still lay on the sofa, but a figure hovered in front of her. Pratt, humming away some opera melody, audible through his crime scene mask.

Over by the door, Reed and Ashkani were arguing, head to toe in crime scene suits, arms jerking around, fingers jabbing at each other. Couldn't tell which was which — they were almost the same height.

'Oi oi.' Fenchurch got between them. 'What's going on?'

'Nothing, guv.' Reed was on the left, scowling at Ashkani. 'And that's the problem.'

'Not sure what you mean.' Fenchurch pointed at the door. 'Kay, I need you to run the street teams. Okay?'

'I thought you wanted me to—'

'This is a higher priority. I need you to be Deputy SIO, Kay.'

Ashkani folded her arms.

'Thanks, guv.' Reed's cheeks plumped up behind her mask, the only sign that she was smiling. 'I'll go and round up some bodies.'

'Thanks.' Fenchurch watched her go. 'It's not personal, Uzma. I know I can trust Kay.'

She still had her arms folded, but at least she wasn't shaking her head any more. 'Meaning you can't trust me?'

'I just don't know I can yet.' Fenchurch stared through her mask, misting with every breath. 'You're shadowing me. I need you to tell me what I'm not seeing. Cool?'

'I think I can do that.'

'Hope you can.' Fenchurch led over to the body.

Dr Pratt stopped humming long enough to look up at them. 'A proper gangland killing, this one.' Instead of his usual plummy tones, he put on a comedy Cockney accent. Fenchurch couldn't figure out why. Pratt got up from his crouch with a series of painful clicks from his knees and exhaled slowly. 'Albanians.'

'What do you mean, Albanians? We know she was.'

'It's not that...' Pratt took a few seconds to compose himself. 'Neither of you have heard of *gjakmarrja*?'

Fenchurch saw his confusion in Ashkani's eyes. 'Why don't you enlighten us, William?'

'Gjakmarrja literally means "blood-taking".' Pratt hugged himself tight, squeezing the Tyvek suit until it rattled. 'In Albanian society, the Kanun is their code of laws. It's informal, passed down orally for centuries. Most of it is fairly innocuous, as I'm sure you can imagine, but the Kanun of Leke Dukagjini is infamous for authorising retaliation killings.'

'Retaliation? She was shot in a gangland style, William. Just like how...' Fenchurch swallowed his words. 'Like how her sister was squashed between a van and a bus. How is this a retaliation?'

'That's the crux of the matter, my dear friend. The Kanun was originally used to control blood feuds, but it has been somewhat overridden by the notion of vengeance over all others.' He pointed at the body, at the foam covering Casey's knees. 'You see the coffee?'

The stale smell crept through Fenchurch's mask. 'So she was having a cappuccino when the killer came in?'

'Very droll.'

'I'm serious.'

'Simon.' Pratt gave a longer pause. 'In Albania and the wider diaspora, they have a tradition known as "coffee under the knee". On feast days or at weddings, say, when coffee is served, those who did not avenge their killed relative have their coffee served on the floor, below the knee.'

Fenchurch stared at Casey, at her dead eyes and her broken face. 'How the hell do you know all of this?'

'This isn't my first rodeo, as they say. Your good friend DI Winter has investigated three *gjakmarrja* killings on his patch, which I also cover. Surprised you haven't had any here, but hey ho.'

'I'm struggling to get what you think is going on here, William. Casey and her sister worked as delivery drivers at a pizza restaurant — cover for prostitution.'

'And, like you said, they're both Albanians.' Pratt gave him a stern look. 'They were taken from their homes by persons unknown and blah blah blah. They didn't come freely, Simon, and they stay because of the Kanun. The threat against their relatives is so severe.'

'Why now?'

'Well, quite. That's something you'll need to get to the bottom of.'

'You think this is the gang who kidnapped her?'

Pratt shrugged. 'Maybe.'

'William, I was hoping for a lot more than a bloody maybe here.' Fenchurch looked at the victim lying there, another life snuffed out in cold blood. 'You're saying this is gang-related because someone's splashed coffee all over her legs?'

Pratt took his time. 'I understand that discovering a body is—'

'This isn't to do with me.' Fenchurch waved at the body. 'This is about *her*.'

'I see. Well, I'll get back in my box.' Pratt crouched back down, humming away as he prodded at the body.

Fenchurch caught a smirk from Ashkani. 'William, I'm sorry.'

A wink was visible through Pratt's mask. 'I'm just winding you up.' A belly laugh. 'Simon, I'm just giving you some advice. It's an avenue you should consider investigating.'

'And I will. You can make up for this by telling us the time of death.'

'And therein lies the rub.' Pratt rested back on his heels, holding himself surprisingly steady. 'Time of death remains a mystery and shall remain unknown.' He pointed over to the street. 'The window was open, so the body got cold. Could've been opened before or after death, hard to tell. And even then...'

'Ballpark?'

'Sorry.' Pratt lifted his shoulders. 'Could be last night, could be this morning. The fact the coffee still has foam on it might indicate this morning, but it could've been placed there independently of the body.'

≈

FENCHURCH LEFT THE CRIME SCENE — DESCENDING INTO A HIVE OF activity, SOCOs and plainclothes officers milling around seeming busy — but he couldn't see much, if any, progress being made. He kicked off his crime scene suit and dumped it in the discard pile.

I shouldn't have let Webster go last night. Should've just killed him.

Sod Holly and the potential witnesses, sod the bloodstains on my clothes. Sod prison time as a cop. I'd give up my freedom to take the man who'd kidnapped my daughter off the street.

A chill ran up his spine as he set off down the stairwell.

Casey would still be alive. Webster wouldn't have killed her.

But my son would grow up knowing his father was a murderer. Chloe would only remember me having killed someone. Would she understand? Would Abi?

The cold breeze bit his cheek. He focused on Ashkani. 'Can you do a little bit of digging into the Albanian stuff? See if there's something in what William's saying here.'

'I thought you wanted me to shadow you?'

'This takes precedence.'

'Sir.' She slouched off towards her car.

A figure waltzed past her. Loftus, lost in thought, leaning against his Audi.

Fenchurch joined Loftus. 'Sir, how do you want to progress this?'

'I know what you're thinking. Webster. Am I right?'

'Am I that obvious?' Fenchurch tried to keep calm. 'Pratt's going on about Albanian blood feuds, sir, but I can't shake the feeling that it's a bit of a coincidence that the night he's released, someone dies in his trademark manner.'

Loftus just looked at him, breathing slowly.

'I don't want to jump to conclusions here, but I certainly want to speak to him about his whereabouts.'

'Evidence first, okay? I need you to keep away from him until you've got a smoking gun, do you hear? Go nowhere near him, without approving it with me first. Clear?'

'Of course.'

REED BECKONED FENCHURCH OVER. SHE WAS STANDING ON THE STREET as Walter Baker gave a statement to a plainclothes officer. 'Mr Baker, can you—?'

'Simon!' Baker recognised Fenchurch like an old friend. 'I was just saying to your colleague here,' he waved at Reed, 'her warrant card needs updating, by the way. We had a batch of 'em where the magnetic strips stop working after a fashion. I did send out an email...' He tutted. 'You've got other priorities, though, I suppose.'

'I'll get onto it first thing. I swear.' Reed gave him a broad smile, but Fenchurch knew she was just humouring him. 'Tell DI Fenchurch what you saw.'

'Yeah, so this was last night, way before you and... What's her name?'

'DS Ashkani.'

'Right. Right, before you and DS Ashkani showed up this morning.' Baker peered up at the top-floor flat. 'I mean, you're probably wondering what I'm doing here all day? Important job like mine? Well, today's a special day. I've got a delivery coming — my new gaming PC. Seventeen packages coming from various vendors and I don't trust the couriers round here, know what I'm saying? Things go missing. Even worse, I don't trust my neighbours. They'll sign for stuff and keep it. And I could get it all delivered to the office, but you know it's not standard policy. So I needed to be in to get my goodies. Good chance I'll be able to sit down with *The Witcher 3* in full 4K.' He grinned at Fenchurch, then at Reed. 'So I'm working from home today. And I am genuinely working from home, pulling together some thoughts on the Strategic Access Programme I've been tasked with leading. Of course, you lot can't do that, but I'm not a cop so I have some leeway. Anyway, as things stand, ten of my lovely little boxes have turned up but I'm not still able to start building the blessed thing until—'

'Just tell the story, sir.' Reed's expression looked more and more strained with each syllable. 'Last night?'

'Right, yes of course.' Baker pushed his glasses up his nose. 'So last night, I was sitting doing the *Sunday Times* cryptic, you know it's not as good as the—'

'And?'

'Right, so the buzzer goes and I thought, hello. I mean, I was thinking of getting one of those doorbell things, you know, where it's a—'

'And?'

'Oh yes, so I answered the door but it wasn't one of my boxes turning up early, just someone needing access to the stairwell. Just like you and your friend this morning. A crying shame, but not to be expected, I suppose. I was thinking it could've been one turning up early, you know? If it was the case and the motherboard, I could've had a head start. I mean, I've had deliveries on a Sunday night round Christmas time. Doesn't happen that often and, of course, I usually—'

'What time was this, sir?'

'Yeah, sorry.' Baker stared at his watch. 'Be about... Ooooh. About half eleven?'

Comfortably in our window of opportunity.

Webster had his bike back. So easy to just come round here and get in, get back to killing ways.

'So I went down to check. Don't want to let anyone in. You never know who it could be—'

'Mr Baker, someone was murdered in that flat last night.'

Fenchurch pointed up at Casey's window, just as a camera flash went off. 'Now can you cut to the chase, please?'

Baker stood there, hands on hips, scowling at Reed. 'Does he want me to help or not?'

'He does.' Reed's fake smile was back, trained on Baker. 'Can you just tell DI Fenchurch what you saw?'

'No need to be so shirty. Christ. So it was a delivery guy. Pizza. Said it was for my neighbours. Got the wrong address. Very polite, I have to say. Not a lot of them are. So I went back to my crossword, but there's a lot of crosstalk on the entrycom, so I heard the buzzer go upstairs.'

'Definitely a man?'

'I couldn't say for definite. It could've been a woman, I suppose, the quality on those entrycoms is terrible. We had the vendors all in a few months back to pitch for upgrading the Met's systems and the quality nowadays is frightening.' He stared into space, then focused on Fenchurch. 'But I think it was a man.'

FENCHURCH POWERED ALONG BRICK LANE, HIS FOOTSTEPS CLICKING AS he checked the parked pool cars. Still no sign of her. 'This fits Webster's MO and he's not got an alibi for it.'

'You think he killed her?' Reed looked up. 'You'd normally have hauled him in for an interview by now.'

'The timeline fits, Kay. But once bitten, twice shy. I'm taking this slow and steady like Loftus asked.'

There she is.

DC Lisa Bridge was in a pool Mondeo at the corner, outside the bagel shop, her forehead creased as she worked away at a laptop resting against the wheel.

Fenchurch got in the back seat. 'Lisa, need your help with something.'

Bridge rolled her eyes, but didn't look round. 'Wouldn't happen to be CCTV, would it?'

Fenchurch blushed. 'I know I keep asking you to but if you could look at last night's—'

'Already on it.' Bridge worked away on her laptop, kneading the soft keyboard. 'Just let me finish— Shit.'

Fenchurch gripped the headrest as Reed got in the passenger seat. 'You got something?'

'See for yourself, sir.' Bridge swivelled the laptop round.

Really bad quality image, grainy and greyscale, and from up high. Did give a good view of the street and all the flats in the block.

Through the murk, someone bent to speak into the entrycom, propping up a road bike, a pizza bag wrapped around their torso. Time 23:26.

'You got anything better than this?'

'Got a lot worse. And this is after I processed it.' Bridge hit a key.

The footage jerked back a few seconds. A bike courier showed up with a big bag, their face obscured by a helmet and shades. Baggy tracksuit, rather than lycras. The courier pressed the buzzer and waited a few seconds, before pushing the door and disappearing inside, lugging the bike with them.

Another few seconds later, something flashed in the front room of the second-floor flat. Another two in quick succession.

'The gunshots.' Fenchurch braced himself.

Moments after, the courier left by the front door and hopped back on the bike. Still couldn't see their face, even as they cycled off.

Could be Webster.

Shit, could even be Kirk. Holly's baby daddy.

'Wind it back.' Fenchurch peered at the screen, rewatching from the arrival.

'You happy with this, sir?'

Fenchurch nodded slowly. 'Slightly.'

'I'm trying my best here.'

'I know. This isn't a criticism of you, Lisa. This is good work. Confirms the timeline. And confirms it was an assassination. We need more evidence to prove it's Desmond Webster, though.'

25

'His name is Pavel.' Fenchurch loomed over the security guard behind the desk in Aldgate Tower, the foyer empty and sterile. 'He works for Loco.' He pointed up. 'Up there. Tenth floor.'

'Okay, sir.' The guard picked at his teeth with a fingernail. 'The problem is the address book runs on surnames. I can't search for a first name.'

'In 2018?'

'Yeah.'

'This is a bloody tech company.'

'Not my problem, mate.'

Fenchurch took a deep breath. 'Can you call the Loco or Travis receptionist and get his surname, then?'

'I suppose I could.' The guard picked up the phone and dialled a number.

Fenchurch's mobile rumbled in his pocket. Three missed calls from Savage, only one voicemail. He tried returning it, but no answer.

How the hell did he find out about this?

The guard pointed at the lift. 'Mr Udzinski will meet you upstairs.'

'Thanks.' Fenchurch marched over to lift and got in.

'Hold it!' A female cyclist jogged towards him, carrying her bike over her shoulder.

Fenchurch hit the open button and kicked a foot in to block the doors.

'Thanks.' She got in, panting hard, sweat dripping onto the floor. Her headphones bled out tinny hi-hat and cymbals, but didn't cover her ears, missing by a good centimetre. She smiled at him and tapped them. 'They're bone-conducting. Means I can still hear street noise when I cycle. I'd *die* of boredom if I couldn't listen to my podcasts, I tell you.'

'Better than dying of being squashed.' Fenchurch grimaced at his own joke.

The door opened and the cyclist wheeled her bike off through the busy office.

Pavel waited by the reception desk, breathing on his shades and rubbing the lenses against his T-shirt. He saluted at Fenchurch's approach. 'I'm afraid I can't help you.'

'I've not even asked what it is yet.'

'I don't care. My hands are tied.' Pavel held them up, pressed together at the wrists. *Annoying git.* 'We've got a new agreement in place with the Met for both Travis and Loco businesses.'

'Mate, a girl's been—'

'You're not listening to me. I can't help. You need to speak to DCI Jason Bell.'

Fenchurch groaned. 'You're kidding me.'

'Them's the rules, mate. DCI Bell has established a process for the information for both businesses.'

'This is about Desmond Webster. I know he's back here.'

Pavel's head jerked round and he sighed. 'How the hell—?' He drummed his fingers on the desk. 'That's supposed to be secret.' He fixed his mirror shades on Fenchurch, no doubt masking a glare. 'After everything you've put him and his family through, you're still victimising him?'

After what he put my family through. Yeah, a million times.

'You know he's a killer, right?'

Pavel laughed. 'He's paid his debt to society.'

No he hasn't. Not by a long shot.

'Right, wait there.' Fenchurch got out his phone. Two numbers for DCI Jason Bell. He tried the desk.

Pavel watched him, arms folded, mirror shades on.

'Simon, how the devil are you?' Bell's Brummie tones rasped out of the speaker. Always that bit louder than everyone else.

'Had better.' Fenchurch turned away from Pavel. 'Listen, I'm just at Loco and I need—'

'Right, Inspector, you need to come to my office. Now.'

∽

FENCHURCH DROVE INTO THE LANE FOR THE SCOTLAND YARD CAR PARK and he joined a three-strong queue. The leafy tree-lined block felt a million miles away from the claustrophobic space it used to occupy just over the river. The famous sign turned round in the breeze to the left.

Two cars ahead, a suit was out of his Audi, shouting at the guard but getting nowhere.

Fenchurch pulled up and waited, drumming his thumbs in time to Roxy Music playing on the radio.

Audi man still shouted, but the guard was getting his way.

Fenchurch picked up his phone and checked the display. Another two missed calls from Savage. No texts or voicemails. And nothing from Loftus. He tried again. Got voicemail again.

Audi man got back in his car with a flounce and swerved round in a tight curve, shouting and screaming to himself.

Fenchurch tried Loftus now.

'This is Julian, but I can't take your call. Drop me a message and I'll call back ay-sap. Okay? Cheers!'

Fenchurch waited for the beep. 'Sir, I imagine you're busy, but I'm about to meet up with DCI Jason Bell. You'll know what that means. Well. I'm not leaving there without access to the data at Loco. Okay?' He killed the call and flashed his warrant card at the guard, then pulled through the gates into the car park.

No spaces.

FENCHURCH STOMPED INTO BELL'S OFFICE IN SCOTLAND YARD. BLOODY empty.

Jesus Christ. Where the hell is he?

He called Bell's mobile. Another clown bouncing him to voicemail.

So Fenchurch sat in his chair and put his feet up on the mahogany desk. *Nice office, have to say.* High up the new building, with a choice view across Victoria Embankment to the London Eye slowly wheeling around in the sunshine.

The door opened and Bell waddled in. Just about as fat as it was possible to get without keeling over on the walk between his car and the lift. He looked exhausted, dark rings around his eyes, either from stress or undiagnosed diabetes. 'There you are.'

'Where did you expect me?'

'Can I get you a coffee, Simon?'

'I just want what I asked for on the call, Jason.' Fenchurch crunched back in the chair. 'Nice office.'

'Comes with the territory.' Bell sauntered over to the window and took a slug of coffee. 'What I'm doing is of strategic importance. There's talk of me getting the knife crime task force.'

'You deserve a stabbing.'

Bell laughed. 'Have a seat. Oh, I see you've taken mine.'

Fenchurch didn't move.

'You'll never change, will you?' Bell rested against the window and took another drink. 'You can't just rock up at Loco, you know?' He left a space, but Fenchurch didn't fill it. 'Last time you were there... July, wasn't it? Heard all about it from Pavel. I was on holiday so you were a little bit naughty, weren't you? We hadn't yet reached a service-level agreement with Travis about their Loco business.' He ripped the lid off his coffee and took a big slurp, getting foam all over his mouth and nose. 'We have now.'

'Jason, I need you to stop getting in the way. I know how easy it is for them to give me the information I need.'

'Well, as ever, you're right in the middle of a clusterfuck.' Bell wiped at his face, removing foam from his nose. 'Two of their cyclists got stabbed last night. One in Croydon, one in West Ham. So, I'm trying to manage the situation with them. Last thing I need is you rocking up like that. It doesn't help me or you. Am I making myself clear?'

'Not really.' Fenchurch leaned forward, resting his elbows on the desk. 'If they've had two stabbings, they should be bending over backwards to help.'

'Who are you framing this time?'

Fenchurch rolled his eyes. 'Jason, you're better than this.'

'Am I?' Bell smiled. 'Had a call from Jules the other day. You'll know him as Superintendent Loftus. That, or sir.'

'I'd love to have been a fly on the wall.'

Bell turned back, his grin gone. 'Jules was asking me if you were ready for a DCI role.'

'Right.' Fenchurch's neck burned. 'You're mates.'

'Go back a long way. Worked together in Shepherd's Bush. I was DC to his DS. Fun times.'

'Before we met.'

'Indeed.' Bell slumped in one of the chairs opposite his desk and tossed his empty cup in the bin. 'Jules asked if I could put in a good word for you.' He paused, licking his lips. 'Or a bad one.'

'Jason, are you going to help me with Loco or not?'

'You need to learn to relax, mate.' Bell smirked. *Prick's enjoying himself here.* His mouth twisted into a sneer. 'But I told Jules that I think you're good enough for that position. High stress, but you've been living in intolerable conditions for years, so I reckon you can cope.'

'I took the role on an acting basis.'

'It's really tough, mate. The transition from street-level stuff to what I do isn't for the faint-hearted. Let me know if you need any coaching.'

Wanker.

'I'll bear than in mind. Thanks.'

Bell raised his eyebrows. 'How's Chloe doing?'

'She's okay.' Fenchurch tried to swallow the lump in his throat, but it stuck there. 'She's living with us again.'

'That must be nice.'

'It's good.' Fenchurch shifted on the chair. Couldn't get comfortable. 'Jason, I've got a dead body on her way to Lewisham, so...'

'Okay, okay. What's the story?'

'Sister of the pizza driver who died last summer. We got Desmond Webster for it last year.'

'Heard he got off last night. You went tonto at the judge, right?'

'What? No. Where the hell did you hear that?'

'Rumour mill. You didn't?'

'Someone came forward and confessed. Thing is, I know Webster did this one and I don't want him getting off this time.' Fenchurch stared over at the window, then back at Bell. 'But before I speak to him, I need his movements from your buddy Pavel.'

'Wise move.' Bell nodded slowly. 'Okay, so you want me to sort this out ASAP, correct?'

'That'd be helpful. Then I know whether I should be speaking to him.'

'You doing it by the book...' Bell looked out of the window. 'Is that a pig flapping its wings out there?' He clapped his hands together. 'Alright, mate, I'll take it up with Pavel. Doubt it'll be quick though.'

≈

STUPID BASTARD... SHOULD'VE GONE SOUTH OF THE RIVER.

Fenchurch inched towards the lights. Tower Bridge was on the horizon, its namesake tower between them, flags whipped by the breeze. The lights turned green, letting the car in front trundle a few feet towards the roadworks.

A constant in this bloody city these days.

His mobile blasted out *Won't Get Fooled Again* by The Who, that line about meeting the new boss...

Fenchurch hit answer and sound exploded out of the speakers, still set at Led Zep volume. 'Sir, I need a—'

'Jason's already called me.' Loftus sighed down the line. 'I thought we had words about your behaviour?'

'We did, sir, and I'm behaving. If it'd been the old me, Webster would be sitting in a holding cell in Leman Street with half his teeth missing.' Fenchurch waited for a laugh, but didn't get one. 'I'm building a case against him.'

'Hmm.' Loftus paused. Sounded like he was driving as well. 'Jason's a good cop. It doesn't stand to upset good cops.'

'I'm not saying he's good or bad, sir. I just need you to apply pressure on him so I can get the data this century.' Fenchurch tightened his grip on the steering wheel as he inched forward into the hallowed slot by the roadworks. 'So, can you speak to him for me?'

'Jason doesn't work for me so it's not like I can give him a direct order.'

'I'm not suggesting it, sir.' Fenchurch set off, racing through the roadworks and pulling up the left lane towards the Minories before a wave of cyclists got there first. 'I need to access their data. I need Desmond Webster's movements.'

'I'll see what I can do.' And Loftus was gone.

Not like I'm asking you to do anything special, sir, just your bloody job.

Fenchurch drove through the lights and slalomed round the roadworks, then cut along the back to Leman Street.

Yet again, Fenchurch wished Docherty was alive and well.

He parked at the back of Leman Street and got out into the cool air. Felt like it was going to rain. He set off towards the back entrance, but spotted Ashkani over by the smoking area, sucking on a cigarette.

She stamped it out and jogged over. 'Sir.'

'Just call me Simon, it's fine.'

'Right.' She held the door open for him. 'Any chance you could have a word with Howard Savage?'

Bloody hierarchies... Why do people have to be arseholes to each other? 'What about?'

'The Albanian angle. He's spoken to Pratt and, well, it's getting murkier by the minute. He's all over their operations in the East End.'

'It's just drugs, right? Why's Savage involved?'

'Drugs are just the start of it.'

'Jesus. Right, I'll speak to him and see what I can do.'

She smiled a thank you. Seemed genuine, too. 'Heard you were over at Scotland Yard?'

'Is nothing a secret these days?'

'DCI Bell, right?'

'Right.'

'That guy's a total prick.' Ashkani snarled. 'Used to rub DI Mulholland up the wrong way.'

Like there's a right way.

Stop thinking like that.

'Well, Uzma, it's with Loftus to fix.'

'You think it's Webster?'

Fenchurch let out a breath. 'I do.'

'Bell's a dingbat. He's going to dick you about for weeks on this.'

'Is there anything in this Albanian blood feud stuff?'

'I don't know what to make of it, sir. I mean, Casey and Amelia are both Albanians, but there's very little to point towards a ritual killing. There's so much stuff on Albanian gangs, it'll take longer than forever to find anything. Needs a lot more bodies on it than just me for an hour, you know?'

'But we know Webster killed Amelia.' Fenchurch stared off into the distance, trying to focus his thoughts. 'Doesn't make sense for someone else to kill Casey, does it?'

'Well, they both worked for that pizzeria, didn't they? Prostitution, drug running, people trafficking. They're evidence. Stands to reason that the Albanians would want to clear their trail.'

Fenchurch nodded. 'Why get Webster to do it, though?'

'You're sure it's him?'

'Not a hundred percent, but...' Fenchurch stared back across the car park, thinking it through. 'Seems so unlikely that some Albanian gangs would pick now to kill Casey. Surely they'd pick her off before she had a chance to speak to Savage. He's had over a year of investigating their operation.'

'Well, here's an idea.'

'What?'

'I'm supposed to be shadowing you, right?' Ashkani got out her phone. 'Got a call from Julian Loftus, told me to make sure it was by the book. We've got some evidence, don't we?'

'What, the CCTV?'

'Correct. It sure looks like Webster on there. Fits his MO. What's more "by the book" than getting a suspect to conflict known movements.'

'Uzma, we don't know it was him on the video.'

'I'm happy to work with you here.'

'What's the play?'

'Nothing to it. We go in, take him in for questioning, then we tear apart whatever bullshit alibi he comes up with.'

'Simple as that?'

'Never is, sir, but I live in hope.'

What's her game? Giving me enough rope to hang myself? Deny any of this was discussed?

Fenchurch shook his head. 'Sod it, let's do it.'

'Thanks.'

'But I've a feeling we're going to need to speak to Holly. Can you track her down for me?'

Ashkani frowned. 'You don't want me in the interview?'

'I do, Uzma, but I don't want anyone speaking to Holly and giving her a chance to alibi her father. Okay?'

'Sir.' Ashkani marched off towards her car, eyebrows raised.

26

FENCHURCH TRUNDLED ALONG MILE END ROAD, PASSING THE ONLY coach full of schoolkids in England where someone wasn't mooning the traffic. He pulled a left and came to a halt a few car lengths away from Webster's house, bumping onto the pavement. He killed the engine and waited, close enough to keep an eye out, but far enough to not be immediately obvious that cops were scoping the place.

Up ahead, on the right, halfway up the road was the man who took my daughter.

His phone chirruped. A text from Ashkani:

GOT HOLLY. TAKING HER TO LEMAN STREET.

Fenchurch thanked her in a reply and got out, the breeze blowing grit and leaves into his face. He crossed the road and skipped up to knock on the front door.

The door opened and Kirk peered out, shrouded in frying bacon smells and thin smoke. Holly's baby daddy, in the same place as last night. *Are they back together?* Either way, Kirk sniffed at him. 'You're Old Bill, ain't you?'

'Well done.' Fenchurch held up his credentials, peering past him into the dingy flat. Sounded like Sky Sports News playing loud inside.

Kirk folded his arms. 'Holly's at work.'

Fenchurch stuffed his fists in his pockets, wrapping his fingers around his warrant card. 'It's her old man I'm after?'

'Give me a minute.'

Fenchurch scanned the street. An old lady struggled against the wind, dragging her wheeled shopping trolley behind her like a reluctant dog.

'Through here!' Webster's voice briefly overpowered the Sky Sports jingles.

Fenchurch entered the flat and walked through to the living room.

Webster sat on the sofa, bouncing his granddaughter on his knee. 'Hello, me old mucker. What can I do you for?'

Fenchurch stayed by the door, blocking the only possible exit route. 'Need to ask you a few questions.'

Webster stared at Kirk and tilted his head over to the kitchen units. 'Pop the kettle on, would you?'

Kirk slouched over to the sink, shoulders sagging.

'Thought he was inside?'

Webster spoke in a low tone. 'Holly's ex. Helping her out while she's at work.' His lips twisted into a snarl aimed at his granddaughter's father, lost in the universe of his phone, thumbs pounding the screen, a deep frown etched into his forehead as the kettle rumbled. 'I had a little word with him before he got out. Came to an understanding, shall we say. He's leaving Holly alone, but doing his bit to help this little rascal.' He tickled Sandy and made the girl squeal. 'Now. What's up with you?'

'We should do this down the station, if you don't mind?'

'And if I do?' Webster sighed. 'Thought you'd have learnt not to blunder in here without any evidence.'

'Who says I've not got any?' Fenchurch gave him a broad grin. 'Get your coat, Desmond. You've pulled.'

'Fine.' Webster got up, kissing Sandy on the head as he rested her on the sofa. 'Kirk!' That got him to look up from his screen. 'Need you to take care of your daughter for a bit.' He trotted off to the stairs and bounced up like a man half his age.

Kirk poured water into a tea cup. 'You still want one, mate?'

'I'm fine.' Fenchurch joined him by the sink. 'You were with old Des last night, weren't you?'

'Yeah. Holly told me to do one about half ten, though. Why?'

'Des here all that time, yeah?'

'Pretty much.' Kirk chucked the teabag in the sink and added a spot of milk, barely enough to make the drink change colour. 'You're asking the wrong fella.'

'What do you mean, pretty much?'

'I don't know. All I know is I left at half ten. Anything else, you need to take me into a station for.'

Fenchurch stared at him for a few seconds. A lightbulb went off in his head.

What if it wasn't Webster who killer her?

What if Kirk's his number two? Robin to Webster's Batman.

Kid's got form, probably still got contacts.

Then Webster thumped down the stairs. 'Come on, then.'

'INSPECTOR.' UNWIN PACED DOWN THE CORRIDOR, COFFEE IN ONE HAND, briefcase in the other. 'I'm a bit taken aback by this.'

'Really?' Fenchurch laughed. 'Your client murders someone and you're surprised I want to speak to him?'

'He's innocent.'

'No, Terry Oldham's innocent. What was it your paymasters offered him? Or did they threaten him?'

Unwin gave a shrug. 'Just doing my job.'

'Thing is, most people's jobs don't involve keeping murderers off the street.'

Unwin held up his coffee, grinning. 'I could throw this over you.'

'Be my guest. Would love to do you for assault.'

Unwin chuckled as he took a drink. He peered over Fenchurch's shoulder and his look darkened, at the approaching footsteps. 'I'll be speaking to my client.' He bundled into the room.

Just in time to avoid Loftus, Reed in his wake.

Fenchurch smiled at Reed. 'Kay, get the preliminaries over, would you?'

'Sir.' She followed Unwin inside.

Loftus stood there, fingers twitching. 'Remember that you have no air cover, Inspector.'

'Always on my mind, sir.' Fenchurch held the door handle but didn't open the door. 'I'm doing this by the book.'

'Glad to hear it.' Loftus got out his cigarettes and flipped the lid. 'You're one hundred percent sure this was Webster?'

'I'm nowhere near that confident, sir. It's just... That assassination method is his hallmark. Head, mouth, heart. Tap, tap, tap. Brain, brain stem, heart. Any of them would kill you, but Webster always did all three, every time, to make sure. A guaranteed kill. And we've got CCTV footage.'

'Are you absolutely sure this isn't to do with the Albanian blood feud, because—'

'This is nothing to do with that. Pratt should focus on his job, not ours. This is a gangland assassination, sir, the sort that happened a lot before Webster went inside. The sort that didn't happen any more as soon as he was in custody.'

'Be careful here.'

'And I've listened. Speak of the devil.' Fenchurch clocked Bridge coming along the corridor. 'Kay's in there. I'll be watching in the Obs Suite.'

'Sir.'

Loftus waited for the door to shut. 'Well, I'm surprised again. I thought you'd be leading it?'

'Not a DCI's job, sir.' Fenchurch gave him a fake smile. 'But whatever alibi Webster gives us is bollocks. I happened to see him getting his bike back last night.'

'You just happened to?' Loftus grimaced. 'Have you been tailing him?'

Shit.

'No, sir. I drove past the Loco office. It's just up the street from here. I was on my way to hospital and there he was, bold as brass, getting his bike back.'

'We need a bit more than that.'

'Which is why I was trying to get the movement data from Loco. Why I called you to chase up Jason Bell.'

Loftus stood there, thinking it through. 'I'll get on top of that.' He marched off.

'Many thanks, sir.' Fenchurch entered the Obs Suite and hung his suit jacket from the back of the chair. He took a seat, focusing on the screen, a far cry from the setup they had in bloody Bethnal Green of all places. The video camera was trained down the middle of the table, splitting Webster and Unwin on the right, Reed and Bridge on the left.

Unwin crumpled his coffee cup and tossed it into the middle of the table. 'DI Fenchurch knows how well this went the last time.' He leaned forward. 'You should let my client go, you know? Save us all the trouble of a second civil court case. I filed the first this morning.'

'Let's see how this goes, shall we?' Reed shifted her focus to Webster. 'How's about you start with your movements between leaving custody last night and my colleagues collecting you?'

'We were going to go to that boozer down the road from the courthouse.' Webster sat there, yawning into a fist. 'Can't remember the name of it. Cock and bollocks or something. Nice place. Supposed to meet a few old lags in there. Dalton here was going to stick a couple hundred quid behind the bar.' His eyes lit up. 'But my Holly was there, outside court. And I thought to myself, "Desmond, you're better than this. You've been so good inside, let your old mates have a treat, but keep yourself away from temptation." So we cabbed it back home.'

'Sounds *really* believable.'

'Sergeant, I cleaned up inside. Cut the booze right out.' Webster patted his flat stomach. 'Lost a shitload of weight. That's something I owe your gaffer for. Fifteen months at Her Majesty's pleasure makes you take stock, you know? Especially on the second time round the board. I'd much rather spend time with my granddaughter than end up staying in there.'

'That why you persuaded Terry Oldham to take the rap for it?'

'Terry told the truth.' Webster sniffed. 'I tried to do time for him, but his guilt got the better of him.'

'A likely tale.'

'Look, darling, all I wanted was to spend some quality time with my daughter and young Sandy. I mean, I'd seen them inside, but it's not the same when you've got an inch of security glass between you, is it?'

'Just the three of you?'

'Nah, that useless lump of coal was there.' A snarl flickered on his lips. 'Kirk.' He smiled. 'Hard to believe lovely little Sandy came from his seed. Light of my life, she is. One in a million.'

'Was Kirk with you all that time?'

'Why do you ask?'

'Well, it's not like I can trust a word that comes out of Holly's mouth, can I?'

'Sergeant, you really need to speak to a shrink or something. I swear, it's like a constant barrage of negativity with you. Lighten up, learn to trust. Didn't your daddy love you enough or something?'

Reed laughed. 'So, when you got back home, you stayed in all night?'

'Feels like you're leading me somewhere. Or at least you think you are.'

'Just answer the question.'

'Alright. We got a pizza in to celebrate my release. Geezer chucked in some non-alcoholic beer, too. Some Scotch stuff, really fruity. Quite nice, have to say. Prefer that German stuff in the purple bottles, but hey ho. Made my day, I swear.' Webster flashed his eyebrows. 'Well, not as much as seeing my daughter. And I wish I'd seen your gaffer's face when I got out of court.'

'You didn't leave the house?'

'Oh.' Webster paused. 'Well, I had to speak to a mate. He'd kept a hold of my bike while I was inside. Got damaged when your gaffer assaulted me, didn't it? He fixed it up, looked after it.'

'This mate got a name?'

'He's not really a mate, I suppose. My boss. Geezer called Pavel. Can't even begin to pronounce his surname. Polish, I think. But he's as Cockney as you or me.' Webster chuckled. 'You're Essex, though, ain't you?'

'So you just went to get your bike back?'

'That's what I said. Cycled straight home. Fifteen minutes tops. Tell you, it was a pleasure to get back on a real bike and feel the wind in my hair.'

Reed whispered something to Bridge, but Fenchurch couldn't make it out. 'When did you go to bed?'

'Half midnight, maybe. Kirk cleared off about half ten.'

Matching the kid's story.

'Holly with you till the bitter end?'

Fenchurch took it as a cue to check his texts. Still no sign that Ashkani had turned up with Webster's daughter. *What the hell is she doing?*

'Nah, she went to bed just after Kirk left. Working today. Shelf stacking, but it's a good start for her.'

'And you just stayed up on your Jack Jones last night, did you?'

'You got some evidence says I did something else?'

'The way it works best is when I ask the questions and you answer, not the other way round.'

'I like the cut of your jib, sweetness.' Webster rocked back in his chair, lifting the front legs clean off the ground. 'Yeah, I watched some really terrible telly, then went to bed. Swear the old gogglebox has got even worse while I was inside. But a night in my own bed. Fantastic. Slept like a log and not one with a chainsaw in it. Holly woke me up when she left for work, gave me Sandy to cuddle while I came to. Kirk was already there.'

Reed checked some paperwork for a few seconds. 'Mr Naughton was inside for robbery, yeah?'

'Something like that. Not armed, though. And it's not like he's a nonce or anything.'

'Okay, let's wind the clock back to last night. After Kirk left and Holly went to bed, did you happen to visit anywhere on Brick Lane?'

'What?' Webster looked over at Unwin, then back at Reed. 'I told you, princess, we had pizza delivered. Why the hell would I go out for a curry?'

'Didn't say anything about a curry.'

'That's all there is on Brick Lane, though, yeah? Curries, curries and more curries.' Webster twisted his mouth into a snarl. 'Couple of Jewish shops, I'll give you that. Couple of bars for hipsters. But anytime someone's on Brick Lane, it's all about a curry.'

'You didn't murder anyone, did you?'

'Excuse me?'

'You heard the question, right?' Reed smiled. 'Or did all those gunshots over the years kill your hearing?'

'Funny.' Webster narrowed his eyes at her. 'No, love, I never killed nobody. The one you framed me for, didn't kill her neither. I've gone straight, princess. Being back in prison while you framed me reminded me how hard it is. I can't go back in there. I'm not even so much as parking in the wrong spot.'

'You confessed to abducting a child.'

'Did I?' Webster stared straight at the camera. 'Or was I just getting a rise out of your boss?'

Fenchurch clenched his fists. *Thank God I'm not in there. His head would've been bounced off the walls a few times by now.*

'You knew exactly what you did, Desmond.'

'Sergeant, my client has answered your questions. I suggest you let him leave.'

Reed looked at Unwin for a few seconds. Then she got up. 'Interview terminated at ten fourteen.' She left the frame and the door clicked as she left the room. Onscreen, Bridge killed the audio feed. Seconds later, the video cut out.

The Obs Suite door opened and Reed poked her head in. 'What do you think?'

'Pretty much as I expected.' Fenchurch got up and put his suit jacket on. 'I don't believe his alibi for a second. Right now, our priority is to speak to Holly and Kirk and drill right down.'

'You really think he's lying?'

'Kay, I know he is. There's a gap in his alibi, from when Holly went to bed through to this morning. You saw that CCTV Lisa found. Whoever killed Casey, did it right in the middle of that gap.'

'I agree. So what now?'

'We hold him until that alibi falls apart, then we arrest him for murder.'

Reed blocked the doorway, stopping him leaving the room. 'Loftus grabbed me in the canteen, said he's not happy about you bringing in Webster. Said if you don't get him by lunchtime, we have to let him go.'

Snide little wanker.

'He should speak directly to me, not pass messages through you.' Fenchurch blew air up his face. 'Webster's staying here until he's got a solid alibi. I don't care about innocent until proven guilty. If we let him go and there's another corpse...'

'Your funeral, guv.'

'Don't joke about that, Kay.' Fenchurch laughed.

Then his mobile blasted out *The Queen is Dead* by The Smiths. Ashkani. He answered it. 'Uzma, what's up?'

'I've got Holly in room one.'

27

FENCHURCH WAITED IN THE CORRIDOR FOR ASHKANI TO JOIN HIM. 'GOOD work finding Holly.'

'Thanks, sir.' Ashkani gave a noncommittal smile. 'Wasn't rocket science. And I've got a good team.'

'All the same. I asked you to find her and you did.' Fenchurch nodded at the interview room door. 'Got her brief in?'

'He was already here...'

Fenchurch groaned. 'Shit.' He opened the door. Dalton Unwin was talking to Holly in a low voice. 'You sure get around.'

'We're okay to start, seeing as how you asked so nicely.' Unwin gave a fake smile. 'Though I am keeping tabs on how much of my clients' time you're wasting.'

'Time spent with friends is never wasted.' Fenchurch focused on Holly. 'Nice to see you again.'

She wore a Tesco uniform, the name badge reading Holly-Ann. 'Saving it for your wank bank, are you? You filthy pervert.'

Unwin brushed her arm and she shut up.

'I see you've got your father's sense of humour.'

'What do you want?'

'You remember spitting on me yesterday? Outside court.' Fenchurch pointed at his cheek. 'Landed right here.'

'You got me in here for that? You got *her*,' she gave Ashkani a disdainful wave, 'to fetch me from my work for *this*? My boss ain't impressed, you know. We could've done that upstairs in the canteen or the boss's office, but hauling me in for questioning like this? Come on, that's messing with my life, mate. That job's all I've got.'

'We just want to check on what happened after your old man got out last night.'

'You messed up, didn't you?' Holly grinned. 'Tried to frame him and you couldn't.'

Keep her thinking she's winning. 'After that, what did you do?'

'We was going to take my old man out for a drink. I mean, I'm earning now so I wanted to treat him. But he's not touching the stuff any more. And Dalton here was going to stick some cash behind the bar for Dad's mates.'

Fenchurch shuffled through his notebook, pretending to be confused. 'Can you remind me how your father can afford to pay for the services of one of London's top lawyers?'

'Inspector...' Unwin laughed, a real throaty one. 'You're overstating my worth. As you know, my firm runs a very cost-effective service for our clients. We appreciate Mr Webster's business. And the bar tab is a standard "thank you" to our clients. We genuinely like them. Wouldn't defend them if we didn't.'

'Very generous of you.' Fenchurch fixed his stare on Holly. 'You stay in that pub a while?'

'We didn't go in. We went back home. My place. Well, Dad's place too.'

'Very cosy.'

'Kirk had been minding Sandy for me.'

'So he left, right?'

'No.'

'So the three of you went out for something to eat?'

'Nah. We got a pizza.'

'From Mario's?'

'Hardly.' Holly got out her phone and fiddled with the screen, her purple nails flashing in the lights. She held it up. 'Got it off Just Eat from a place round the corner. Two pizzas, a veggie one for me and Dad. Kirk had some meat thing.' She slid her mobile across the table. 'There. Plus some beer.'

Fenchurch checked the screen. All seemed to be on the level. He passed it to Ashkani. 'Take a note of that.' Then to Holly. 'So when did this pizza arrive?'

'I can't remember.' Holly tapped her screen. 'Says on there. I learnt to keep a record when it came to you lot.'

'When did you go to bed?'

'About half ten, I think. Kicked Kirk out around then.'

Fenchurch made a note. 'How was Kirk when he left?'

'He was fine. Hadn't been drinking, if that's what you're getting at.'

And the plot thickens... Sober enough to get on a bike and shoot someone.

'You hear anything during the night?'

'Got up a couple of times to go to the toilet. All quiet.' Holly smiled. 'Checked my old man's room. It was great to have him back in his own bed.'

'He was there all night?'

'You got some evidence to suggest he wasn't?'

'You tell me.'

'You've got nothing on him. He ain't done nothing.'

The door clattered open and Loftus paced over to Fenchurch, scowling as he leaned in: 'Let him go. Come see me outside.'

FENCHURCH WALKED OVER TO THE SMOKING AREA, BLINKING AS THE FUG engulfed him. 'Sir.'

'Well.' Loftus stamped out his cigarette against the box and managed to squeeze it in. 'I'd like to commend you for sticking to my rules, Inspector.' He flipped open his carton and pulled out a fresh cigarette, offering the box to Fenchurch. 'But I get the feeling you're not.'

'No thanks.' Fenchurch leaned against the side of the shelter. 'I'm playing fair here. We've got reasonable suspicion. We shouldn't be letting him go.'

'Simon, you haven't got a smoking gun.' Loftus raised his eyebrows as he lit his second cigarette. 'Unwin's suing us, too. I can't have you acting like a cowboy again.'

The back door opened again, and Webster sucked in the fresh air. Holly followed him out, grabbing hold of his hand. Webster swaggered up to them. 'Inspector. Or should I say, Chief Inspector?'

'Desmond.' Fenchurch stood his ground, trying to keep his face neutral even as Loftus blew smoke across him.

'I was just saying to my girl here,' Webster hugged Holly, 'how it's nice to constantly get reminded of what freedom tastes like.' He sucked in the air again, deep like he wasn't tasting stale cigarette smoke. 'Although I expect I'll get many more reminders from you. Every time you've got a crime in your manor, Fenchurch, you'll be thinking of your old mate, Desmond Webster.' He held his gaze. 'Thing is, I've changed. I'm a new man. I want to see my granddaughter grow up, unlike what happened with Holly here. All that time I lost, I'm never losing another second.'

Fenchurch stared hard at him.

A taxi honked its horn.

'Well, as nice as this is, Fenchurch, I've got to get on.' Webster grinned at him. 'Come on, love.' He walked off with Holly, hand in hand, then helped her into the cab.

'We'll get him, sir. Make sure he never gets out again.'

'Make sure you behave yourself.' Loftus snapped off his cigarette and put it back in the box. He clapped Fenchurch on the arm and walked off. 'Show me those extra stripes aren't just for Christmas.'

'Have you spoken to Bell yet?'

Loftus stopped. 'He's busy.'

'We need that data if you want to make sure Webster never gets out again.'

'Right, right.' Loftus sneered. 'I'll speak to him.'

Fenchurch walked back across the car park, watching Loftus get into his car and put a phone to his ear.

Webster's taxi pulled out onto the road.

'Sir?' Ashkani was waiting in the middle of the car park, arms folded. 'Everything okay?'

'Not really.' Fenchurch looked over at her. 'We jumped the gun here.'

'Sorry, sir. I suggested we did this.'

'This isn't on you, Uzma. We had to check that it wasn't Webster.'

'You think he's in the clear?'

'No. But until we get that data, he's my main suspect.'

'In the interview, why did you ask Holly about Kirk?'

'Sometimes pays to back more than one horse in the race.'

'Are you thinking he did it?'

'Maybe. He wasn't in the house when Casey was shot. Maybe Webster's training a protégé.'

Her forehead creased as she thought it through. 'I mean, it could've been Kirk. He had the opportunity, didn't he? He left their house around the time where Casey was murdered. Could've been him on that CCTV. Should we bring him in?'

'No point. I spoke to him, told me the same story. He could've done but, until we do what Loftus says and get solid evidence against, we should leave him be.' Fenchurch got out his Airwave Pronto and pulled up the PNC for Kirk Naughton. He clicked through to his arrest report, his bleary-eyed mugshot staring out of the pixelated screen. Convicted of robbing a post office in Colchester.

Long way from home.

Ashkani brushed her hair out of her eye. 'So?'

'Sometimes we need to keep our powder dry. We need this data from Loco. Then we'll either bring in Webster and squeeze him like a lemon, or focus on Kirk.'

'Right. Good plan.' Ashkani grunted. 'Can I get you a coffee?'

'Tea would be smashing. Milk.'

'Okay.' She trotted off, her shoes clicking off the tarmac.

Fenchurch stared up at the clouds, a burst of blue breaking through.

Kirk had an opportunity, sure, but is he in the same league as Webster? If Kirk did kill her and we go after him without evidence, he'll know. And so will the people he works for. And Desmond Webster. They'll all be on guard.

But maybe that's the angle. Play them off against each other, draw out who's really behind this whole thing.

A horn honked behind him.

Fenchurch swung round. Loftus was behind the wheel, face like thunder as he hammered his horn again. Another car was trying to get into the car park, stuck in a Mexican standoff with Loftus.

Loftus won, his Audi bumping the kerb as he rounded the oncoming Vauxhall. It took the space Loftus had just vacated.

Nelson got out. 'Simon.' He walked over and held out a hand. 'You holding out on us?'

Fenchurch scowled at him. 'What are you talking about?'

'Casey Nicholas.' Broadfoot got out of the passenger side and rested against the roof, grinning. 'Didn't think to let us know she'd been murdered, did you?'

'I don't see how it's relevant to—'

'You're a piece of work, ain't you? She was a witness in our prosecution of Mario Esposito.' Broadfoot rapped his thumbs on the car roof. 'But the good news is that we're taking over this case.'

28

'IN HERE.' FENCHURCH HELD DOCHERTY'S OLD OFFICE DOOR. INSIDE, IT still lay empty. Cold too, with the window still open from the summer heatwave.

'Thought you'd have set up in here.' Nelson gestured for Broadfoot to enter first. 'Acting DCI and all that...'

'How did you hear that?'

'No secrets in this place.' Nelson nodded into the room. 'Loftus told Broadfoot that you're SIO.'

'He offered me the full role, but I don't know...'

'I can't understand you.' Nelson laughed. 'You used to moan about getting turned over for promotion, now you won't accept one. It's worth a few grand a year, if nothing else.'

'And I need to see if it's something I can put up with on top of the shitload of hassle I've got right now. The stuff with my boy, with Chloe... Seriously, I've not got the time.'

'Bloody hell.'

'Jon?' Ashkani paced along the corridor, smiling as she passed Fenchurch a tea. She leaned in to kiss Nelson on the cheek. 'How you doing, mate?'

'Good, Uzma.' He returned the kiss. 'You?'

'Getting there.' She took a sip of coffee. 'You want me in here?'

'No. Catch up with Kay and see if she needs anything.' Fenchurch shifted his tea to the other hand. 'And do some more digging into Kirk's background for me.'

'Sir.' She walked off with a smile. *Probably pleased that I'm finally listening to her.*

Nelson watched her go. 'You two still at loggerheads?'

'Wouldn't go that far.' Fenchurch took a sip of tea through the lid. 'She's just not someone I can necessarily trust, you know?'

'I can vouch for her.'

'You *could* vouch for her, Jon. Back in the day. But she's had Mulholland's poison in her ear for the last five years.'

'Like I've had yours.'

'Exactly.' Fenchurch laughed. 'So I'm keeping an open mind about her. You're welcome to take her over to your team.'

'And put up with her bleating about becoming a DI? No chance.'

'You two just going to stand there?' Loftus waltzed past them.

Fenchurch let Nelson enter first, and stayed standing by the door as it click shut.

Broadfoot was over by the whiteboard. 'Right, we'd better get down to business, I suppose. So.' He clicked his tongue a few times. 'Casey Nicholas was our key witness against Mario Esposito. One of you arseholes should've told us that she's dead.'

'We caught the case, Derek.' Loftus took Docherty's old chair, swivelling round to face Broadfoot. 'Simon's the SIO.'

'But you should've called me, Julian. Common courtesy and all that.'

Loftus held his gaze. 'Derek, I took this through the MIT's Operational Command. They rubber-stamped it an hour ago. If you'd done your job properly, I would've seen that Casey was a person of interest in your case.'

'So that's how you're playing it?'

'Playing what? This is our case. End of.'

'This isn't just a murder case, okay?' Broadfoot drummed his fingers on the back of the whiteboard. 'We're prosecuting Mario for drugs, prostitution and people trafficking. And I don't mean the royal "we". This is a cross-Met case.'

Fenchurch joined him by the board. 'You think Mario's involved in her death?'

'You don't?' Broadfoot rounded on Fenchurch, staring up at him. 'You think he's innocent?'

'I didn't say that. I know he's caught up in this. But he's not the big bad guy here. He's not the one paying people to bump off his girls. Last I heard, he's just a pizza guy getting extorted or coerced into this. He isn't the one bringing them over here.'

'Inspector, the guy was sticking coke in the crusts of his pizzas.' Broadfoot paced off, arms raised. 'How the hell can you think he's innocent?'

'I think he's as guilty as a puppy in a puddle. But he isn't the big bad here.'

'Right.' Broadfoot leaned back against the far wall. 'And we're back to DI Fenchurch thinking he's better than the rest of the Met put together.'

'Have I ever given that impression?'

'Constantly.' Broadfoot left a pause, probably for a laugh. He got nothing. 'Okay, so we know Mario's behind this. The people trafficking, the prostitution, the drug running, these assassinations. Everything.'

'And you have evidence that you'll share with us, yes?'

'You're not cleared for it.'

'Is Superintendent Loftus?'

Broadfoot glanced over. 'Naturally.'

'Fine, but you can't seriously be telling me that Mario's behind this whole plot.'

'He's—'

'Not too late, am I?' Savage barged into the room, shifting his focus across the four occupants.

'Never too late, Howard.' Broadfoot pointed at the free chair next to Nelson. 'Have a seat.' He waited for him to sit. 'As you should know, Julian, DCI Savage is investigating the people-trafficking angle, as per his remit.'

'Indeed.' Savage crossed his legs and rested his hands on his knees. 'My team had been working very closely with Casey, ensuring her co-operation with regards to Mr Esposito's prosecution.' He shot a glare at Loftus. 'So, it would've been nice to learn of her death from friends.'

'Why was Casey still here, Howard?' Loftus folded his arms. 'She should've been taken back home and reunited with her family.'

'Because she wanted to stay. After her sister's death, we found her family back in Albania and broke the news to them. As suspected, they were indeed under threat from some local gangs. I don't know how well you know Albanian culture, but—'

'Pratt's given us all a detailed lecture series.'

'Well, yes.' Savage gave a knowing chuckle. 'Anyway, Casey wanted to stay here. Told us she'd built a life.'

Fenchurch sighed. 'Did she say who with?'

'Back off, Simon. I mean it.' Savage smoothed down his trouser legs, taking great care with it. 'We set her up with a clean job at Loco.'

'Seriously?' Fenchurch felt his gut plunge through the floor. 'She was working *there*?'

'Very easy to get employment and Casey enjoyed the work.'

'Even though Mario hired them?'

'I'm aware he employed them, yes.' Savage shared a withering look with Broadfoot. 'Loco run a hefty chunk of London's local deliveries. Am I to assume that all of them are corrupt or employing murderers?'

'They employed Desmond Webster.'

'Ah, I see. The crux of the matter.' Savage recrossed his legs. 'And you think Webster killed Casey?'

'That's one of my working hypotheses. We're awaiting some further evidence.' Fenchurch shot a look at Loftus. It just bounced off him.

'But Webster has an alibi, yes?'

'Two. We're checking them.' Fenchurch reached over to shut the window.

We should've brought Kirk in. At least to shut up these arseholes.

Savage leaned forward, clamping his knees. 'But you're getting your officers to hassle the poor man, correct?'

'Howard, have you seen Casey's body?'

'As a matter of fact, I have.' Savage got to his feet. 'I was at the crime scene this morning. Dr Pratt and I had a long conversation about it.'

'Then you'll agree that it's a tell-tale Webster hit.' Fenchurch pointed a fake gun at him and shot fake bullets. 'Tap, tap, bloody tap.'

'Gjakmarrja.' Savage brushed himself off like Fenchurch had actually shot him. 'This case bears all the hallmarks of a *gjakmarrja* revenge killing. An Albanian blood feud. I believe William Pratt mentioned it to you? The coffee under the knee?'

'William shouldn't be speaking to you without a murder detective there.'

'This is *our* case, Simon.' Savage joined him by the window. 'Not just yours.'

'Howard, you're not taking over.' Loftus wagged a finger at him, then did the same to Broadfoot. 'Same with you.'

'I mean this case is all of ours.' Savage held up his hands. 'The whole of the Met. Murder. Drugs. Prostitution. People-trafficking. We can cover all bases in this room. We need to work together.'

Fenchurch clamped a tight grip on Savage's shoulder. 'Howard, you coming in here and talking about a load of Albanian hocus pocus is not us working together, is it?'

'Hocus pocus?'

'This isn't a blood feud, Howard, and we're not ignoring anything.' Fenchurch threw his arms in the air. 'It just doesn't appear to be a... whatever you said. Listen to me. We've got two suspects for her murder. Desmond Webster and his daughter's kid's father. Who have you got?'

'You're missing the point. Sometimes it isn't just a simple murder. Sometimes it's not someone getting pissed off enough to stab someone else. Sometimes it is one of my elaborate people-trafficking plots, okay? Sometimes it's a guy running a pizza parlour as a front for drugs and prostitution. Sometimes he's trafficking people. Sometimes he's working with a transnational organisation. Sometimes those people are Albanians who rely on traditions to enforce their terror.'

Fenchurch let him have his glory for a few seconds. 'Howard, you should be focusing on how they got poor Amelia and Casey into the bloody country in the first place. How they kept the pressure on them. Not pissing on my chips. This is a murder case and I'm the SIO. So back off.'

'I'll do nothing—'

'*Howard.*' Loftus was on his feet. 'Simon's right. You need to let my guys do their jobs.'

'But this isn't even related to—'

'If it's not related, then you can bugger off.' Loftus pointed at the office door. 'And if it's one of these blood feuds, we'll find out. If it's not, we'll still find out.' He stepped close to Savage. 'You're here as a courtesy, okay? Both of you.' He gave Broadfoot a sideways glance. 'Now, I've listened to you all and this is how it's going to be. This is *not primarily* a drugs case and it's *not primarily* a people-trafficking case. This is *primarily* a murder case. Someone's dead and we're investigating. DI Fenchurch is in charge.' He let it sink in. 'Now, if you're not happy with that, then take it up with your superior officers. We all talk, you know. All the time. You should see the state of our inboxes. But as the ranking officer in this room and with the approval of the Ops Command, this case is staying with the East London MIT. End of. Am I clear?'

Broadfoot shrugged. 'Very far from happy, but I doff my cap to thee, Julian.' He went through the motion.

'Less of that.' Loftus focused on Savage. 'Howard?'

Savage's nostrils twitched. 'I'll discuss this further back at base.'

'But you accept this for now?'

'For now.'

'And you'll both support our investigations?'

'Sure.' Broadfoot nodded at Nelson. 'Come on, Jon.'

Savage joined them by the door. 'I advise you keep your mobile on, Julian.'

'Always is, Howard. Morning, noon and night.'

Fenchurch stopped Savage leaving. 'I want to speak to Spencer.'

'What the hell for?'

'You need to get your memory tested, Howard.' Fenchurch moved out of his away. 'You know he was shagging Casey, right?'

Savage lost control of his nostrils, the twitching extending to his lips. 'You're still on about—'

'Christ, Howard, what else has he done?'

'Nothing, I hope.'

'You know where I can find him?'

29

'YOU'RE A BLOODY IDIOT.' FENCHURCH GOT IN THE LIFT AND THUMBED the button for the eighth floor. The Empress State Building hung above the lift controls, the eighth floor marked for Savage's Trafficking and Prostitution Unit. 'How the hell is he back working here?'

'That's rich coming from you.' Savage leaned back against the rail as the doors juddered shut and the lift rumbled up. 'Christian was cleared by the DPS. He never had a case to answer.'

'What about sleeping with a witness? Hiring a car in his own name?'

'They made me remove him from the undercover operation.'

'That's it?'

'Someone had discovered DS Spencer's true identity. We don't know who, but we took him out of harm's way. He's had no contact with Casey since.'

'As far as you know.'

'I trust him.'

'So why do you look about as pissed off as I usually feel?'

'Derek sodding Broadfoot... We had an agreement. I wanted to prosecute Webster for the abduction of your daughter. But we agreed to defer until we prosecuted him for Amelia's murder. Now that's fallen apart, it's all up in the air now.'

'You don't think anything will stick?'

'You heard them back there. They're set on Mario as the big bad here. He just isn't. And Webster won't face justice for what he did to you and your family.'

Fenchurch smiled through the pain. 'I appreciate it, Howard.'

'I'm not doing it for you, Simon. I'm doing it for your daughter.'

'You didn't exactly stand up for yourself, though. You had a pop at me.'

'You try facing off to Derek Broadfoot and see how you cope.' The door opened and Savage set off, marching through Empress State Building towards the Trafficking and Prostitution Unit's desks by the windows looking west. He grabbed someone's shoulder and hauled them to their feet. 'Come with me.' He dragged them to a glass-walled meeting room.

Fenchurch followed them in, closing the door behind him. 'DS Spencer, nice to see you again.'

'What the hell is going on?' Spencer tried to shove Savage away, but the DCI had him, bunching up his navy suit in his fist, creasing pristine material. It fitted him like it had been tailor-made that morning. 'Come on, what—'

'*Sit.*' Savage pushed him over to a chair at the head of the table. He blocked one side, while Fenchurch was covering the door. 'Casey Nicholas was found dead this morning.'

'Shit.' Spencer collapsed back into the chair, sitting on the counter. 'Shit.'

'Someone shot her last night.'

Spencer looked up at Savage. 'Who?'

Fenchurch sat next to him. 'We wondered if you might know, Chris.'

Spencer's mouth hung open. 'You think I did it?'

'You telling us you didn't?'

'I was on a stakeout in Southend, last night. How the hell could I have done that?'

Savage frowned, exhaling slowly. 'Of course.'

'That the truth?'

Savage nodded at Fenchurch. 'We're running an operation out there.'

Fenchurch let Spencer make eye contact. 'You okay, son?'

'Had better lives, you know?'

'Want to talk about it?'

'No.' Spencer stared at the floor. 'Casey had a really tough life. Taken from her home and... To just die like that? Her sister and all. Jesus Christ.' A strand of oily hair slipped down to dangle across his forehead. 'I never told her, you know? Wanted to. Wanted to be honest with her, open my heart to her, but... this job. Man...'

'I hear you.'

'I listened to you.' Spencer looked at Fenchurch. 'What you said. I don't want something like this hanging over my career. So I broke it off and I was waiting until this whole case was finished, then I was going to tell Casey the truth.' He brushed away tears. 'But it just kept going, didn't it? Then you lost him, right?'

'I don't know what you're going through, but I hope that her death is nothing to do with you.'

'Seriously?' Spencer laughed, harsh and bitter. 'You're still banging on about that?'

'I'll bang that drum until people like you listen. I saw what happened to Casey. If this is—'

'This has *nothing* to do with me. Nothing.' Spencer smoothed down his slicked-back hair. 'Casey stopped working there the day Mario got taken away. That bullshit investigation into me kicked off round about then, so I had to clear off too. Howard, tell him.'

'It's right. We cleared out all the Albanian nationals from the business. The few that stayed, we got them jobs at Loco.'

'Mario's is still trading?'

'Correct. It's clean now. Under new ownership.'

'Okay, Spencer. We need your help in finding who killed Casey. Our colleagues in the drugs squad are operating under the impression that this was all Mario.'

'That's bollocks. He was a front. If he's taking the rap for it, then more fool him.'

'Who was it then?'

'That's the thing. I don't know. Mate, since Flick Knife vacated the premises, there are loads of upstarts trying to get on the scene. Gangs from south London, from Tottenham — they all want a piece of the East End pie.'

'You think this is one of them?'

'All I know is that Mario was dealing drugs and running hookers from there, doing it under Flick Knife's watchful eye, paying him a cut. Now Flick Knife's gone, some new arsehole is thinking they can get hold of Flick Knife's cut. Or maybe they got wind of how Mario staffed his operation. Could even be the people-traffickers, cleaning up.'

'You're waist deep in shit here. Webster's killed Amelja and Kesja. Who is he doing it for?'

'I don't know!'

'There's a parallel explanation here, of course.' Savage looked over at Fenchurch. 'Casey's body had all the hallmarks of a hit by Desmond Webster. But there was also coffee under her knee.'

'Shit.' Spencer shut his eyes.

'You know about that?'

'The Albanian blood feud business.' Spencer leaned close to the table, keeping his voice low like there was anyone around connected to a gang. 'There was this Albanian used to come in and speak to Mario. Came in for an onion pizza with filo pastry. Absolute bastard to make. Gunged up the oven like nobody's business. Tasted good, but took an age of man to clean the oven.'

'You got a name?'

'No, but Adrian will know him.'

~

FENCHURCH PICKED UP A GIANT DRUM OF INSTANT COFFEE FROM A market stall, pretending to price it up. Over the lane, Mario's Pizza was doing a brisk lunchtime trade. Market traders popping in for a quick slice, maybe, or office drones from nearby as the City sprawled ever outwards. 'You believe this story about an Albanian?'

Savage picked up a pair of fluorescent pink socks. 'As far as I see it, there must've been people pulling Mario's strings.'

'You got any idea who it could be?' Fenchurch picked up a smaller drum of coffee. 'You must've—'

'We debriefed and resettled all of the affected workers. None of them contradicted the evidence. We resolved any threats hanging over them. Seven of the nine have returned home, two are staying until their visas expire next year. Helps to have witnesses down the road, rather than in Albania.'

Fenchurch watched the pizza place again. 'You've no idea who this Albanian is, do you?'

'I have too many ideas, that's the problem. But I remain unconvinced.' Savage snatched the coffee tin from Fenchurch's grasp. 'Are you sure this is the right move?'

'Positive.' Fenchurch set off towards Mario's. 'And you heard Loftus. This is my case, so keep quiet in here.' He crossed the lane and opened the door.

Adrian Hall appeared in the doorway, his hipster beard halfway to his waist now. He gave Fenchurch an up-and-down as he entered. 'We're full just now, sir.'

'You clearly don't remember me.' Fenchurch smiled, showing his warrant card. 'Just a few questions, sir.'

Adrian waved around the room. 'Can you come back later?'

'Wish I could.' Fenchurch put his ID away. 'Unfortunately, I've got a dead body in the mortuary.' He gestured through to the kitchens. 'Can we do this through the back?'

'Fine.' Adrian grabbed a passing waiter. 'Dean, can you run the shop for a few? Cheers.' He headed off into back room and shut the kitchen door. The TV screen was frozen on that American comedy show Chloe loved, with a Range Rover stuck in the river. Adrian picked up a remote and turned it off. 'What do you want to know?'

'Casey Nicholas was murdered last night.'

'Jesus.' Adrian slumped into the chair, rested his head in his hands. 'What happened?'

'You saying you don't know?'

'Of course I don't!'

'See, I remember something that happened last year. You ordered a pizza from here, which Casey's sister was to deliver. She worked here, if you recall. Next thing I know, someone followed her to your home, but squashed her on the way.'

'That was nothing to do with me.'

'You saying you didn't order it?'

'No, I did. It's just...'

'What? You called your mate up and he—'

'I've no idea what happened!'

Fenchurch stared hard at him. 'Casey knew what was in your pizzas, didn't she?'

'They're clean now, I swear.' Adrian huffed out a sigh. 'I'm running this place now. I took it over from Mario when he got put away. It's clean as a whistle. All above board.' He smiled at Savage. 'And we're co-operating with your colleagues in prostitution and drugs.'

'Glad to hear it.' Fenchurch picked up a DVD case for 'King of Comedy', and took his time pretending to read the back. 'So who was doing all that nasty stuff, then? The previous owner?'

'He was. All of it. The drugs, the prostitution, you name it.'

'Just Mario? All on his own?'

No response.

'Because the way I hear it, there was an Albanian geezer...'

'How'd you hear about him?'

'Doesn't matter. He put you up to it?'

'No. But that guy was bad news.'

The door slid open and a waiter came in. Behind him, a chef stood in the kitchen. 'Sorry, boss, but Tomas has cut his finger. I need to take him to hospital.' The waiter scuttled back through.

'Ah, shit on it.' Adrian shot to his feet and charged over to the kitchen door.

Fenchurch stopped him. 'We were in the middle of something here.'

'Were we?' Adrian squeezed past and nudged the door open. He started washing his hands as the door shut behind him.

Cheeky bastard.

Fenchurch followed him through. It was melting in there. 'We can do this down the station, if you'd rather.'

'Can't you see how busy I am?' Adrian was whipping a pizza base round in front of him. 'I'm down a chef and a waiter now.' He crouched down in front of the oven, the wood burning inside, and slid a pizza in on a paddle. Then another two in and he shut the door. He got up but still didn't look at Fenchurch.

Fenchurch joined him by the oven and started sweating almost immediately. 'I need to know who this Albanian geezer is.'

Adrian got a pizza out, checked it, and stuck it straight back in. 'Why?' He took the three pizzas out and hit a bell. 'This place is clean, mate. I ain't paying nobody nothing.'

A waiter came through and started slicing them with a pizza wheel. He dumped them on big plates and took them through.

Fenchurch watched him leave. 'Two Albanian girls connected to this place are dead, okay? Now, I've got a ton of theories as to what's happening, but one of them says that whoever abducted those girls from their homes, they're cleaning up now.'

'Mate, when I said this place was clean, I meant it.' Adrian smeared tomato paste on three fresh pizza bases. 'We don't even do a stuffed crust any more. They're all like these ones. Romanica, I call it.' He finished sprinkling mozzarella on then gave it a dusting of herb, oregano by the smell of it. 'Clean as a bloody whistle.' He shovelled the first pizza into the oven. 'Now, you need to get out my hair, mate, because I'm up to my beard today.'

'Just tell me and I'll leave.'

'Fine.' Adrian took another lump of dough and started whipping it. 'This geezer used to come in and get a tomato and onion Albanian. It's like any other pizza, but you swap the usual base for filo pastry. Mario ran it as a special a few times. This bloke heard about it, so he comes in and gets chatting to Mario. The rest is... You know how these things go. It's incremental, little bits here and there. Mario started taking a side order from this guy, ended up with a whole operation full of whores and drugs.'

The first thing anyone's said that makes the slightest bit of sense.

Adrian stuck a second pizza in the oven and wiped sweat off his forehead.

Fenchurch stared at him, watching him load the final pizza in the oven. 'This Albanian geezer still around?'

'Came in a few weeks back, but I refused to serve him.'

'Brave.'

'Big brute, he is. You could tell he was trouble just from looking at him.'

'Even braver. He threaten you?'

'Just with silence. I think he had some sort of extortion thing going on. But I don't pay anyone except my staff and my suppliers. Like I said, this is an honest business now. I'm passionate about pizza, not about enriching thugs.'

Fenchurch refocused on Adrian. 'I suggest you get yourself to a police station and you tell them what you just told me.'

Adrian dropped a paddle on the floor. He reached down and tossed it in the sink. 'Shit.' He darted over and opened the oven door. Black smoke billowed out. He found a second paddle and got the pizzas out. Only slightly charred, despite that. 'Can't sell these.' He shut the door and deflated.

'You can get ahead of this. Come with me, give a statement. We'll look kindly on you.'

Adrian took a deep breath and darted over. 'Mate, these pizzas are ruined. Need to make another three. There's no way I'm getting out of here before eleven tonight.'

'Give them here.' Fenchurch handed over a tenner. 'I've got an Incident Room full of hungry cops.'

Adrian pocketed the money. 'There's no case to answer here, mate. I'm innocent.'

'Then come with me. Tell your story.'

'I can't. Look, I'll do it when my chef gets back. Okay?'

'Good lad. Now, what was this Albanian's name?'

'Zamir.'

30

FENCHURCH CHECKED HIS MOBILE — STILL RADIO SILENCE FROM THE powers that be. One message from Ashkani:

ON MY WAY.

No sign of her, though.

He rested the stack of pizza boxes on the roof of Savage's car. 'Am I supposed to know who this Zamir is?'

'Zamir Selinaj is responsible for about forty percent of the brothels in the UK, at a rough guess.' Savage plipped his locks but didn't get in. 'He's been running Soho like it's the Seventies all over again. The place is awash with drugs and vice.'

'So you know about him?'

'Not everything, but between myself and Derek Broadfoot, we know enough.'

'How do we speak to him?'

'You don't just *speak* to him, Simon. It's not that simple.'

'Never is.'

'Listen to me. The Albanians run most of the illegal activities in this country, split with the Turkish gangs. London, the Midlands, even stuff in Scotland. And they are *vicious*. And they cover it up well. Which is why I'm concerned that this is a blood feud, after all.'

Fenchurch scanned the street and spotted Ashkani's pool car trundling towards them. 'That again.'

'I'm serious. It's how they hold power over these people. The gang is based in Southend.'

'Southend? That's where—'

'Yes. Spencer is working the case against them.'

'Sure that's wise?'

'It's my operation, Simon. This gang runs about three quarters of the heroin entering the UK, plus they traffic people. Chinese, Syrian, you name it, so long as they can pay, they'll bring them here.' Savage's expression darkened. 'As for their own people, well they just force them to do their bidding, as you've seen. Like I say, a blood feud. The power they hold over their people is astonishing.'

Fenchurch gave Ashkani a wave, then leaned back against Savage's car. 'So if this isn't Desmond Webster's handiwork, or even if it is but he's working for these Albanians, we need to speak to this guy, right?'

'Listen, I've got some undercover operatives working at a betting shop out in Barking. It's possible they might have some leads on this.'

'Two seconds.' Fenchurch got in the passenger seat of Ashkani's car and dumped the pizza boxes on her lap. 'Take these.'

She picked them up, face like thunder. 'What the hell?' She lifted the lid and peered inside. 'These are all meat. I'm vegan.'

Well, either way, they smell really good and I'm bloody starving.

'Listen, I've got to see a man about a dog.' Fenchurch waved at Savage. 'Need you to keep an eye on Mr Hall there. Make sure he doesn't scarper.'

'Need I remind you that I'm a DS?'

'Sergeant, that guy is possibly up to his armpits in Albanian gang crime. Seems like the drugs and prostitution didn't end with the previous owner. If this all pans out, it'll be good for your career.'

'Oh, there's a margarita in here.' She pulled out a slice and bit into it.

'I thought a vegan couldn't eat cheese?'

'Well.' Ashkani shrugged and kept chewing. 'There's nothing much mmf mmf at base. Though mmf mmf probably mmf you.'

'Probably what?'

'Kill you, sir.' Ashkani held the slice in front of her mouth. 'She's climbing the walls. All that CCTV.'

Lisa Bridge. Right.

Ashkani folded the slice in half and took another bite. 'I did some digging into Kirk Naughton. Spoke to his probation officer. Reckons he's clean.'

'You agree with him?'

'Her. She said nothing to make me disagree.'

'But nothing either way on Kirk?'

'Right.' Ashkani put the crust back in the box and took another slice. 'Starving.'

'You okay to do this, then?'

Ashkani bit into a slice. 'Mmf mmf fine.'

~

They passed a Shell on the right, followed by an almost-adjacent Esso. Fenchurch gestured at a cemetery on the left, rows upon rows of tombstones basking in the fresh wash of sunshine. 'That's where Docherty's buried.'

Savage took his eyes off the road to focus on Fenchurch. 'You okay?'

What I'd give to bring him back... To stop the cancer eating away at him.

'Here we go.' Savage powered on down the road and pointed at a betting shop just round the bend. 'Zamir runs it as a cover.' He pulled up in a spot that gave a decent-enough view of the shop.

The sort of chain bookies you'd find anywhere. Grimy decor, loud adverts in the window. Two punters lurked outside, smoking and chatting. A cluster of cars and vans outside. Maybe they belonged to the gamblers still chatting away, still smoking.

Or maybe not.

Fenchurch waved at a van, Shrimper Flowers. 'Well, there's a Southend connection right there.'

Savage squinted at it. 'I don't follow.'

'Southend United's nickname is the Shrimpers.'

'Shit.' Savage got out onto the street, heading over to the van.

Bloody hell...

Fenchurch got out and tracked behind him, catching him at the van. A florist's, with a giant cartoon shrimp holding a bouquet of flowers. Really badly done. 'What's up, Howard?'

'This is how Derek's lot suspect they distribute the coke. Flowers and plants.' Savage slapped a hand on his bald head. 'Bloody football.'

One of the smokers kept looking at Savage. He wore a navy polo shirt with the betting shop's logo embroidered in pale yellow. Not a punter, but an employee.

And maybe even an employee of Savage, one set on blowing his cover.

Inside the shop, a man peered out at them through the smoked-glass entrance. Evil eyes, narrowed. He came out onto the street. Guy was like he was cut from granite, and a big slab of it at that. Squared-off shoulders, bulging muscles, and the sort of neck you just couldn't strangle, no matter how hard you tried. 'Can I help you, gents?' Slight accent to his Estuary English.

Savage pointed at the shrimp cartoon. 'This your van?'

'It's a mate's.' He pointed at the other smoker, the one in overalls. 'Tell him, Dave.'

'That's right. You want some pansies, or something?'

Savage stepped closer. 'Zamir Selinaj, isn't it?'

'Who the hell are you?' Zamir frowned at Savage, then at his employee. 'Wait, I know you.' He nodded, then again. 'You and Stefan here, I've seen you, ain't I?'

'Sir, this is—'

'No, this is bullshit.' Zamir rounded on Stefan, towering over him. 'You Old Bill, are you?'

'Come on, mate. I'm—'

'You're filth!' Zamir pushed him back against the flower van. 'You think you can get something out of me, eh?'

'Stop!' Savage reached into his pocket. 'I'm a police officer, sir. We need a—'

Zamir snapped a punch at Savage and sent him flying across the van's bonnet. Zamir pinned him down, wrapping his long fingers around Savage's throat. Savage struggled, trying to reach Zamir's own throat, but the big man had him where he wanted.

Stefan, the employee, lurched to Savage's defence, but Dave, the overalls guy, took him out with a trip.

Fenchurch launched himself at Zamir, fists raised. He caught an elbow in the face and bounced off the side, sliding down until he crunched off the pavement.

Dave grabbed Fenchurch's collar and pulled him up. Then crumpled into a heap, with Stefan standing over him.

Heavy footsteps pounded away from them, Zamir running off, past the bookies and the row of shops.

Got to get him.

Savage was sitting up, dizzy and swaying around.

'Stay with him!' Fenchurch got up and ran after Zamir, tugging his phone out of his pocket as he gave chase. He hit dial and put it to his ear. 'Control, this is DI Fenchurch. Send an ambulance to my location.' He rounded the end of the row and stopped. No sign of Zamir.

Shit, where the hell is he?

Fenchurch continued on down the road, slowly, still searching the place.

Zamir was in the cemetery, his straight-backed run pounding through the gravestones, laser focused on getting the fuck out of there.

Fenchurch hopped the low fence and sprinted after him, his throat on fire as he powered past the first row of graves, a much straighter row than the one Zamir was on. Fenchurch slipped onto the grass edge to dampen his footsteps and knew he'd catch Zamir where the paths merged if he just sped up that little bit. And he dived forward, crunching into Zamir with a rugby tackle.

Zamir went down, but slipped out of Fenchurch's grasp. He rolled over, onto the grass, and used a grave to haul himself up. He kicked Fenchurch, connecting with his arm.

Fenchurch swept out with his feet, but Zamir jumped, landing on Fenchurch's ankle with a sickening crunch.

Then he went down in a blur.

Savage lay on top of Zamir, heavily out of breath, and grabbed his wrist, pressing him face-first into the grass. 'We should never have approached that shop.'

'Well, we've got him now.' Fenchurch limped over and passed his cuffs to Savage. 'He assaulted you, so he's going down for that.'

Zamir was a dead weight. Savage couldn't shift him.

Fenchurch tried to help, gripping the big man's armpit and hauling him up to standing. 'Come on, sunshine, let's get you somewhere nice and warm.'

'I'm going nowhere.' Zamir slumped against a gravestone, focusing his reptilian gaze on Fenchurch. 'Staying right here.'

Fenchurch crouched in front of him. 'You know anything about Casey Nicholas?'

'Who?'

'She died last night. Could be a gangland hit, or it could be one of you Albanians doing some sort of blood feud shenanigans. Either way, you're in the frame for it, matey boy.'

'You can't do this to me.'

'Oh yeah?' Fenchurch pointed back towards the bookies. 'Just wait till I get into that van and find all that lovely heroin.'

'I don't know what you're talking about.'

'Coke?'

'No.'

'People?'

'No.' Zamir laughed. 'I tell you, my friend, if you want to get some good cocaine, speak to Adrian at Mario's Pizza. He will sort you out. He's selling drugs. I hear you can just go in there and buy them off him. At the table. Very simple process. Keeps it in the family.'

'What do you mean?'

'Well, he's Mario's son, isn't he?'

31

BLUE LIGHTS DANCED OFF THE BOOKMAKER'S, WHICH WAS SURROUNDED by squad cars and an army of uniformed officers. One of them dipped Zamir's head as he pushed him into the back seat.

Savage seemed to relax, his shoulders slumping. 'This isn't how I wanted it to play out.'

'Didn't think it would be.' Fenchurch leaned against Savage's car, arms folded. 'How long have you been after him?'

'Two years.' Savage shook his head. 'We've got nowhere near enough evidence to put him away.'

'He assaulted you, Howard. The old Al Capone trick. If you can't get him for people-trafficking, drugs, prostitution, you can at least get him off the streets.'

Savage nodded slowly. 'Trouble is, he'll still control things from in there.'

'But it'll inconvenience him. Try and take this as a win.'

Savage laughed. 'You're right.' He smiled across at Stefan, doling out orders to some uniform. 'Steve there knows where some of the bodies are buried. The florists too. We might get something there.'

'That's more like it.' Fenchurch clapped him on the back. Made him wince. 'So, what's the plan?'

'Well...' Savage exhaled. 'I'm going to tail that car to ESB, along with at least five others. I want make sure nothing happens on the way.'

'And that bombshell about Mario?'

'You believe it?'

Fenchurch shrugged. 'We need proof.'

'I'll let you take lead on that.' Savage set off towards his car. 'Catch you later.'

Fenchurch leaned back against the wall and got out his phone. He had a few missed calls from Loftus, but he dialled another number. He set off towards his car. And realised Savage had driven. He flagged down a uniform and held out his hand for the keys.

'Guv?' Reed, sounded like she was in an office somewhere.

'Kay, need to meet you at that factory in Hackney.' Fenchurch got behind the wheel of a Volvo. 'Bring a hunting party.'

∼

MARIO'S FACTORY WASN'T IN HACKNEY AT ALL. ONE OF THE FEW remaining warehouses in Harringay that wasn't turned into a loft. Triangular roofs, the right-angled peaks off-centre. The sign above the door read Espo International, but Fenchurch couldn't miss it. Place was swarming with uniformed officers, a few shifty plainclothes guilty by association.

Fenchurch got out of the squad Volvo and tossed the keys to an older uniform. 'Make sure this gets back to Barking station.'

'That'll be tough.' The uniform smirked. 'Closed it, didn't they?'

Fenchurch grunted at him. 'Well, get it to Dagenham or Romford or wherever the hell it's come from.'

'Sir.' He pocketed the keys, but didn't look like he was going anywhere in a hurry.

Fenchurch walked over to the factory, calling Loftus. He bounced the call yet again. Fenchurch marched over to the door, shoving his warrant card into the face of the bum-fluffed uniform guarding the door. 'DS Reed around?'

'She's inside, sir.'

'Thanks.' Fenchurch entered the factory, stepping back into the Eighties. Bare brick walls on three sides, the fourth a pair of wooden doors either end of a security desk. The guard was chatting to a pair of uniforms. The left door read MANAGER'S OFFICE so Fenchurch took that.

Inside, Spencer was going through paperwork. He looked over with a smile that turned into a frown.

'What the hell are you doing here?'

'DCI Savage told me to get out here.'

Fenchurch got up close. 'Well, I'm telling you to bloody clear off.'

'You know where to look, do you?'

'What?'

'I was undercover in this organisation for a year. I know where they keep stuff.' Spencer stood his ground, puffing his chest out. 'You honestly think Zamir's telling the truth? That Mario is Adrian's old man?'

'I don't know, son. I like evidence. Earlier, you said his place was clean.'

'It is. Spotless. Adrian's cleaned up.'

'Just because it's not baked into the crusts any more, doesn't mean Adrian wasn't dealing, wasn't selling it at the tables.' Fenchurch took a step closer. 'Did you know?'

'Of course I didn't.' Spencer stared at the floor. 'I've been stuck behind a desk, ain't I?'

Fenchurch took another step and grabbed Spencer's shirt, the material bunching around his fist. 'This pizza business was a front for people-trafficking. Drugs, prostitution. Assuming Adrian is still selling coke and ketamine from that restaurant, then either you know and you're involved, or you don't know and you're incapable of doing your job.'

'Guv!' Reed pushed them apart, and split Spencer off. 'What the hell?'

'Kay, I've been looking for you. What is he doing here?'

'Savage's orders.'

'I want him out of here.'

'Guv, he's been helpful.' Reed held out a document, shaking it like a lawyer in the Old Bailey. 'Proof. Adrian is Mario's son.'

Fenchurch took the page and scanned it. 'Go on?'

'Adrian Hall's not his real name. It's Adriano Esposito. His mum remarried, I think. Changed his name.' Reed nodded at the page. 'Ownership deeds for the restaurant, plus this place. Adrian was co-owner, fifty-fifty split with his old man. Then last summer, just after Flick Knife died, Mario switched full ownership of this place to Adrian. Made it appear to be a sale, but I doubt we'll find a financial transaction.'

Fenchurch tried to process it. He turned on Spencer, pinning him against the grubby wall without touching him. 'How much do you know?'

'Nothing!'

Fenchurch focused on Reed. 'This is a complete disaster, Kay. Get him out of here and keep him away.'

※

Mario's Pizza was still open, still trading. The lights glowed in the lingering lunchtime gloom as a young couple inspected the menu, no doubt trying to decide where to spend their precious pennies on their one date-night meal out this week. Maybe this month. It wasn't to be here — she was pointing inside and scowling, her ski-jump nose twitching. Her boyfriend grabbed her hand and they waltzed off in search of somewhere else.

Their absence gave Fenchurch a better view of the restaurant, of Adrian Hall working the front of house.

And selling drugs, if Zamir was to be believed.

Fenchurch opened the back door of Ashkani's car and slid in. 'Evening, Jon.'

'Nice to see you, Simon.' Nelson stayed focused on the restaurant, chewing away.

Fenchurch reached between Nelson and Ashkani to grab a slice of pizza out of the box. 'Well, Adrian is Mario's son.' He held the slice ready to eat, his mouth watering. 'Kay found proof.'

Nelson shared a look with Ashkani then craned round to stare at him. 'Broadfoot said him and Savage are going to interview Zamir.'

'Two DCIs in an interview...' Fenchurch laughed. 'They'll spend the first hour figuring out how to switch on the recorder.'

Over the road, Adrian opened the door and passed some pizzas to a delivery driver. A man on a moped, old and fat.

Ashkani pointed at him. 'He's clearly not a prostitute.'

'Rule thirty-four.'

She scowled at Nelson. 'What?'

'Rule thirty-four of the internet.' Nelson finished chewing his pizza. 'If it exists, there's porn of it. Someone somewhere will get off on fat men on mopeds.'

'Jesus, Jon. You need to get away from the drugs squad before they eat the rest of your soul.'

'It's not all bad.' Nelson pointed at Mario's. 'Think we should arrest Adrian?' He chewed. Sloppy eating noises came from the back seat. 'This is *really* good pizza. The guy's got a gift.'

Fenchurch reached round to take a second slice. Slightly burnt, but it *was* really good pizza. 'Him being Mario's son is one thing. Means it's more likely that he's continued to deal after we took him down. But it'd be useful if we had something else on him.'

'Thing is, our snouts tell us someone round here's dealing coke, ketamine, heroin, MDMA, spice, you name it.' Nelson took another bite. 'Just not got a name.'

'So it could be Adrian?'

'Right.'

Fenchurch took his time chewing his pizza. 'You want to move now?'

'Waiting on Broadfoot's orders.'

'So we're just sitting around, waiting?'

'About the size of it.' More chewing. 'You got anything to drink?'

'This isn't a drive-through, Jon.'

'You bastard.' Nelson stared out of the window.

Over the lane, a man left the restaurant, rubbing his nose, snorting.

Fenchurch recognised him, but couldn't quite place him. 'Jon, who's that?'

'The geezer who bought coke from Mario.' Nelson leaned across Ashkani, pressing her back in the driver's seat. 'Had a stuffed-crust pizza, didn't he? Chicken and banana or something. Lived down by St Kath's Docks, remember?'

'The gym bunny.' Fenchurch nodded. 'Colin Dunston.'

Nelson clicked his fingers. 'That's him.'

Dunston stopped in the street, patting his suit jacket pocket a few times, like he was searching for some lost family heirloom. He seemed to relax as he set off down the lane, heading towards home.

'Tenner says he's been buying some product.' Nelson opened the back door. 'Stay here and keep eyes on Adrian. I'll tail Dunston, then arrest him.' The door clicked shut.

And I'll just sit here. A DCI, staking out a pizza restaurant. SIO, my big hairy arse.

His phone blasted out the crashing opening of that Who track. He answered it before the second beat. 'Sir.'

Loftus yawned. Sounded like he was outside somewhere. 'Listen, I'm out at ESB and Savage is still interviewing this Zamir character.'

'Getting anywhere?'

'Lawyer's obfuscating things.' Loftus sighed down the line. 'Do you believe that Zamir's behind this?'

'Could be.' Fenchurch played it through. 'We know there's a connection to an Albanian gang. People-smugglers, drug dealers. When Zamir spotted Savage, he knocked his block off. It was brutal. You don't do that if you're innocent.'

'I'd expect a professional approach. Deny it, get lawyers involved. Not violence.'

'We spooked him. It was an accident, sir.'

'Still, I don't like him just telling you that information. Feels staged.' Loftus's breath rattled the speaker. 'Despite acting like the big man earlier, let's just say that I've got orders to defer to Drugs on certain matters.' Another sigh, deeper. 'And to Howard ruddy Savage on anything pertaining to Mario's Pizza.' Sounded like Loftus was smoking, sucking a deep drag into his lungs. 'Don't you ever want to take a nice, quiet job out in the countryside? Get away from all the politics and the games?'

'Every five minutes, sir.'

A female delivery driver cycled up to the front door and hopped off her bike. Adrian opened the front door and gave her a stack of pizzas. He watched her go, taking a moment to himself as he looked up and down the lane.

'I've got eyes on Adrian Hall. I want to bring him in, sir. At the least, he's got information. Given we know he's Mario's son, his involvement in Amelia's murder seems a lot likelier. Possibly Casey's too.'

'Stay put until Howard gives us confirmation. And I need you to await further instruction from DCI Broadfoot's team. DI Nelson should be there.'

'Already been here, sir. Aside from eating most of my pizza, he's chasing down a fresh lead.'

'I know it's difficult taking orders from someone who was once a subordinate—'

'It's not that, sir. Someone bought drugs from there.'

'Proof?'

'Maybe. I just—'

'Stay there.' Another drag. 'I'll keep you apprised, Inspector.' And he was gone.

Fenchurch stared at his phone. So much for being an Acting DCI.

≈

THE RESTAURANT DOOR OPENED WITH A TINKLE AND TWO MEN LEFT, hands in pockets, locked in a deep conversation. No sign of any drugs on them.

Fenchurch clutched his mobile tight, keeping a watch on Mario's. His legs were locking. *Need to get out and stretch.* He rubbed at his quads, finding a tight knot halfway down. A few seconds of pressing and it popped. Bliss.

Ashkani scowled at him. 'That doesn't sound good.'

'It's very far from good, Uzma.' Fenchurch let the relief wash over him. 'We're getting nowhere fast. How do you see this?'

'If you're asking me my advice, I say let Jon Nelson do most of the damage, sir. Then you can take the glory.'

'Not my style.' Fenchurch leaned back and tried to massage some energy into his dead legs.

That Nirvana song blared out. The one from the second album, with the name he could never remember, not even when he read it. Nelson loved it, though. Fenchurch answered it.

Nelson was out of breath. 'Simon, I've arrested Dunston outside his office.'

'Quick work.'

'He's a fast walker.' Some muffled shouting in the background. 'Got a pair of uniforms taking him back to Leman Street just now. I swear, the quantity he's got on him, it's like he was going to deal.'

'To his colleagues?'

'Maybe. Even though he got off with a warning last time, this is twenty grams of coke and at least the same in ketamine. Like I say, dealing.'

'He say where he got it?'

'Guy's hardened and smart. Not even said "no comment".'

Fenchurch rasped the stubble on his head. 'Broadfoot want us to move on Adrian yet?'

'Not yet.'

'Come on, Jon.'

'He's speaking to Loftus and Savage now. I'll let you know, okay?'

'Well, keep me updated.' Fenchurch killed the call, but held onto the phone.

Fenchurch spotted Adrian through the restaurant window, nodding his head in time to the music blasting out of the open door. He pulled on a heavy coat and scarf, then left, heading off along the lane away from them.

'Sod it.' Fenchurch opened his door and got out. 'Stay here, Uzma. Something's spooked him.'

'STILL GOT EYES ON HIM, JON.' FENCHURCH WEAVED THROUGH HEAVY foot traffic, keeping a good distance behind Adrian, twenty or so metres ahead. He followed along Goulston Street, passing the spot where Amelia was killed all those months ago.

Adrian acted like nothing had happened or like he'd blotted it out of his mind. He crossed the road, heading for Aldgate East tube.

Where are you going?

Fenchurch stopped, waiting on the traffic island.

Adrian passed the tube entrance and cut down Leman Street.

Fenchurch let out a sigh of relief. 'He's heading to the station.'

Nelson sounded out of breath down the phone line. 'Aldgate East?'

'No, I mean Leman Street. I told him to give a statement. Maybe he's listened.'

'Is he going to confess? Maybe he knows that Dunston's been nicked so he's going to give it all up. Shit. He can't know…'

'Not the first time we'd have a leak, Jon.' Fenchurch rounded the corner and spotted Adrian taking a side lane behind the construction site. 'He's not heading to the station.'

Nelson groaned.

Fenchurch quickened his pace, the wind rattling down the lane between the two-metre high boards and the adjacent building, a Sixties tower currently being renovated by the site's developer.

Adrian paused halfway along and looked behind him.

Fenchurch knelt down to tie his laces, resting his mobile on the slabs. Gave himself a count of three, then he looked back up.

No sign of Adrian.

Shit!

'I've lost him, Jon.' Fenchurch jogged along the lane, bursting out onto Commercial Road, busy with vans and lorries.

Adrian was jogging over the road, narrowly missing being clipped by a white van. He set off down a back street.

'It's okay, Jon. He's going to his flat.' Fenchurch rounded the van, waiting for a car to power past on the other lane. 'Any orders from on high?'

Nelson paused, voices muffled in the background. 'Broadfoot says take him.'

'Just as well I followed him, isn't it?' Fenchurch set off into a run and shot off down the street.

Adrian stood in the path leading to his flat. He turned towards Fenchurch. 'You stalking me or something?'

'I need a word with you down the station, sir.' Fenchurch grabbed his coat and walked him away from the block of flats, onto the wide pavement. 'Thought you were on your way to the police station, but no.'

Adrian stopped dead, his gaze shooting around the street. 'I ain't done nothing!'

'Oh yeah?' Fenchurch blocked his exit. 'We had a little chat with your mate. Zamir. Said you're dealing drugs from the restaurant.'

'Complete bollocks. I told you, Zamir's been coming in and threatening me. Asking for protection money.'

'We arrested Colin Dunston. It's over.'

Adrian slumped back against the garden gate.

'We know you're Mario's son.'

Adrian looked up, the relief of years of lies and extortion seeming to ease off his shoulders.

'Come on.' Fenchurch grabbed his shoulder and led him down the street.

Adrian elbowed Fenchurch in the guts, pushing him over onto his knees. Something hit the back of Fenchurch's skull, something hard, and he stumbled forward, struggling to stay upright. He tripped and fell, smacking his head off the pavement.

Adrian sprinted off, heading back the way they'd come.

A loud crack and Adrian fell over.

A gunshot. Came from behind.

Fenchurch pushed up to standing, dizzy, wheeling around like he was on a waltzer. Everything was a blur.

Another shot. Then another.

Adrian lay on the pavement at his feet. Blood spilled onto the slabs, his head burst open like a dropped melon. A crimson stain spread out from his heart, soaking his beige coat.

Movement to the left.

Fenchurch wheeled round, swaying.

Someone got on a bike.

But the world spun and Fenchurch fell forward again. He tried, but just couldn't make them out.

The bike sped off.

Fenchurch tried to get up, but landed on the ground, the concrete biting at his cheek.

Everything went black.

32

'Simon?' Ashkani loomed over him, her mouth open. 'Are you okay?'

Fenchurch tried to stand up, but stumbled back again. His skull felt like it'd been caved in, but he couldn't feel any damage. He looked back at Adrian's house, breathing hard. At the body on the ground. At the pool of blood. 'What the hell happened?'

God, I sound wasted.

'I was just behind you... I saw it all.'

'It's okay, Uzma.' Fenchurch got up at the fourth attempt. Had to brace himself against the wall.

'Simon...' She grabbed him in a hug, wrapping herself around him. 'He was shot in front of me. Of us.'

'Hey...' Fenchurch tried to step away, but she was clinging tight. He saw fragility in her eyes, misted by tears. 'Why did Webster kill him?'

'You saw Desmond Webster?'

'I... I don't know who I saw.' Fenchurch's head thudded. 'Did you see them?'

Her hands balled into fists. 'I...' She shook her head. 'I just saw Adrian fall over. You were in the way. I...' She brushed away her tears and sucked in a breath. She stared at him, her steely resolve reappearing. 'Simon, you've been concussed, you need to get to hospital.'

Fenchurch focused on the body in the doorway.

I need to find out who killed him and why.

A wound had opened Adrian's skull. A second in the windpipe. Then a third over the heart.

Jesus. Like there's any doubt about who did it.

He turned to Ashkani. 'I need to bring Webster in.' He called Savage.

'We're sorry, but—'

Fenchurch held the mobile away from his head, listening for the beep. 'Howard, it's Simon, call me back immediately.'

He fired off a text:

CALL ME. URGENT.

Fenchurch pocketed his phone and swayed. He set off towards the main road.

Ashkani grabbed him. 'You're going nowhere except hospital.'

Fenchurch stared at her for a few seconds. 'Fine, but I need you to manage this crime scene.'

FENCHURCH BLINKED HARD. THE LIGHT DISAPPEARED, LEAVING A GHOST circle in his vision. Then it shone into his other eye. He struggled against shutting his eyelids, against even blinking.

The doctor removed her thumb from his cheek and let his blink reflex return. 'Okay, well, you're not concussed.'

Fenchurch shut his eyes until both circles of light faded. He reopened them, blinking quickly.

The doctor sat back, legs crossed. 'But you've got to stop doing this to yourself.'

'It's other people doing it to me.'

'I'm not being funny. You're a police officer, you're not a prop forward. Take better care of yourself and you can keep going, otherwise you'll have to retire early. And it won't be much of a retirement. No long cruises or pottering in the garden. You'll be limping to the toilet in the middle of the night. Sitting on the settee all day, watching *golf*.'

'Point taken.'

'You're not listening, are you?'

'I am, it's just...' Fenchurch got up. Had to stabilise himself on the edge of the bed. But the fug was clear, just an aching pain at the back of his skull. He patted it, felt a cricket ball lump there. *Someone certainly hit me for six...* He looked over at the doctor, tried to give her a serious stare, make her accept what he was saying. 'There's a killer out there and I've got to catch them.'

'You don't have to solve every single crime in London, you know?'

'Feels like it.' Fenchurch gave her a smile as he grabbed his jacket. 'I take your point, though. I'll change. Promise.'

'Glad to hear it.' The doctor picked up her tablet computer. 'Now, can I get someone to collect you?'

'I'll walk.' Fenchurch swallowed hard. 'It's just round the corner and I could do with some fresh air.'

~

CARS AND TRUCKS STILL THUNDERED PAST ON THE MAIN ROAD AS Fenchurch walked back to the crime scene. His head felt like it was turned inside out.

Adrian's street was filled with police vehicles and associated officers. The SOCO van was right outside, the flash bulb pulsing in the gloom. A pair of uniforms stood either end, managing entry through the wall of crime tape flapping in the breeze, a wide expanse blocking most of the street.

Fenchurch took a clipboard and signed in. He passed under the tape, catching his growing lump, making him gasp. The area around the house was split off again, the inner locus thrumming with suited SOCOs and William Pratt's tell-tale stoop as he walked away. *Guy must be getting fed up with all these bodies.*

In the middle, a pair of SOCOs assembled a tent next to where Adrian Hall still stared up at the sky, a hole in his forehead and throat.

Assassinated. Webster's hallmarks. His MO.

Ashkani left a uniform with a pat and came over. 'You okay?'

'I'm cleared for duty, if that's what you're asking.' Fenchurch waved at the body. 'Amelia, Casey and now Adrian. They all worked at Mario's. Who paid Webster to kill them?'

Ashkani nodded along with his logic. 'You're sure it was Webster?'

'He killed Amelia and Casey. Now Adrian. It's him, I know. And he's covering up for the bad guys. Last year, Adrian ordered a pizza, right? He lured Amelia Nicholas here so that Webster could murder her. Now he's dead. Someone's closing off loose ends.'

'You want to speak to Webster again, don't you?'

'No. We've done that already and he's got answers for everything. Alibis too. We need to build a case here.'

'We're getting nowhere with the CCTV.' Ashkani turned back to the road. 'No cameras on this street and the three nearest ones are all due for replacement before year end in April. Until then they're broken, not recording anything.'

'So whoever shot him just gets away?'

'We could scan the whole area's CCTV, but it won't prove anything.'

'Might give us some clues, though.'

'Fine.' She got out her mobile and tapped out a message. 'Let's see what it gives us.' She put the phone away and stared at Fenchurch. 'What now?'

'Not sure.' Fenchurch called Nelson, listening to the ringing. 'Right, stay here and run things for me.'

'What's up?'

Fenchurch set off. 'Need you to meet me at Belmarsh, Jon.'

~

MARIO SAT IN HIS CHAIR, ALL CASUAL LIKE HE WAS BACK IN HIS restaurant with a De Niro film playing, and not on remand for drug dealing, prostitution and people-trafficking.

Fenchurch waited for him to look across the table. 'Mr Esposito, a man called Adrian Hall worked for you, didn't he?'

'Adrian? What's he got to do with anything?'

'Did he or didn't he?'

Mario's lips settled into a grimace. 'He *did*, before all this cock and bullshit.' He waved around the room, like it was his restaurant and not a prison interview room. 'But now he runs the place for me.'

'And Adriano's your son, correct?'

Mario gripped the table edge like he was holding on for dear life. 'What?'

'We found some paperwork up at your office. You transferred the business into his name, made it look like he'd bought it.'

Mario slumped back in his chair, deflating like a punctured beach ball. 'My boy... He took my wife's new surname when we divorced. *Bitch*.' He bared his teeth. 'Adriana married this faccia di culo.'

'I've watched the Sopranos.' Fenchurch smiled at him. 'Face like an arse, right?'

Mario shrugged. 'My boy was fourteen when... when she, she left me and married this *banker*.' Said with more venom than faccia di culo. '*He* made my boy change his name, tried to own my son. Adriano Esposito sounds magnificent. Adrian Hall sounds so vanilla. So plain.'

'We know he's been dealing drugs from the restaurant.'

'That's bullshit.'

'We've got proof. Now, I need to know who you and your boy have been working for.'

Mario rasped the stubble on his chin. 'Nobody.'

'Not Zamir?' Mario looked up. 'Zamir Selinaj.'

'I don't know who you're talking about.'

'You got into bed with him. Knew exactly what him and his gang were doing, didn't you? Took the money, took your cut. You gave *them* cover. And your son helped.' Mario stopped scratching, his mouth twitching. Still kept his peace. 'These Albanians, the people behind this, they don't just back off.'

'I'm keeping quiet. I don't want anyone going after my family.'

Fenchurch left a pause, let Mario think he'd won. 'Sorry to be the one to tell you this, but Adrian's dead.'

'Shit on it...' Mario collapsed back in his chair. He slouched forward, head in his hands. Tears filled his eyes, slid down his face. 'How?' He wiped at his cheeks. 'How did this happen?'

'He was shot outside his home.'

'Who did it?' Mario smashed a fist off the table. 'Who did this to my boy?!'

'Wondering if you had any ideas.'

'I'll kill them with my own hands!'

'That's going to quite difficult for you in here, sir.'

'You've arrested someone?'

'We have a few suspects.'

'Desmond Webster, yes?' Mario smashed a fist off the table again. 'That... He... My son... My Adriano...'

Fenchurch gave him a few seconds space. 'Why him?'

Mario kept quiet.

'Tell me about Webster.'

'He delivered pizzas. This, this Loco company, they sent him. But it's all cover. He killed Amelia, drove that van into her.'

Fenchurch left him all the space he'd need.

'We needed to cover our tracks, make it all go away. A series of accidents.'

'We've got Zamir in custody. He's no threat to you in here.'

'It's not him. He's not behind this.' Mario pleaded with him. 'Listen to me, you need to catch Webster, you need to bring him down for what he's done.'

'I'm working on it. Trouble is, you covered for him, didn't you? Last year, Adrian ordered some pizza. And you sent Amelia out to deliver it. You told Webster. Then,' Fenchurch clicked his fingers, 'she's not a problem any more. And we think he killed her sister.'

'Kesja too?' Mario pinched his nose. 'Shit on it...' He stared off, shaking his head. 'I know what I've done. But these people... They have people inside. If I talk, that's it.' He ran a finger across his throat, like he was slitting it.

'We can see what we can do for the man who testifies against them.'

Mario swallowed, his Adam's apple bobbing under the salt-and-pepper stubble covering his throat.

'Assuming we get enough evidence, we can potentially offer immunity. Maybe a new identity. You're no spring chicken, Mario, but this is a chance to start again. Somewhere new. You don't have to be Mario any more. You don't have to have all this baggage.' Fenchurch pointed at his face, then rubbed at his own smooth skin. 'You can even have a shave without fear that some big Albanian's going to slit your throat.'

Nothing from Mario, not even a twitch.

Fenchurch glanced at Nelson. Something tickled at the back of his brain.

Back in court, what did he say?

Oh yeah.

'It's maybe nothing, but we've been through Younis's financial records. We found a payment that came from Mario's Pizza.'

Fenchurch rested on his elbows and waited for eye contact from Mario. 'What were you paying Younis for?'

'What?'

'We know you paid him. Slipped up, didn't you? What happened? Run out of cash and have to put it all through the books?'

Mario slumped back in his chair. 'I'll tell you. Then you show me how much that's worth.'

33

'This is beyond a joke.' The warden stuck his hands on his hips and scrunched his face tight like it was old newspaper, his focus shifting between Fenchurch and Nelson. 'Mr Younis has a ludicrous number of visitors as it is. Now you two show up. Flaming Nora.'

'I feel your pain.' Fenchurch offered a sympathetic smile. 'But it's really important we see him.'

'It's always like that.' The warden focused on him, giving a look that meant no bullshit. 'You know he's still awaiting trial, right?'

'Same with Mario Esposito.'

'Heard you offered him a deal?'

'That's right. We'll see how it all pans out.'

'You sure you want to—'

'Not much longer before I get out, Fenchy.' Younis walked past, led by a guard. 'Clock's ticking, my love.' He followed the guard into a room where a female lawyer waited, tapping her pen off the table.

The warden's gaze lingered on Younis's lawyer. 'Inspector, I don't want to be the one giving you advice, but the sooner that creep's in general population, the better.'

'We'll be quick.'

'You lot never are.' The warden skulked off, shaking his head. 'Ten minutes, then I'll be back. Okay?'

'Appreciate it.' Fenchurch locked eyes with Nelson. 'He always this helpful?'

'This is him on a good day.' Nelson entered the room, taking the seat opposite the lawyer.

Leaving Fenchurch to face off against Younis. He entered the room and took his time shutting the door. He didn't sit, just rested against the seat back. 'Okay, Younis, we know about those murders.'

Younis shoved his hands in the pockets of his navy trousers and sat there like that, like he was going to say something, but he just leaned over to whisper to his lawyer.

She started tapping her pen again, then nodded at him.

Younis smiled at Fenchurch. 'You'll have to narrow it down a bit, my love.'

'Amelia Nicholas.'

'You must be a special kind of stupid, Fenchy, because I heard on the radio that Des Webster got done for that.' Younis clicked his fingers and pointed at Fenchurch. 'Oh, yeah. You cocked it up, didn't you? He got out, didn't he? Someone else did it. Tut tut.'

'We know you're behind it. You paid him to kill her, didn't you? A good chunk of money, enough to pay for his daughter and her kid for a bit.'

'You should write novels, Fenchy. You've got an incredible imagination.' Younis laughed. 'Though the things I'd like you to do with me, now *that* requires an imagination.'

'What about her sister, Casey? And Adrian Hall?'

'If you're just going to read out names from the phone book...'

'AKA Adriano Esposito. Son of Mario Esposito.'

Younis stared at him for a few seconds. 'Two things.' He wet his lips, his lizard-like tongue flicking across his lips. 'Nah, it's just one. Fuck off.'

❧

FENCHURCH DUG HIS KEY INTO THE IGNITION AND STARED BACK AT Belmarsh, looming in the evening light.

Nelson lurched across the car park, toking on his vape stick, taking his time as ever. He got in and pulled the door shut with a loud crack. 'Well?'

'Well what?'

'You get anything out of that?'

'It's Younis. He's the one who's behind all of this. We've got him, Jon. We can start building the case.'

'You don't think Mario's just dangling something in front of us? Throwing us off Zamir's scent?'

'Could be.' Fenchurch turned the ignition and the car roared to life. 'But Younis runs so much of the East End. He's got to have his fingers in that pie. I think they're in league.'

'Simon, you've let him get in your head. You'd fit him up for assassinating JFK if you could.' Nelson gave him a look, but Fenchurch didn't give him anything in return. 'Tell you, I'm starving. That pizza didn't hit the sides. You want to talk this through over a burrito?'

'Be just like old times.'

CHILANGO WAS IN THAT QUIET SPELL BETWEEN LUNCH AND DINNER, THE cooks frying up trays of beef, chicken and veggies.

Smells gorgeous.

Fenchurch tapped his card against the reader and got the all clear.

'Thanks, sir.' The waitress hummed along to the flamenco cover of Johnny Cash as she stuffed the receipt into the bag and held it out for him, careful not to spill either lemonade.

'Thanks.' Fenchurch took it from her and headed out, waiting for an office drone to come in, a fat guy dressed in a navy suit, red tie like he thought he was the president. Fenchurch let out a sigh as he blocked the way, then the guy took a hint and moved to the side.

The cold hit Fenchurch's cheeks, the night just darkening. Spitalfields was thriving. The Pret was still open, the place where they'd met Chloe's social worker so long ago.

The street was pretty quiet, just a young couple arguing about something. At the other end, Christ Church Spitalfields pierced the gloomy sky. And there was Nelson in the car, talking on the mobile to someone. Laughing.

Fenchurch set off towards the car, passing a man dressed in black.

Someone grabbed his shoulder from behind. A foot lashed his shin, and he went down, losing his grip on the bag. Sticky lemonade splashed over his cheek, the tang hitting his mouth. Fabric touched his forehead. Then everything went black. A squeal of tyres. He was hauled to his feet. Then his knees hit something hard, and he tumbled forward. A van door shut behind him. An engine revved and they shot off.

THE VAN STOPPED. STILL DARK IN THE BACK. FENCHURCH MOVED HIS wrists, making the cable ties bite deeper into his skin.

Someone pulled him to kneeling, then tore the mask off. Bright lights blinded him.

A man walked over to the light, outlined, his gun just visible, the rest of him shrouded in darkness. 'Don't move.' A London accent, but with a slight Jamaican twang. Could mean something, probably meant nothing.

'I wasn't planning to.' Fenchurch tried a smile. Something stung his cheek. 'Who are you?'

The man reached down and picked up a tablet, then tapped at the screen. Sounded like it was dialling. Then he rested the tablet on the floor.

Younis's face filled the screen. 'Hello, lover.' He was in a prison cell, but lying in his bed. Head on the standard-issue pillows, photos of muscle boys pinned to the wall behind him.

Fenchurch felt his forehead twitch. 'What do you want?'

'You, of course.' Younis leered at him. 'Take your top off, Fenchy.'

'What?'

'Come on, lover. I spend a hell of a lot of time thinking about how sexy you'd look out of a suit. Bet it takes years off you. I like to imagine you in a nice polo shirt, good chance to show off those strong, strong arms of yours.'

He's just messing. Call his bluff.

'Let me go, or I'll—'

The masked man shot forward and put the gun to Fenchurch's head. 'Get up.'

Fenchurch used the side door to pull up to standing. 'I'm not doing anything.'

'I'm doing you a favour 'cos I like you, Fenchy.' Younis blew a kiss. 'A lot. So get your kit off. Now.'

Bloody hell.

The gunman reached over and started unbuttoning Fenchurch's shirt. He pulled it wide, tearing at the buttons, but only one popped open.

'Phwoar. You still work out, don't you? Even with that dodgy knee of yours.' Younis grinned. 'Now your trousers.'

'No.'

Younis pointed at his lips.

The gunman undid Fenchurch's belt and hauled his trousers down to his knees. 'Happy?'

'I'm standing on end, Fenchy. And I can see you ain't got nothing in your pants cos they are *tight*, man.'

The gunman moved behind Fenchurch. He was close enough to ram back against the van door, but he was armed and probably not alone.

A hand ran over Fenchurch's stomach, slow and careful, but tugging at the hairs.

'I wish that was me, with you.' Younis bit his lip. 'This is like virtual reality, I tell you. So I gather Mario's been talking, has he?'

The gunman shifted to Fenchurch's underpants, running his hand over material.

Fenchurch swallowed.

Younis gave a little grunt. 'But you're right. I'm behind those deaths, all three of them. I paid that prick Webster. Half up front. But he did such a good job. Might even give him a bonus, especially as he kept shtum.'

Fenchurch held his breath as the gunman caressed him.

'Webster's a good guy. Old-school, like they say.' Younis's face started blurring on the screen as the gunman stroked Fenchurch's inner thighs. 'I sometimes worry about geezers like him. You know? They act all hard and that, but have they got a soft centre?'

The gunman grabbed Fenchurch's left nipple and tugged on it.

'Yeah, I like that.' Younis was barely visible. 'Only time you can tell is when you lot put them to the test. They've got a code, ain't they? Their word is their bond. Some of Flick Knife's old crew. Well you'll never find the bodies. Webster got caught for killing one girl, didn't he? Years ago. Crime of passion, that was his mistake.'

The gunman moved to the other nipple, pinching hard.

'Stupid bastard.' Younis shifted angle, but the screen kept wobbling. *Christ, he's masturbating.* 'But it was proof, wasn't it. He didn't grass. So I gave Webster a chance. Got him to kill Amelia.'

Fenchurch struggled to keep his cool. Tried to process the calculus of taking the weapon off the guy. Everything came up blank. He shut his eyes, trying to imagine he was on a beach with Abi. 'Why?'

'You know why, Fenchy. Those girls... what happened to them? That's barbaric. Amelia and Casey, taken from their homes, brought over here. It's not good. Everything I've ever done is with consent.'

The gunman was stroking Fenchurch's buttocks.

'Except this.'

The gunman cupped Fenchurch's balls.

'Why did you want her dead?'

'Evidence, my good friend. They were beyond helping. The things they'd done. The things they'd seen. I tried to get Webster to make it look like those Albanian wankers had done it. Throw you clowns off the scent.'

'It didn't work.'

'Well, it did. Way I hear it, that idiot Savage has brought in some Albanian for questioning.'

Fenchurch flinched as the gunman squeezed his left ball. 'How the hell did you know that?'

'Don't kid yourself, Fenchy. I know everything. Selinaj Zamir isn't a nice man. Him and his organisation, what they do to people. I found he was linked to Mario, so I spoke to him about it. Bloke said he had no idea, said that Zamir just bought pizza from him. Just think, though, if I hadn't paid Webster, good old Mario would still be making his pizzas. And his girls would be out shagging people and selling drugs on my patch. I didn't know who those girls were and, quite frankly, I'm sickened by it. Zamir and his gang... what they do... it's just not cricket. And it happened on my watch, not Flick Knife's. So I had no choice but to end the operation. Just a shame that Webster didn't get to kill Mario before it all fell apart.'

'You weren't running those girls?'

'Bite him.'

The gunman nibbled Fenchurch's left ear.

'Harder.'

Fenchurch clenched his jaw tight. 'You weren't behind this? You didn't kill them to make sure nothing blew back against you?'

'You know that Mario was, what's the word, boffing Amelia?'

'What?'

'No idea what she saw in him, but, you know, beggars can't be choosers, I suppose. If I was you, and believe me I've spent hours thinking about that, then I'd be connecting the dots differently. Like maybe he was a bit too loose-lipped to her. Talked a bit too much. So someone had to take them all out, stop it spreading.' Younis nibbled his lip. 'If it wasn't for me, Fenchurch, you wouldn't know what was going on round the corner from your nick. I've done you a favour. Brought all this shit out into the open.'

'Why did you have to kill them?'

'I just wanted to kill Amelia and silence Mario. But then you had to go and arrest me, didn't you? You and your big mate Jon Nelson. Started poking through my stuff. You know, he came in here and started asking me about Mario, about this payment. That got me thinking. It's why I had to act now, get someone to take out Casey and Adrian. I mean, they were close to Amelia and Mario. Who knows what they told them.'

'You got Webster to do it?'

'Got him out of jail, yeah. Took a lot of hard graft to do that. See, that geezer... The beauty of him is he's so old-school it bloody hurts. He took a hit for us, went down for Amelia. But I needed someone like that, so I got him out, put him to good use.'

It all makes sense. Perfect bloody sense.

Why's he telling me? What's his plan?

Fenchurch laughed through the pain and the humiliation. 'I'd say

I'm going to take you down. But you're already down. I don't need to do anything.'

'Oh yeah? I saw you in court, wanking away. I'm getting off with whatever bullshit you're throwing at me. And when I get out of here, which will be very soon, we should go for a real date, yeah?' He shut his eyes and his breathing increased. Then he gritted his teeth, focusing on Fenchurch's crotch. A deep exhale. 'I'd say the pleasure's all mine, Fenchy.' Breathing hard. 'But I know you enjoyed it.' Younis kissed the screen. 'You can get rid of him now.' The screen went blank.

The gunman pointed the weapon at Fenchurch's neck. Then the hood went back on.

The door slid open and Fenchurch was shoved out into the cold night, bracing himself against hard tarmac. Something soft landed on him. His clothes.

The van drove off and Fenchurch wrestled against his bonds to shrug off the mask. Dark, just distant streetlights. The van's lights were off, and he couldn't make out the licence plate.

A plane roared over his head, low like it was coming in to land.

London City Airport.

Fenchurch rummaged through his clothes and found his phone in a pocket. Powered off. He turned it on and shivered, waiting for it to power up. It tried to connect to a network. Then notifications flew in, fifteen missed calls from Nelson, twenty texts.

Fenchurch hit the first one. Answered first time. 'Jon, pick me up.'

34

HEADLIGHTS TRAILED ACROSS THE CAR PARK.

'We're sorry, but the person you've—'

Fenchurch killed the call. *Bloody Loftus.* He kept on walking, still felt Younis's hands snaking over his body, like they were his and not the goon's. His balls shrunk back inside his stomach. He stopped and took a series of deep breaths, trying to calm himself.

A car pulled up on the rough tarmac and Nelson peered out. 'Simon? What the hell?'

Fenchurch got in the passenger seat. 'Drive.'

'What on earth are you doing here?'

'I don't want to talk about it.'

'No.' Nelson stuck it in neutral. 'You were in Chilango's five minutes, next thing I know you've dropped the burritos and there's no sign of you. Then you call me half an hour later. Come on, Simon. The truth. Now.'

Fenchurch stared into the footwell and let out a breath. 'Younis abducted me.'

'What? We just saw him inside.'

'One of his goons did it. Had a gun.' *And he ran his fingers all over my body...* 'He told me that Webster's working for him.'

'What, he just told you?'

'It's inadmissible in court, Jon. But it's intel. Webster took them all out, clearing them off the streets. Blaming Mario and Zamir.'

'So he's using the Met to clean up this mess?' Nelson chuckled. 'You believe him?'

'I do. Younis... He's an odd one. I mean, Christ, I'm going to have nightmares about this...'

'What happened?'

'I...' Fenchurch felt his balls tighten again. 'I don't think he was lying.'

'You're playing it like that, yeah?'

Fenchurch's nipple still ached. 'Thing with him is it's not about truth or lies, is it? He'll tell just enough truth to throw us off the scent. Or put us on someone else's scent.'

'You think he's throwing us Webster as bait?'

'Either way, we don't have anything against him. It's just his word, off the record. But he knew about us arresting Zamir.'

'What? How the hell could he?'

'Half of Albania must know by now, Jon.'

'You look white as a sheet, Simon. You sure you don't want to talk about it?'

'Sure.'

'Suit yourself.' Nelson set off across the car park, following the spiral round to the road back to central London. 'Where are we heading?'

FENCHURCH STARED INTO THE PRISON CELL.

Two heavy-set guards lifted up the mattress and chucked it on the floor. Younis's possessions lay scattered on the floor. They ran their batons down the bedding, inch by inch. Then the bigger of the two shook his heads. 'Not in here.'

'I don't know what you're hoping to find in here.' Along the corridor, Younis grinned like the cat that owned the place. The adjacent cells were occupied, but silent. They knew him, knew his reputation.

The warden noticed Fenchurch and stepped up close. 'We've done an intimate search of him. Nothing there, either.'

'He was on the screen. Must've been Skype or FaceTime.'

'I believe you.' The warden winked at him, then looked around the silent prison. 'These lot will never give him up. Probably up one of their arseholes. And it'll have been wiped.' He grimaced. 'Sorry, that was a horrific pun.'

The first guard came out with a shrug. 'It's clean.'

His mate scowled. 'All we've got is a sock covered in...' He cleared his throat at the sight of the warden.

Fenchurch walked over to Younis. 'Where is it?'

'Where's what?'

'You know.'

'I know nothing, mate.'

'I'll get you for this. You paid Webster to murder Amelia, Casey and Adrian. You're going down for it.'

'You've got some wild fantasies, my friend.' Younis puckered up for a kiss. 'I'm disappointed that you had to get these guards to do your dirty work for you. Big guy like you, you could've probed me yourself.'

∿

NELSON WAITED BY THE CAR AND GOT HIS VAPE STICK OUT OF HIS POCKET. 'You mind?'

Fenchurch stared back at the prison. At Younis. He felt filthy fingers on his balls again. 'Whatever.'

'You know, Broadfoot's got all of Webster's financial records and most of Younis's. The ones we know about, anyway. If we're lucky, we'll find a transaction.'

'Unless it's cash.'

'Won't be cash. Someone like Younis, most of their operation is online. Cam shows and all that dark web shit. Hard to launder. Trouble for them is, if you want someone to do a job, you've not got a ton of cash sitting around you can just use. You've got to be very creative. It'll be Bitcoin or Ethereum or God knows what else. Not that easy to track, but we've got ways and means.'

'You were lucky with the Mario payment. Won't get lucky again.' Fenchurch stopped. Cars whizzed past on the road, headlights blurring in the night. 'Fed up with this bullshit, Jon.'

'You want his blood, right?' Nelson let out a puff of vape. 'Going after Webster won't bring Younis to justice.'

'I'll settle for Webster.' Fenchurch stared hard at him. 'He kidnapped Chloe, in case you'd forgotten. And he's out there, still killing people. We should head round there, get him to take us through his movements.'

'We've run out of leeway with that. Unwin's already put in a complaint. Proving anything against him is going to be hard, especially after the Amelia case. Especially after bringing him in to question about Casey.'

Fenchurch thumped the car roof with the heel of his hand. 'Have you got any better ideas?'

'I do, as it happens.'

∿

'I'll lead here.' The lift door slid open and Fenchurch got out first, soaking in the office din. He led Nelson over to the security desk, but the receptionist was on the phone and refusing eye contact.

Someone hurried past, pulling their coat on.

'Oi!'

Pavel waited by the lift, hitting the call button with his thumb. 'I've got to get home, mate.'

'You're not done, son. Not by a long stretch.' Fenchurch blocked entry to the lift. 'I need Desmond Webster's movements for the last twenty-four hours.'

'You know that this isn't how it's supposed to work. All requests are to be routed through DCI Bell and/or his team.' Pavel took off his mirror shades, but his eyes were already shut. 'Have you approved this with him?'

Fenchurch glanced at Nelson. 'We have.'

'Well, you shouldn't be here without him.'

Fenchurch thumbed behind him. 'He's just coming up now.'

Pavel opened his eyes, as bloodshot as a three-day hangover. 'Am I supposed to believe that?'

Sweat trickled down Fenchurch's back. 'I know Webster was on that bike when Casey was murdered. She worked for you as well, right?'

'Come on, man. You know I can't approve this without DCI Bell.'

Fenchurch tried to stare him down, but the little bugger kept looking away. 'Just give me—'

'This is another rogue exercise, isn't it?' Pavel thumped the lift button again and it started whirring. 'You haven't approved this with DCI Bell, have you? You know how much shit I got into the last time you pulled this trick? You've met our CEO. You don't get to that position without—'

The lift doors clunked open and Bell sauntered out, his belly hanging over his trousers. 'Evening, Pavel.' He winked like they were old mates. 'Simon here's a very needy customer, never off the phone.'

Pavel took a deep breath. 'You've approved this request?'

'Let's just say that this isn't a standard one, Pavel mate.' Bell winked at him again. 'Simon needs an urgent answer, so whatever we can do to speed this up, yes?'

'Whatever.' Pavel marched through the office, shaking his head in time with his footsteps.

Fenchurch walked lockstep with Bell. 'Thanks for that, Jason.'

'Saved by the Bell, eh?' He laughed like it was the first time he'd ever used it. 'You sure this fella's your killer?'

'I just need the information. Then we'll be in a better position to work out if he is or not.'

'Not like you to be doing your homework before the last minute, Simon.'

'This *is* the last minute. Webster's back on the street and people are dying.'

Bell stopped Fenchurch, not far from Pavel's desk. 'Have you got any other suspects?'

'Well, Howard Savage thinks it's this Albanian geezer we picked up.'

'Zamir?' Bell started counting on his thumb and fingers. 'He's got drugs, he's got sex trafficking and prostitution, and he's got a gang of Apple-pickers nicking iPhones and those silly bloody earphone things. So Broadfoot, Savage and myself — the trifecta, as we call it — we've been investigating Zamir. And we think his lot stabbed a couple of Pavel's cyclists the other night. Nicked their bikes and their mobiles. It never ends, I swear.'

'These are happening on my patch, though. I should've been made aware.'

'Julian's been sent the minutes of the meetings, Simon.'

'Has he read them?'

'You know what he's like. So many comments and clarifications. My secretary's going spare at him.'

'You've got a secretary?'

'I'm important, mate.' Bell smiled. 'You know he hasn't called me, don't you?'

'Crossed my mind, yeah. But thanks for helping anyway.'

'What are mates for, eh?' Bell clapped his arm with another wink. *The guy's lost it.* 'Now, why is Uzma Ashkani calling me about someone called Kirk Naughton?'

'He's another suspect. Webster's daughter's baby daddy.'

'Oh, Simon, you really need to learn to focus your case. By now, you should have one suspect, not two plus an Albanian.'

Fenchurch frowned. 'You know Kirk?'

'Simon, as part of my arrangement with Pavel, we vet any potential employees.' Bell tutted. 'Co-signs. I swear, the legal hurdles this lot jump through just to not pay their staff properly... Anyway, Pavel passed him through, said Webster put him up to a job here.'

'Did he pass?'

'Just. I mean, armed robbery. He's lucky this lot get so much of a kickback from the government for taking on ex-cons.'

'So he works here?'

'Three weeks, yeah.'

'Interesting.' Fenchurch walked over to the desk. 'How you getting on?'

Pavel was sliding over the keys. 'Well, I can tell you that Webster wasn't working today. He hasn't clocked on.'

'Shit.' Nelson looked as disappointed as Fenchurch felt. 'That's not what we wanted.'

'There's some good news, though.' Pavel clicked the mouse and pointed at one of his screens. 'After the events of last July, we've updated the system so it's always tracking. And Desmond collected his bike from our storage last night. Fresh from a service and a tracker update.'

Fenchurch rested on the back of Nelson's chair. 'So you've got his movements?'

Pavel nodded.

'Let's start with two o'clock today.'

Pavel clicked the mouse again. The screen traced a path through East London.

At the time of Adrian's death, Webster was outside his house.

35

THE STREET WAS MOSTLY DARK, THE STREETLIGHTS NOT YET ON. Fenchurch waited across the road from Webster's house, crouching behind a car. Lights on downstairs and up. He patted the back of his head, at the receding bump. Still hurt like hell. Then he looked over at Nelson on the pavement. 'Ready?'

'Like old days.' Nelson cracked his knuckles, but scanned around nervously.

Fenchurch led him up the path to the house and knocked on the door. Loud music played inside, inane kid's stuff. The sort of nonsense Fenchurch was getting used to all over again.

The door opened and Kirk Naughton peeked out, yawning like he'd not slept in years. 'Whassup?'

'Police, sir.' Fenchurch flashed his warrant card and barged past him into the flat. 'Desmond Webster in?'

'Upstairs.' More yawning. 'What's he done?'

'Jon, stay here.' Fenchurch crossed the living room and headed upstairs. Dark, but light surrounded a door frame. The air was damp, smelling of lavender.

Fenchurch opened the door and got a wave of damp heat.

Webster was on his knees, leaning forward as he bathed Sandy. 'Here, Kirk, pass me a towel.' His eyes widened. 'Shit. You again, eh? Not happy with my answers?'

'Shouldn't use that sort of language in front of a child, Desmond.'

'You can't even let me have five minutes with my granddaughter, can you?' Webster jabbed a finger at the door. 'Get out.'

'Helps if you don't shoot people.'

'I said, get out!'

'I know what you did.' Fenchurch crouched next to him, his thighs burning as soon as he started. 'Took money from Younis. Killed Amelia, took the rap for it. Then you got out and killed Casey, then Adrian. Just like old times, yeah?'

'We've been through this before! I ain't killed anyone!'

'Where were you at two o'clock today?'

'I've been here all day, I swear. Since you let me go, anyway.' Webster lifted Sandy out of the bath, splashing water on the floor. 'Kirk, get me a bleeding towel!'

'You got any evidence you were here?'

'Holly's got to work though, ain't she? Check with Kirk. He's been here all that time too. Supposed to be minding Sandy, but I swear he just plays on that computer game.'

'You've honestly been here all day?'

'Christ, you can see why people hate coppers, can't you?'

'It's because people like you lie. And I pick holes in those lies.'

Webster laughed. 'You're my hero.'

Fenchurch stared at him, feeling his balls squash tight again. 'Stay here.'

'Not going anywhere.' Webster knelt down and helped Sandy back into the bath.

Fenchurch thundered down the stairs, motioning for Nelson to swap with him. 'Keep an eye on him.'

Kirk perched on the edge of the sofa, clutching a game controller, headphones on.

Fenchurch waved in front of his face.

Kirk eased off his headphones. 'Whassup?'

'Has he been here all day?'

'Most of it, yeah.'

'What does that mean?'

'Had to pop out for a bit, didn't I? Need to collect this bike for this job he's got me.'

'When was this?'

'Lunchtime. *Bargain Hunt* was on.' Kirk frowned at the TV like it could answer him. 'Or was it *Doctors*?'

Fenchurch got out his mobile and found the day's schedules. *Doctors* meant 13:45 onwards, meaning right when Adrian was shot. *Bargain Hunt* was quarter past twelve. 'Which was it?'

'I don't know.' Kirk was playing the game again, eyes darting around the screen. 'Wait a sec, the news came on and I put Holly's PlayStation on for a bit. Sandy was on my lap as I shot a load of these South African geezers. Des wasn't too happy, told me to put my headphones on. So here I am. Shit, is that the time?'

On the screen, a man in a grandad shirt took cover to shoot at a load of mercenaries. 'So he was here at two o'clock?'

Kirk clicked his fingers. 'Fo' shizzle.'

So someone's lying. Either Kirk is or Pavel's system was wrong.

'What's up, anyway? You think he's killed someone?'

'Why, he say anything?'

'Nah. Not to me, mate. He thinks I'm a cunt.' Kirk laughed.

Fenchurch's phone blasted out The Who again. Loftus.

I could just bounce this, then head upstairs and grab Webster. Dunk his head under the water, get the truth out of him.

But he answered it. 'Sir?'

'Simon, what the hell are you doing at Webster's house?'

Nelson stopped outside Docherty's old office. 'You okay?'

'Not really, Jon.' Fenchurch pinched his nose, squeezing hard. 'I'm away to get slaughtered here.' He pushed inside to face the music.

Loftus, Broadfoot and Savage loitered by the whiteboard, talking over each other.

Loftus held up a hand to shush them. 'Simon.'

'Sir. Just thought you should—'

'Spare us. Dalton Unwin's been in touch.'

'Right.'

'Simon, you need to let this go.' Savage recapped the pen and put it in the tray under the whiteboard. 'You can't just—'

'I can.' Fenchurch stepped into the small room and tried to dominate the space. 'Webster's killed at least two people, probably three. And we're letting him slip away. Again.'

'The problem is that Webster is alibied to the hilt.'

'Wouldn't go that far.' Fenchurch took the pen from under the whiteboard and put a cross on Savage's timeline where they'd marked "Adrian Hall's death". 'He's got a shaky alibi for this time. But we can also place him there.'

Loftus took the pen and scored out Fenchurch's cross. 'We think it's likely to be someone in this people-trafficking organisation, tidying up any links to them.'

'Younis told me it's Webster.'

Broadfoot scowled at Fenchurch. 'What?' He laughed. 'He just *told* you?'

'He was messing with me. Made me...' Fenchurch swallowed hard.

'He told me off the record that he paid Webster to kill them, trying to clean up his mess and pin it on Zamir. He was sickened by the people-trafficking.'

Broadfoot laughed again, louder this time. 'Love to have seen that little creep sickened by anything.'

'Hold on a sec.' Savage stared at his whiteboard. 'Do you believe Younis?'

'He's honest with me. I don't know what game he's playing, but I believe him.'

Savage started drawing a mind map in the corner of the board. 'Zamir... Hmm.' He stared out of the window like he was going to jump through the glass.

Loftus clapped his hands together. 'Come on, lads, let's take a step back. We've all been hard at it all day. Two dead bodies is... Well. We need to regroup and come up with a clear strategy here.'

'Right.' Broadfoot scanned the room like he was looking for excuses as much as looking at people. 'And here was me hoping I could avoid dinner with my husband's sister tonight.'

Loftus laughed. 'Like you need a reason to avoid people, Derek.'

'Tomorrow, then.' Broadfoot grabbed his coat from the rack near the door. 'Jon, come on. We've still got Colin Dunston in custody. Let's lean on him, see what he can give us about Adrian's operation.'

'Sir.' Nelson held the door open for him. 'We should check the money trail. If we can pin the Webster tail to the Younis donkey, then...'

The door shut behind them.

Loftus exhaled slowly. 'Howard, keep me updated on how this Albanian chap pans out.'

Savage was still peering out of the window. 'Of course.'

'I'll see you tomorrow, then. Call me if anything urgent happens.' Loftus gestured at Fenchurch. 'Simon. A word?'

Fenchurch joined him out in the hall. 'Sir, you're making a mistake.'

'I need a cigarette.' Loftus was hurrying like the four horsemen of the apocalypse were on his heels and the only thing that would stop him was that one last smoke. 'You made a fool of yourself back there.'

Fenchurch followed him into the stairwell and clattered down after him. 'We need to bring in Webster.'

Loftus took out his cigarette carton as he burst into the long corridor. 'You blundering into his home for the umpteenth time... What the hell were you thinking?'

Fenchurch opened the back door and held it for Loftus. 'I should be breaking his alibi, not—'

'Let me give you some friendly advice.' Loftus set off across the car park, lighting his cigarette as he walked. 'On a case like this, we need to bide our time, okay?' He took a long drag, barely losing pace. 'We need to play the long game. This isn't just two idiots fighting and one stabbing the other. This is a strategic case. Three different Met units have to work together. Something will break, somewhere in Younis's organisation. Mark my words.'

'It's Webster, sir. Mario and Younis have told us now.'

'I'm not asking, I'm telling.' Loftus blew out held smoke, emptying his lungs. 'We've got no leads, no suspects.'

'Apart from—'

'No. Keep the hell away from him. I know it's personal with you and I trust you to not go wild here. Okay?'

'Sir, I—' Fenchurch snorted. 'Okay.'

'I need results tomorrow.' Loftus rested the cigarette on his lip. 'Now, Chief Inspector, it's time for you to get out of here and clear your ruddy head.'

36

FENCHURCH GOT INTO HIS CAR AND RAN HIS FINGERS OVER THE STEERING wheel, practising like it was Younis's neck. Or Loftus's.

It's Webster. Clear as day.

And politics are getting in my way, yet again. So much for being a DCI. Waste of time.

His phone chirruped and he got it out. A text from Chloe:

HEY DAD, I'M GOING OUT TONIGHT. MATES HAVE CANCELLED ON ME. CAN I GET THAT LIFT? X

He tapped out a reply:

OF COURSE. WHAT TIME?

The dots appeared below his message.

I FINISH AT SEVEN. X

SEE YOU THEN. DAD

Fenchurch stared out at the night and breathed away all the stress.

Forty minutes to kill...

~

FENCHURCH TOOK A DEEP BREATH AND STEADIED HIMSELF. *OKAY, HERE we go.*

Through thick safety glass, a nurse in protective clothing tended to a young man, a large chunk of his dark skin faded to light pink. A fresh acid victim, yet another casualty of the virus spreading through London. The nurse applied a light gauze to his cheek, making the kid flinch.

Fenchurch continued on, trying to avoid looking at any other victims. Fury burned in his veins. He stopped at the end, avoiding the glass, daring himself to not just focus on the cheese-wire grid.

Dawn Mulholland lay on a bed, her face covered in bandages, staring at an e-reader.

'Ah, Inspector.' Dr Lucy Mulkalwar squelched down the corridor, her crocs kissing the flooring. She picked up a chart, then sniffed. She looked up at him, a good foot and a half shorter. Her dark skin had taken on the pallor of her Glaswegian accent. 'Long time, no see.'

'Doc.' Fenchurch felt his gut rumble. Hunger? Or just guilt? He nodded at the glass. 'How's she doing?'

'She's on the mend.' Mulkalwar joined him. 'To be perfectly frank, while she's on the list for a skin graft, it's going to be a long, hard road for her.'

'She's strong.'

'And then some. But she might not get through this alone. You can have a quiet word, if you wish. She's quite lucid.'

Can I speak to her?

After all she's put me through?

And after what's happened to her? I could've saved her from this torment, if only I'd acted quicker.

But I didn't.

'Thanks.' Fenchurch pushed through the door into the room. 'How you doing, Dawn?'

Mulholland stared at him, her mouth hanging open. 'I've never felt this sore in my life.' She locked her e-reader and set it aside. 'Everything hurts. It's been weeks now and it's...' She exhaled slowly. Then gasped. She patted her bandages, her eyes doing enough wincing for her whole face.

The sterile room looked out across the car park towards Leman Street station and her old life. Two chairs, but he wasn't sure he was welcome. Wasn't sure he wanted to stay, even if he was.

'The doc says you'll make a good recovery.'

'But not full. The acid burnt my nerves.' She touched the pink skin on her face. 'I'll never be able to smile.'

You were never much—

Stop it.

Let her grieve.

'I'm sorry to hear that, Dawn. It must be horrendous for you.'

She finally looked at him, her ice-white eyes burning. 'Like you care.'

'I...' Fenchurch rubbed his fingers off his palms. *Shit.* He took a breath and sat, committing himself to whatever she wanted to give him. 'I'm going to be here for you, okay? I'm going to be a friend. I want to help you through this.'

'A friend?' She said it like an insult. 'Simon, you—'

'Dawn, can you hear me out?' He raised his eyebrows and held her fiery gaze until she looked away. He blinked hard, trying to get rid of the ghosts. Not just the ring of light from the doctor's torch, but faces. People now gone. He refocused on Mulholland. 'I'm sorry for being an arsehole to you, Dawn. For the last year, I...' He focused on the ceiling. 'I knew about you letting Desmond Webster go.' He stared at her. Tried to let his ice beat back her fire. 'The man who took Chloe.'

She swallowed.

'You know I found out that you questioned him and that... That you let him go. That you didn't check his alibis.' He gripped his thighs tight, hard enough to hurt. 'And I held it against you. For over a year. You didn't deserve that.'

'You've been a complete arsehole to me, Simon. A complete arsehole. Do you know what it's like sitting in the same office as someone who hates you? Do you know what that's like?'

'Trust me, I know.' Fenchurch let his grip soften. 'Dawn, I want to put it all in the past.'

'Do you know what it's like to see a glare every time you enter your own office and not know why? When you try to help, all you get is hate? When you offer sympathy it's like you abducted their child? Do you know what it's like to have to fish your scarf out of the bin?'

'Dawn... I've made mistakes and I seem to be able to get away with them. You should be able to.'

'Mistakes?' Her lip quivered. 'What the hell are you talking about?'

'You let him go, Dawn. The man who kidnapped Chloe. You... You let him go.'

'I didn't want to.'

'What?'

'He was guilty of something, I just didn't know what. I wanted to keep him, but my boss at the time, DI David Shaw, he told me to release him. Didn't even want me to check his alibis. Both were under surveillance from another squad, didn't want to risk upsetting that.'

Fenchurch let a slow breath out. 'I didn't know.'

'No, you didn't. You didn't ask me. You just held this grudge against me.'

'I'm sorry.'

'Was that why you didn't help me?'

'What?'

'When this happened.' She pawed at her bandages. 'You were there. You could've prevented what happened.'

'Dawn, that's—'

'Do you know what this feels like?'

Fenchurch gripped his thighs again. 'I'm truly sorry for what's happened to you, Dawn. I want to do whatever I can to get you back on duty. If that's what you want.'

'How dare you?'

'Because—'

'You could've saved me.' She pawed at her face. 'You could've stopped this, Simon. It's all your fault. All your fault!'

Fenchurch let her have her rage. *God knows I've had mine.* 'Dawn, I wouldn't wish what happened on my worst enemy. And you're very far from that.' He leaned forward in the chair. 'I thought you were. Thought you were the devil. In my head, I built you up to be this witch. Pure evil.' He rubbed his forehead, squeezing at his bones. Causing pain, worse than the throb from the back of his head. He gave her a warm smile. 'You're just a person, Dawn. You've got flaws, like everybody, but you've also got good qualities. I overlooked them. And I'm sorry I wasn't there to prevent the attack. I'm sorry it wasn't me going into that room, I'm sorry it was you who...' He took a long breath through his nostrils. 'And I want to change all of that, Dawn. I want to help. I want to be your friend.'

The room was silent. A drill started up nearby. Someone screamed, coming from down the corridor — probably the fresh victim.

Mulholland reached out and took his hand. 'Thank you. I know how hard it was to say all of that.'

'I mean it, Dawn.' Fenchurch clenched his jaw, clamping his teeth together. 'When you're ready, I'll be there for you, when you come back to work.'

She pulsed his hand. 'I don't know if I can, Simon. Any... any time I'm in danger, how am I going to react?'

'That's a long way off.' Fenchurch clutched her hand even tighter. 'You've got physical scars, I get that. But they're good at helping with the mental ones. After what I've been through, what Abi's been through too... I had counselling for it. It didn't completely fix me, but it got me out of the woods. It got me out of my cave, got me back with Abi. And it made me strong enough to find Chloe, to go through that whole process. She lives with us again. I don't have PTSD, but I've got the next best thing.'

She let go, wincing. 'It's not funny.'

'If you can't laugh, then it means they've won.'

'I know.' She nodded. 'Uzma told me you're after Webster again.' She pursed her lips. 'Is that why you're here?'

'Indirectly.' Fenchurch patted at his skull, the lump feeling closer to a football. 'I think he just killed again. You remember Adrian Hall?'

'Worked at Mario's. I remember.'

'Shot three times. Usual pattern. Day after Webster got out. Day after he shot someone else.'

'Dear God.'

'Tell me. Am I wrong in assuming it's him?'

'What do you think?'

'We talked to him. He was all about how he's changed. How being back on remand reminded him that he couldn't hack prison.'

'A leopard seldom changes their spots.'

'Has he, though?'

'I knew him back in the day. Interviewed him. Got inside his head.' She shook her head. 'I just don't think he'd stop killing. It was a job for him. One he was so good at that we never caught him, but it becomes a compulsion. And London's still as murky as it was when Blunden ran things. Just because it's someone else writing the cheques, it doesn't stop someone like Webster from cashing them.'

Fenchurch got to his feet. 'Thanks.'

'Was that helpful?'

He shrugged. 'It's always good to get other opinions on things.' He reached over and took her hand again. 'Thanks for listening to me.'

'I'm here for you, Simon.'

'Thanks.' Fenchurch felt a knot in his gut. *Christ, I do mean it.*

She didn't let go of his hand, even though he tried. 'I hear you've taken Alan's job.' She winked. 'DCI Fenchurch, is it?'

Fenchurch got his hand back. 'It's just Acting. I don't know if I want it or not, Dawn. I'm happy as a DI, but...'

'I know you, Simon.' She chuckled, a trace of a smile lighting up her broken skin. 'You're never happy.'

'See. You can still laugh.'

37

FENCHURCH PARKED AT THE SOUTHWARK TESCO AND WAITED, LISTENING to Pink Floyd playing on the radio. Never really a fan, but it was on and it stopped him thinking. *Wish You Were Here.*

Damn right.

The car park was busy, the road blocked off by a red-faced dad two cars over, trying to stop his three kids from killing each other. A taxi trundled up to an old woman with a rammed trolley by the front door.

Still no sign of Chloe.

He checked his message again.

Five minutes is all.

She's just late. Like those people in the news who worked at that sports warehouse place who get searched every night. Tesco aren't that bad, but there's always something. Can never just get away on time.

So he sat back in his seat and watched the car park, listening to Pink Floyd.

He jerked awake.

Christ.

The Beatles were playing now, *Back in the USSR.*

Ten past seven now.

And no sign of my daughter.

Fenchurch killed Paul McCartney mid-stutter. A deep breath and he got out into the cold air. He yawned, but it was starting to wake him up a bit.

Chloe was over by the entrance, talking to someone. A man, roughly her age. For once. She tucked her hair behind her air and laughed, touching his arm.

Flirting.

Fenchurch felt proud. But also felt weird.

Need to check the guy's background. Find out if he's on the level. If he's a threat.

The guy walked off with a brush of Chloe's arm and Fenchurch set off towards his daughter.

But she was staring at her phone, oblivious of him. Then she turned around, facing away from Fenchurch, and hugged someone else, laughing. They talked, nodding vigorously.

Fenchurch couldn't see who she was talking to. And then he did.

Holly, wearing a Tesco uniform.

'Chloe!' Fenchurch started running, almost fumbled his mobile as he hit call. Feet pounding the tarmac, down to the last hundred metres, and she wouldn't bloody answer her phone.

Chloe just kept talking to her friend, then disappeared round the corner.

Shit!

Fenchurch tried to speed up, but his tank was close to empty. He swung round the corner to the back of the store. Giant plastic flaps guarded the entrance. To the right, a compactor ground away on some cardboard boxes.

Nobody there.

His mobile rang, blaring out *Daughter of a Child* by the Auteurs.

CHLOE

He answered it. 'Get away from her!'

But Chloe was gone.

He shot over to the trash compactor and jumped up the ladder, tugging the rungs until he could see inside.

Just boxes, getting squashed flat.

So where the hell is she?

'Dad?'

Fenchurch swung round and jumped down.

Chloe was scowling at him. 'What the hell are you doing?'

'Looking for you.' Fenchurch rushed over and grabbed her in a big hug. 'Come on.' He led her back to the car park.

She pulled her hand away. 'What the hell?'

Fenchurch reached for her hand again, but she slapped it away. 'Chloe...' No sign of Holly. 'Where is she?'

'What the hell?'

'Chloe, the woman you were with. Holly. Whatever she told you, she's—'

'Who is she?'

'She's the daughter of someone your grandfather put away.'

She tilted her head to the side. 'What aren't you telling me?'

'Her old man...' Fenchurch held out a hand to her. 'He's the one who—'

'Desmond Webster?' Chloe swallowed. 'Her old man's Desmond Webster?'

Fenchurch still held his hand out for her. 'Come on, I need to get you away from here.'

She took his hand. 'Jesus.'

Fenchurch led her back through the car park, keeping a constant search for Holly. No sign of her. 'Where did she go?'

'I answered the phone and next thing I knew, she wasn't there.'

Maybe I spooked her.

The red-faced dad slammed his trolley into the bay, then stomped back to his people carrier full of misery.

Fenchurch tossed his keys to her. 'Get in the car and lock the doors. I need to find her.'

'Dad, what are you going to do?'

'I'm going to warn her to stay the hell away from you.' Fenchurch stared into her eyes. 'Now, I need you to—'

'What does she want?'

'I don't know. Could be a coincidence.' Fenchurch got a tingle at the back of his head, round the lump on his skull. 'But I don't like coincidences. I need you to stay in the car. Can you do that?'

'Right.' She opened the passenger door.

'Keep your phone on. If you see someone approach the car, drive home. Okay?' Fenchurch shut the door and stormed back across the car park. He got his mobile out and hit dial.

Answered immediately. 'Guv, you okay?'

'Kay, I need you here. Old Kent Road Tesco. As soon as you can.'

'What's up?'

'Just get here.' He put his phone away and turned the corner back to where he'd last seen Holly.

The compactor was whirring to a stop now. Through the flaps, the radio blared out Buzzcocks, *Ever Fallen In Love.*

Fenchurch felt something hard in his coat pocket. The knife. *Christ, I forgot about that.* He pulled it out and grabbed the handle, the blade riding his wrist, hidden.

Where the hell is—

A gun pressed against Fenchurch's skull, digging into the bruise.

'Stay right where you are.'

Fenchurch recognised the voice. 'Holly, this—'

'Drop the knife.'

Fenchurch let it clatter to the ground. He raised his hands. 'Don't do this.'

'Get down on your knees.'

Fenchurch got on one knee, still facing away. Then he put the left down, unsteady and painful. 'Holly, think about your own daughter. Sandy. Her life isn't ruined right now. If you kill me, your daughter will have the same life as you. You can break the circle. Get out of this bloody city. Take her away, miles away. Go and get a job that makes you happy. Make her happy.'

'If I was going to kill you, you'd be dead already.' She pressed the barrel against his neck. 'No, I'm going to kill your daughter. Your precious Chloe. See how you like it...' The gun slackened off.

Fenchurch started shuffling round, his knees scuffing on the tarmac.

Holly raised the gun and aimed at his forehead. 'Sod it.' Then she stumbled forward and tripped over Fenchurch, falling flat.

The gun skidded away, over towards the trash compactor.

Chloe stood over Holly, holding out an extended police baton. 'You don't shoot my father!'

Holly scrambled to her feet.

Chloe walked towards her, still gripping Fenchurch's baton.

'Stop!' Fenchurch tried to stand, but his knee burnt with pain. Took three separate movements to get upright.

Holly pulled out a knife. Fenchurch's blade, catching the light. 'Get back.' She reached to the side and wheeled a bike over, a racer.

Webster's bike.

Shit.

It was tracking her. She was the killer.

Chloe closed on her, the police baton raised.

Holly held the knife out. 'I trust my skill with this more than you should yours.'

'Stop!' Fenchurch hauled Chloe away from Holly. She struggled, kicking out, but he had her. His baton dropped to the ground.

Holly got on the bike and cycled off, back to the front of the supermarket.

Fenchurch watched her go, quickly losing her in the crowd of shoppers.

'I had her...' Chloe broke free. Looked like she wanted to race off after her.

'*Chloe.*' Fenchurch grabbed her arm. 'I need you to go inside the store and wait for your auntie Kay, okay?'

'But I want to help!'

'No. You've already messed up.'

She frowned. 'Dad, I saved your life!'

'Chloe! She was pointing a gun at me! Do you know how dangerous that was?'

She stared at the ground, jaw clenched.

'I told you to stay in the car and you should've, okay? Whatever happens to me, I don't want your mother losing you again. You hear me?'

She nodded.

'Can I have my keys back?'

She passed them. 'I'm sorry.'

'Don't be.' Fenchurch walked her round to the front of the supermarket. 'But tomorrow, I'm booking you into a self-defence course.'

She followed him over to the entrance. A giant display pushed Terry's Chocolate Orange at punters, getting ahead of the Christmas rush.

'Wait inside, okay?' Fenchurch jogged off, heading round the back, towards the compactor and started searching the place.

Where the hell is the gun?

38

FENCHURCH DROVE PAST HOLLY'S HOUSE, TAKING IT SLOW. NO SIGN OF her bike, but the lights were on inside.

Could she have got here quicker than me? She could've done Tower Bridge instead of the Rotherhithe tunnel. Five minutes faster. Maybe. And those bikes go at a fair old lick.

Fenchurch parked and got out. Music played inside Holly's house, Desmond Webster singing along to Tom Jones. He got out his mobile and checked for any missed calls. Nothing. So he called Pavel.

'I'm still running it.'

'It was instant last time.'

Pavel huffed. 'Having a bit of an issue just now.'

'That's very convenient.'

'Do you want my help or not?'

'So long as you actually help. I really need that location. Now.'

'Fine. Webster's bike is at his home address.'

So she's here.

Fenchurch let out a deep breath. 'That's all I wanted to hear.'

The phone rang. Reed.

'I've got to go, but thanks.' Fenchurch switched calls. 'Kay, you okay?'

'Guv, I'm with Chloe. She's fine.'

Fenchurch charged over to the gate and peered in the garden. No sign of her bike, no tell-tale wheel ruts in the fresh mud. 'Take her to Leman Street, okay? And don't let her out of your sight until Abi or I get there.'

'Guv.'

'Can you get a search going at the back of the store. Holly dropped a gun by the trash compactor. I need to know if she's armed or not.'

'Holly pulled a gun on you?'

A car parked up behind him. Ashkani got out.

'Kay, I'll speak later.' Fenchurch ended the call. 'Thanks for coming. I appreciate it.'

'No worries. Is she here?'

'Not that I can see.' Fenchurch snapped out his baton. 'It's all falling into place, Uzma. She had her old man's bike. It wasn't his movements we were tracking, but hers.'

Ashkani snapped out her own baton. 'Have you called in SCO19?'

'On their way.' Fenchurch looked around the street. 'But I hate waiting.'

A BMW saloon turned off the main road and headed their way, silver but marked with Met signage, a blue siren above. Low to the ground, like some drug dealer's pimped-up ride, but that was just the modifications.

'Speak of the devil.' Fenchurch waved down the Armed Response Vehicle and waited for them to park up and get out. He showed his warrant card. 'DI Fenchurch.'

The two officers looked like the sort of couple you'd see in the gym, him pushing it hard on the weights, her pounding the treadmill to within an inch of its life.

'She's Sergeant Smith, I'm Constable Roberts.' The male officer opened the boot and set about the armoury, enough guns to start a coup. He got out a Heckler & Koch assault rifle and passed it to his colleague. 'You two firearms-trained?'

Fenchurch passed him his warrant card.

Roberts checked it and passed him a Glock pistol.

'Thanks.'

'Don't mention it.' Roberts got out another carbine and wrapped the strap round his bulky shoulders. 'What have we got here?'

'Possibly armed suspect.'

'Possibly?'

'I've got someone searching for a pistol. She dropped it, but I couldn't find it.' Fenchurch pointed at the house. 'Suspect might not be present, but I urgently need a lead on her whereabouts.'

Roberts nodded at Ashkani. 'Uzma, can you guard the street? Any approach, give a rasp on the Airwave.' He tapped the radio mounted on his chest.

She held hers out. 'Got it, Glyn.'

'Come on, then.' Roberts pointed at the house and set off, breaking into a slow trot, but keeping low. He went left, Smith took the right, and they mapped out a wide pattern until they converged on the house. Roberts pointed at Fenchurch, then Ashkani, then held up a fist at ear level.

Wait.

Fenchurch gripped the pistol, his palms sweaty.

Roberts headed round the side of the house, leaving Fenchurch with Smith. Seconds later, he was back. He pointed at Fenchurch then put two fingers up to his eyes.

Look.

Fenchurch followed his footsteps on the muddy garden and rounded the side of the terrace.

Inside a new-looking lean-to shed, a shiny road bike rested against the house wall, the pale brick just catching the light. A Mizani Swift 500. This year's model, too.

'She's here.'

Roberts raised his hand and made a walking motion with his fingers, then led back to the front. He raised his eyebrows at Smith and made a gun with his thumb and forefinger, then pointed the thumb down and the finger at the house.

Smith approached the door, training her gun on the glass. She took a sharp breath, then knocked on the wood.

The door opened and Webster peered out. Tom Jones blasted out, loud as hell. 'What the hell?'

Smith trained the gun on his head. 'Need access, sir.'

'Jesus Christ.' Webster nudged the door open. He wore his cycling gear, tight and garish. 'What is it now?'

Fenchurch aimed his pistol at Webster. 'Where's Holly?'

'What?' Webster scowled. 'Well, you can piss off.'

'She just pointed a gun at me.' Fenchurch stepped closer to him. 'Where the hell is she?'

Webster moved aside to let Smith and Roberts past. 'She won't speak to you, you filth. Her head's screwed on proper.'

'She killed them, didn't she? Casey and Adrian. Where is she?'

'At work, you pillock. Sandy's with her old man. I've got to head out.'

'She's been using your bike, hasn't she?'

Webster laughed. 'Mate, I've got to work tonight. Those cheese toasties won't deliver themselves.' He peered back into the living room.

Smith reappeared. 'House is clear, sir.'

'Okay.' Fenchurch set off and got out his mobile, hitting dial as he paced up the path. 'Tammy, it's Fenchurch.'

'Can this wait? It's just, I've got a ballistics expert coming in to—'

'It's urgent and you're going to need that expert. I need you to get a team over to an address off Mile End Road, urgently. I'll text you it. Need you to search the property. You're searching for any loose-fit cycling gear. The suspect was wearing it when she shot the victim.'

'She?'

'Could be male clothing. Check it for residue, that kind of thing.'

'I'll send someone.'

'Make it your best officers.' Fenchurch joined Ashkani on the street. 'Where the hell is she?'

Ashkani frowned. 'His bike's here, right?'

'Right. But she had it at the supermarket. It doesn't make any sense.'

'Could she be riding Kirk's bike?'

~

'ALL OF THEM!' FENCHURCH SPED ALONG MILE END ROAD, WEAVING IN and out of traffic. 'Any cars out on the streets, get them to Southern Grove. Get them all round there *now*.'

His Airwave crackled. 'Will be a few minutes, sir.'

'Thanks for nothing...' Fenchurch killed the call and followed the sign for Tower Hamlets Cemetery by pulling a hard right into a long street, four-storey brick buildings on both sides. *Bloody useless.*

Fenchurch parked outside a block of flats on the left, a Sixties brick building, but already needing to be torn down. Opposite was a new build on the corner with balconies, the new primary school next door. An old Victorian primary school was at the end, already swallowed up by property developers. He pulled up in a parking space, two rows of bike racks in an L-shape. Some garages filled the ground-floor level. He got out and calked Ashkani. 'Any sign of her there?'

'Negative.'

'Keep Webster there.'

'Will do. Out.'

The BMW pulled up, double parking next to him, but leaving him a clear run if he needed to get out of there. Roberts got out and popped the boot. 'She's definitely here?' He passed the Glock back.

'I think so.' Fenchurch checked the pistol and stared over at the block of flats. 'Hang on.' He jogged over the bike rack and scanned up and down. No sign of any black road bikes, let alone a Mizani.

Could be inside.

'Come on.' Fenchurch led Roberts over to the flat.

Fenchurch hopped over the low wall and peered through the glass. Curtains drawn, with a thin crack in the middle. Kirk Naughton sprawled on the sofa, one hand down his trackies. 'Here, Sandy, stop doing that!'

The girl was in a cot by the far wall, crying and wailing.

Roberts pointed at himself then motioned for the front of the building.

Fenchurch waited with Smith, watching Kirk struggling to pacify his daughter. He swapped the Glock to his other hand to give it a rest, but it didn't feel right.

Two clicks on Smith's radio. She set off towards the door.

Fenchurch took a deep breath and followed. Did a double take. Through the crack, Holly came into the room, still wearing her Tesco uniform. She picked up her daughter and hugged her.

Smith thumped the door and waited, rifle drawn.

Wide-eyed, Holly passed their kid to Kirk, who walked over to the flat door and opened it, rocking Sandy in his arms. The baby was still crying, her face like it belonged in the deepest circles of hell. Kirk grimaced. 'What?'

'Need to speak to Holly.'

'She ain't here.'

'I just saw her, you pillock.' Fenchurch entered. 'Is she armed?'

'Not doing anything for you—'

Smith barged past into the living room. 'Clear!'

Fenchurch stared at Kirk. 'Where the hell is she?'

'She ain't here!'

'Is there a back door?'

Kirk was distracted by Sandy's screaming. 'Get the fuck out of here!'

Sod it.

Fenchurch joined Smith in the small living room. He tried the first door. A bedroom, the tiny bed unmade. On the far wall a door hung open. He nudged the gap wider with his gun. A shower room with a toilet and a sink.

No sign of Holly.

He went back through and put his Airwave to his lips. 'Roberts, have you got eyes on her? Over.'

'No. Over.'

'Shit.' Fenchurch walked over to the settee and stood over Kirk, who was finally nursing Sandy with a plastic bottle. 'Is there a back door here?'

Kirk pointed at a door in the far wall. 'Laundry's that way. Get out front through the lock-up.'

'Stay here.' Fenchurch jerked the door open and put his radio to his mouth. 'Meet me out front.' He inched through.

A dark corridor, stale and musty, with multiple doors coming off. An old sign above a door read 'LAUNDRY'. It was lit up by a too-bright bulb. He crept over and nudged the door. Low lights glowed on a bank of stainless steel washing machines. Another door at the far end, criss-crossed by security wire. He sneaked over and raised his gun.

A cat screeched at him.

Fenchurch felt his pulse jolt up another fifty BPM. He kept going and pushed the door open. Into a garage, filled with boxes of old Nokia phones. Burners, no doubt.

Jesus Christ.

The door was open at the bottom, a wide crack letting in yellow street light and wailing sirens.

Fenchurch lowered himself, aiming the Glock where his gaze went.

Someone was cycling off down the main road.

Fenchurch rolled through the gap and set off towards the flashing lights. He flagged down the first car with his warrant card. 'Follow that bike!'

~

'WHERE THE HELL IS SHE?' FENCHURCH GRABBED THE 'OH-SHIT' HANDLE above the door as the uniform driver pulled out to overtake the bus. He put his mobile back to his ear.

'—are you?' Sounded like Pavel was typing.

'Bloody hell.' Fenchurch looked around. 'Solebay Street.'

'Okay. As far as I can tell, Kirk's bike is on Mile End Road. Same block as you.'

'Take a right here.' Fenchurch held on again as the uniform hurtled round a corner. 'Left!' Another tight turn onto Mile End Road, cutting in front of a bus just outside the Bancroft Arms. 'Which way is she heading?'

'Up that street. Can't quite make out the name.'

'Got it.' Fenchurch leaned forward. 'She's heading home.' He got out his Airwave and called Ashkani.

No answer.

Shit.

'Pull in here!' Fenchurch jumped out of the car before it stopped, drawing the Glock as he raced across the road, vaulting the wall into Holly's front garden.

Ashkani lay on the ground, groaning.

Fenchurch rushed over and crouched over her. 'Are you okay?'

'She got me.'

She's been shot!

Fenchurch scanned across her body with his fingers.

'Get off!' Ashkani sat up, rubbing her head. 'Ow.'

'You're okay?'

'No.' She got up to all fours but fell back again. 'What the hell happened?'

'Stay here.' Fenchurch left her and shot back towards the car, putting his phone back to his ear as he ran. 'Pavel, have you got a location yet?'

Pavel paused. 'Hang on.'

Fenchurch got in the passenger seat. 'Hurry up!'

'I'm trying, I'm trying... Pool hall. The pool hall on Mile End Road.'

'Back where we were.' Fenchurch waved at the road. 'Go, go, go!' The car screeched forward, pressing him back in his seat. 'She still there?' He wrestled with his seatbelt and got it to click.

'I think so.'

'Pavel...'

The uniform swung them right, crossing the path of another squad car, and bore down on the pool hall.

No sign of Holly.

'Pavel, she's not here!'

'She's heading that way!'

Fenchurch squinted and saw Holly powering along Mile End Road. She bumped up onto the pavement just after Stepney Green tube.

The uniform slowed, unable to follow.

Holly bumped back down and shot across the road. The uniform floored it, but just missed her, almost hitting a car. She took the back road towards the pub. The uniform reversed back and chased her along another back road.

She powered along, wobbling into the left, towards a big park, the kind of place where it'd be easy to lose her.

The uniform hit the floor and jerked forward, clipping Holly's back wheel. Sent her flying across the grass.

Fenchurch jumped out and aimed the Glock at her. 'Holly Ann Evans, I'm arresting you for the—'

Thump.

Something hit Fenchurch on the head, right on the lump, and he fell back, white-hot pain exploding in his skull. He landed on his elbows and knees, next to Holly. He reached over for her, but a kick in the back pushed him flat on his face.

A hand reached down to help Holly up. Desmond Webster. 'Let's get out of here.' He booted Fenchurch in the side. 'Oh, this'll be useful.' He picked up the Glock. 'You, get out of the car!' He aimed at the pool vehicle.

Fenchurch rolled over, harsh pain searing his side, and could only watch them go.

The uniform got out and sank to his knees, hands clasped behind his head.

Webster helped Holly onto her bike. 'You okay, love?'

'I'm fine.' She sped off, hurtling along the road.

Webster got on his bike and raced after her.

Fenchurch forced himself onto his feet. He staggered over to the squad car. Engine still running. He got behind the wheel and drove off after them. Everything was woozy, like he was following a whole peloton rather than just two cyclists.

The first two versions of Holly and Webster cut through the gardens.

Fenchurch hit the floor and raced up to the end of the road, tugged the wheel left, then again, rounding the square.

They were over on the residential street, both pounding away.

Where the hell are they going?

They'll want Sandy. But they know we have her.

So where?

Fenchurch hared after them, bashing the horn as he ploughed towards them.

Two buses barrelled down the road.

Webster looked round then shouted something at Holly. They both shot off across the road.

Only Holly made it to the far side.

A screech of brakes and the two buses came to a halt either side of the junction.

Fenchurch got out of the car and ran over.

Holly screamed on the other side of the road.

Desmond Webster lay on the road, bleeding and broken, his eyelids flickering. He coughed up a mouthful of blood and fell back.

The Glock lay in the middle of the tarmac, sparkling in the headlights.

Fenchurch lurched at the gun and picked it up.

Holly rushed over to Fenchurch, clawing at his face. 'You killed him!'

Fenchurch pointed the gun at her. 'You're under arrest.'

39

'A GUN.' CHLOE PACED AROUND FENCHURCH'S OFFICE. 'I MEAN, IT WAS A real handgun. Jesus.'

Outside, Reed was talking on her mobile.

'This isn't something you should be excited about.' Fenchurch sat behind his desk, hunched tight. He kept looking at the door, wary of Holly walking through and killing his daughter.

But she wouldn't.

She was downstairs, grieving for her old man, waiting on her lawyer. She wasn't going to kill anyone else.

He looked Chloe in the eye. 'She was going to kill you.'

'Dad, I saved your ass.'

'It's arse, not ass.' Fenchurch gritted his teeth. 'And you almost got me killed.'

'Shut up...'

'Chloe, if the gun had gone off, I'd have been shot.'

She wouldn't look at him. 'Dad, admit that I saved your life.'

'Chloe, I'm serious. Charging into someone who is pointing a loaded gun pointed at someone, with their finger on the trigger... It's going to cause it to go off. You get that, right?'

Chloe swallowed hard and finally looked over. 'I didn't think.'

'No.' Fenchurch shot to his feet. 'You didn't think. I'm serious about this, love.' He walked over to her, eyes wide. 'We lost you once, we can't lose you again.'

Chloe just shook her head, like she was annoyed at him for not liking the birthday present she'd bought him.

'Look, I'm taking you to krav maga classes tomorrow.'

'What?' She glared at him. 'Self-defence?'

'You need to be able to protect yourself.'

'I do?' She laughed. 'I wasn't the one on my knees in front of someone with a gun, Dad.'

Fenchurch didn't have an answer. His mouth went dry.

'Look, Dad, I—'

Abi knocked on the door, Baby Al resting in a shawl. She stepped into the room and wrapped Chloe up in a tight hug. 'Come on, let's get you home.'

Fenchurch wrapped his arms around all three of them and just stood there. His whole family, safe. He whispered into Abi's ears. 'Keep her safe, love. She's going to crash, hard. Be there for her.'

'Can't you be there too?'

Fenchurch broke off from the hug. 'I'll be home before you know it. Okay?'

'Fine.' Abi led their daughter along the corridor.

But Chloe stopped and shrugged off her mother. She stomped back to the office. 'Dad, I'm joining the police.'

Fenchurch looked around, his gut churning. 'What?'

'You heard. I applied last week. When I graduate, I want to join the Met.'

Over my dead body.

In the line of fire, day in day out?

Arresting scumbags with knives. Chasing scumbags down train tracks. Staking out scumbags' operations.

Danger and death at every corner.

Stop being a prick. Get over yourself.

It's her life. It's her choice. Support her, otherwise you're only her father genetically.

Fenchurch grinned at her. 'Okay.'

She smiled. 'I thought you'd go apeshit at me.'

'I'm very far from happy about it, but...' He shrugged. 'You're my daughter.' He smiled at Abi. 'What's worse, you're Abi's daughter. You won't take no for an answer. Or you'll just do it yourself.'

She hugged him tight. 'Thanks, Dad.'

He gripped her tight. 'But I mean it, you're joining a krav maga course tomorrow.'

'Fine.' She pecked him on the cheek. 'I've got to see Granddad, Mum. See you downstairs.' She walked off along the corridor.

Abi stood there, eyebrows raised, Al wriggling in her arms. 'I thought you'd—'

'You knew, didn't you?'

She nodded with a sigh. 'She told me a few weeks ago.'

'You should've told me.'

She smiled. 'I guess I should've done.' She kissed him on the lips, careful not to squash their son. 'She's a lot stronger than you think.'

'So I see. Just don't keep things from me.'

She looked down at their son, then nodded at Fenchurch. 'Okay.' She patted his arm and walked off.

Fenchurch joined Reed outside his office and watched her go. 'Can you follow them, Kay?'

'Are you sure, guv?'

'Long story. Just help me.'

'Okay, I'll keep an eye on them. It doesn't feel right, but you're the boss.'

'Thanks.' Fenchurch watched her follow.

Bloody hell. She's only just back in our life and she's throwing herself into danger like that.

Just like her old man.

Someone cleared their throat behind him. Loftus. 'I heard what happened. Are you okay?'

'I'm fine.'

'Sure? You had a handgun pressed to your forehead.'

'Not my first rodeo, sir.' Fenchurch went back into his office and picked up his tea. 'I'm more worried about my daughter.'

'Not about DS Ashkani?'

'Is she okay?'

'She's fine. But still, this is on you.'

'I wanted to but... I made a snap decision. Sir, Holly's been—'

'You think that *Holly's* been killing people?'

'Holly was stalking Chloe. Worked at the same Tesco store. That's not something that happens quickly. Someone wanted her to act, then pulled the trigger.'

'Mario?'

'Hardly. It's Zamir.' Fenchurch shut his eyes. 'Or Younis.'

'What? Him?'

'He's got fingers in all of these pies.'

'Right, well, that's for Broadfoot and Nelson to progress.' Loftus stank of cigarettes. 'Come on, Dalton Unwin's not a man you keep waiting.'

HOLLY SAT THERE, CRYING. HER EYES WERE RED RAW, LIKE SOMEONE HAD taken a knife to the lids and started cutting away. But her gaze was as cold as packed snow, and trained on Fenchurch.

Crocodile tears.

'This is completely unacceptable.' Unwin threw his notebook on the desk. 'My client has just witnessed the death of her father and now you're treating her like this? You really think any of this will stand up in court?'

Loftus held up a hand to stop Fenchurch jumping in. 'Your client has murdered two people. Both gang-related murders. Assassinations. Like the sort her father was famous for before he was put away.'

Holly looked at him, mouth hanging open. 'Don't you *dare* bring him into this.'

'He's always in this, Miss Evans. Did he train you?'

'Jesus Christ.' Holly focused on the table, shaking her head.

'What were you planning on doing with my daughter?'

She didn't look up, just kept her focus on the table.

Fenchurch gripped the edge of the desk. 'You were playing a long game, trying to lure her as a friend, weren't you? Got yourself a job at the same Tesco. Fifteen months in the making.'

She shook her head again, harder this time, more defiant.

'Who was it for?'

'You don't know what you're talking about.'

'Was it for your old man?'

Holly laughed.

Fenchurch leaned forward, trying to make eye contact, but she didn't look over. 'How about Younis?'

'You don't know what you're talking about.' Still focused on the table. 'It's a coincidence. I needed a job, I got one. She just worked there.'

'A coincidence. Right.'

But I've got her. She's scared of Younis. Meaning he's got something on her.

Holly glanced up at him, then back down. 'Kirk got out of prison just after you put...' She tugged at her ponytail. 'After you stitched up my old man. Meant I could get someone to look after Sandy for me. He's pretty far from perfect and we're not an item, no matter how much he wants it. But he took her for a couple of days a week, let me get a job.'

'Holly, I don't believe you.'

'It's the truth.'

'No, it's not. Someone knew where my daughter was working. Someone who could get you a gun. Someone who wanted revenge on me.'

'It's a coincidence.'

Heard enough of this bullshit now.

'Listen to me, Holly.' Fenchurch got another glance. 'You're going to prison for a long, long time. Two murders, you're probably looking at a minimum of thirty years, with time served. Sandy will grow up without you.'

She shot him daggers with her eyes.

'Sandy will grow up without a mother. Imagine what it'll be like for her visiting you in prison. She'll want to stay with you, you'll want to stay with her, but you won't be allowed to. Then she'll start to resent you. Thirty years, Holly. Minimum. She'll be thirty-two when you get out. You'll be, what, fifty?'

Real tears started to flow. 'You don't know what you're talking about.'

'You're repeating your mother's mistakes. You and Kirk having a kid, then him going inside. Just like your own mother. Except you're the one inside. You'll be the one repeating your father's mistakes, too. Sandy will grow up with Kirk, as long as he's not in trouble. Only a matter of time before we find out who he's stashing those burners for.'

Holly brushed away her tears.

'You remember how hard it was growing up without a father, do you? Imagine what it's going to be like for Sandy without her mother.'

Holly stared at the table, tears dripping into the scarred wood.

'That what you want for your daughter? The love of your life?'

She looked up at him, with glistening eyes. 'What do you want out of me?'

'I know you killed Casey and Adrian. I know.' Fenchurch left it hanging for her. 'I want to know who it was for.'

She kept quiet.

'Was it Younis?'

'Who?'

'Don't play that game.'

'I've no idea who you're talking about.'

'Really? Because I'm sitting here, processing all that's happened today. Your old man passed his profession down to you, didn't he? Younis got him to kill someone. Now, if you're not dealing directly with him, that's by the by, but he's writing the cheques. Doesn't matter how you hear from him. Smoke signals. Morse code curtain twitches. Maybe a call from one of those burners in Kirk's garage. But you hear from him. You kill for him.'

'This is such bullshit.' Holly started pleading with Loftus. 'I'm just a mother.' Her pleas bounced off Loftus. So she rounded on Fenchurch again. 'Thanks to you, Sandy'll grow up without her grand-father.' She shot to her feet. She brushed off Unwin's hand and stabbed a finger at Fenchurch. 'You killed him!' She thumped the table. 'You've been victimising him! He never killed nobody, but you got it in your head that he kidnapped your daughter.'

Fenchurch felt his mouth go dry.

'There's no proof he did anything, but you wouldn't let go. You just kept on coming to the house, picking him up, bringing him here, getting him to answer your questions. He's got a bloody parole officer. You should've asked him, but you didn't. You just kept harassing him. Then you chased me and him on our bikes. And he died.' She thudded back in her seat. 'You. Killed. Him.'

Fenchurch sat back, letting the words rattle around his head.

Is she right?

Was I victimising Webster? Because I think he took Chloe? Because my old man thinks he did?

No way. He's guilty. Chloe recognised him, even said Webster visited her parents... Those maggots who wanted to be her parents.

And Webster killed Amelia, got Terry Oldham to take the rap. Younis got them out.

But Casey and Adrian... I was wrong. Holly did them. Getting into the family trade.

'I'm sitting here with two unsolved murders.' Fenchurch sat forward and stretched out his thumb. 'Casey.' Forefinger. 'Adrian.'

'My old man killed them.'

Fenchurch looked at Loftus. Hard to read his expression. Even harder than usual. His fingers twitched, like he needed another cigarette.

'Inspector.' Unwin drummed his thumbs on the table. 'Here's the thing. Mr Webster gave you alibis for all three murders. The first one, you've got Terry Oldham on the record saying he did it. My client's father told you that he was somewhere else during all three events. But my client can give you something in exchange for immunity from prosecution.'

That's how he's playing it, then. Getting Webster to take the rap. A dead man.

Loftus leaned forward, eyebrows raised. 'I'm listening.'

Fenchurch crunched back in his chair and shot a glare at Loftus. 'Sir...'

Loftus waved him off. 'Give us what you've got on Younis and we'll see what we can offer.'

Fenchurch whispered: 'This is a trap.'

Loftus smiled at Unwin. 'Continue.'

'I have in my possession a signed and witnessed document where Mr Webster took credit for all three murders. In addition, Mr Webster has a recording of a meeting with representatives of Dimitri Younis, including transaction detail regarding payments for the murders of Casey Nicholas and Adrian Hall.'

Holly shivered but stared right at Fenchurch.

He didn't let her look away. 'You killed them, Holly. I know.'

Loftus gripped Fenchurch's arm. 'Miss Evans, I need your testimony against Younis.'

'I can't...'

'Superintendent, my client doesn't need to add to the evidence. It's comprehensive.'

'Holly, I can offer you a way out of this.'

'I can't go in court and—'

'Holly.' Loftus snorted. 'It's only a matter of time before we find enough evidence to prosecute you. We can match your movements with your father's bicycle. Then it's a case of a jury believing our version of events over yours.' He smiled at her again. 'I reckon this'll take us about a year to bring to court. Your father's case was fifteen months. That's time you'll be on remand. No chance of bail. At least a year without your daughter.'

Holly looked at Unwin, then whispered in his ear.

Unwin drummed his thumbs again, longer, faster. He leaned over and whispered.

Fenchurch looked round at Loftus, trying to get him to stop this, but he wouldn't even look at him.

Unwin smiled at them. 'Give me a minute with my client.'

Fenchurch checked the wall clock and leaned forward into the mic. 'Interview paused at 21:43.' He got up and walked over to the door.

Loftus glowered at him as he followed him into the corridor. 'What the hell are you playing at?'

'This is a big mistake. Can't you see what they're doing?'

'Can't you see what you're doing? We're getting a confession here. Two murders. Possibly on the Oldham case.'

'They're playing us. Getting a dead man to take the rap.'

'Simon, I don't know what's going on inside that head of yours but it needs to stop. We've got her. With what she'll give us, we can get Younis.'

'And what if she doesn't?'

Loftus didn't have an answer. He grabbed the door handle. 'Do I need to bring in someone else to shadow me here?'

'She's guilty. She pulled a bloody gun on me.'

'And there's no bloody proof of that.'

'What?'

'DC Bridge has been combing the CCTV for that supermarket.

The cameras out the back where you allege this incident happened were offline.'

'She did it.'

'Simon...'

'Ask my daughter. She was there.'

'And that's going to stand up in court, isn't it? Unwin's not going to try and tear a hole in her testimony? Are you happy to let your daughter go through that? Are you?'

Fenchurch stood there, shaking, trembling. 'Like I said, sir, I think this is a mistake.'

Loftus narrowed his eyes. 'Then it's my mistake, Simon.' He went back into the interview.

Prick.

Fenchurch joined him but couldn't sit at the same table as the woman who'd tried to kill his daughter, so stayed standing.

Loftus hit record again. 'Interview recommenced at 21:45.' He refocused on Holly. 'Well?'

Holly trained her teary gaze on Unwin and got a tight nod. Then she nodded at Loftus. 'Okay. I want to set the record straight.'

Loftus sat back, twisting round to rest his elbow on the chair back. 'Let's start with Casey.'

'Dad knew Casey from the cycling cafes around London. You know, the places you can get a posh coffee while they fixed your bike. He wasn't happy that he had to kill her.' She swallowed hard. 'Dad got someone to place an order for a pizza. Went round and shot her. Tap, tap, tap.'

Loftus gave Holly a new smile. 'Why?'

'Someone knew she was talking to you lot.'

Loftus sat there, his tongue flicking over his lips. 'Who?'

She shut up, staring into space as she brushed her hair.

Fenchurch stepped round the table towards her. 'We've got CCTV of the murder.'

'Then you'll know it was Dad who killed her.'

'It could be you.'

'It's not me.' She brushed her hair back. 'Dad said he needed to shut her up. She was going to make things difficult for people.'

Loftus waved a hand at Fenchurch. 'And Adrian Hall?'

'Adrian was Mario's son, but you knew that.' Holly wound her hair round a finger. 'Dad knew him, said he was a good kid. Got to know him from delivering for Mario's. Adrian told him that Mario was dealing drugs with the pizzas. Little bags of coke baked in the crust. Nobody would blink an eye, perfect. Except, well, Dad told some people what Mario was up to and they weren't happy.' She glared at

Fenchurch. 'Certain people saw you flitting around that restaurant, asking too many questions. They didn't want anyone talking. Mario had been talking to his son.'

'You need to tell us who.'

'It's Younis. Okay?' Holly sneered at him. 'What am I getting for that?'

Loftus looked hard at her. Then he walked over to the door and left the room.

'Superintendent Loftus has left the room.'

Unwin sat back and let out a held breath.

Holly leaned over the table, blocking the mic with her hand. 'I should've killed your daughter when I had the chance.'

Fenchurch felt the old rage rising.

'I see the men she flirts with at work. They all have something in common. They look like you.'

'That's rich.'

'What?'

'You and Kirk. He's just like dear old Desmond, isn't he? A criminal. What's he doing with all those phones? Whose are they? Younis's?'

Holly ran a finger across her throat.

Fenchurch held her gaze. 'Chloe can handle herself.' He smiled through the pain and the bile building in his gut. 'Last July, your old man tried that same trick. Enraging me. Getting me to lash out. I didn't work then, and I won't work now.'

The door opened. Fenchurch looked round then spoke into mic: 'Superintendent Loftus has entered the room.'

Loftus sat down and smiled at Holly. 'You write all that down, sign it and we'll let you walk out of here with a caution for possession of a firearm. And you'll stand up in court and testify against Younis.'

Holly smiled at Fenchurch. 'Deal.'

40

'THIS IS A HUGE MISTAKE, SIR.' FENCHURCH STOMPED ALONG THE corridor ahead of Loftus. '*Huge.*'

'Simon, we'll use her testimony to secure the prosecution of Younis. Isn't that a price worth paying?'

'Sir, she's killed two people. She attacked me. She tried to kill my *daughter.*'

'And her father died after you chased him.'

'They were getting away.' Fenchurch punched the wall. 'Jesus fucking Christ. He's—'

'Simon!' Loftus brushed at the battered plaster. 'Control yourself.'

'Control myself?' Fenchurch wanted to punch Loftus now. 'She killed them and now you're letting her get off with it?'

'Simon, this is above your pay grade. We've solved three murders. Desmond Webster killed those three people.'

'This is all bollocks. This is all to tick some boxes. Close off three murders to make your spreadsheet look better.'

'Think strategically, man.'

Fenchurch shook his head. 'We've got Younis anyway. He's going down.'

'It's not a done deal. This tips the balance in our favour.' Loftus took a breath. 'I've wrestled with this, but this is the best way forward. DCIs Savage and Broadfoot agree with this approach.'

'We should be putting *her* away.'

'Simon, we've got answers. And that's good. I understand your frustration. I do. This distracts from your role in Webster's death.'

'That was an accident.'

'Was it? You really want to go through an inquest, do you? I have and it's a horrendous experience. I've saved you that.'

Fenchurch couldn't speak. Everything felt numb.

'Look, we've got Zamir for a few things now. Howard and Derek will process that, they've got a solid evidence trail. And we can secure the conviction of Younis.'

'I wish I had your hope, sir.'

'It's not hope, it's faith in our process. But we need to play the long game.'

'And let a killer go free?'

Loftus jabbed a finger at him. 'I'm warning you, Inspector.'

Fenchurch shoved his hands deep into his pockets. 'Fine.'

'Simon, I know this isn't easy, but you're a DCI now. Okay? I don't know how you got it, but we've got solid intel on Younis. We've got a witness. Do you know how important that is? All the evidence we've got, his drugs, his underage camgirls and camboys, it's all been hidden behind layers and layers of bollocks. He's an expert at throwing us off the scent. But you...' Loftus smiled, but it was more like a snarl. 'You cut through it all. You've got this result for us. If Holly killed those people, then so be it. Younis is a price I'm willing to pay. I'm prepared to give her a second chance. We've got her on the firearms charge. She's going to get a fine and a suspended sentence. We'll keep an eye on her, keep her on the straight and narrow. I want to give her the chance to break free of this cycle of death and misery her father created. Don't you?'

Fenchurch stared down the long corridor. Felt like it turned in on itself, the ceiling becoming the floor, twisting inside out.

But he's right.

So many times we've let people repeat mistakes. Pass on the murder to another generation. Sandy doesn't deserve to become another Holly, just like Holly didn't have a choice about her own life.

Fenchurch nodded at Loftus. 'Okay... Let's play it your way.'

'Excellent.' Loftus looked down at his shiny shoes. 'Simon, I've got a bit of a conundrum.'

'What?'

'The powers that be, my bosses and their equals, well. They're pushing me to bring in a new broom as the DCI, Simon. You as Acting DCI isn't cutting it when we've got assassins and what have you. They've asked to transition Jason Bell over to head up the East MIT and sort this mess out. Starting on Monday.'

Fenchurch tasted bile in this mouth. 'Bell?'

'I'm afraid so.' Loftus looked back up, locking eyes with Fenchurch.

'Of course, if you were to sign on as DCI permanently, then we wouldn't have to bring him in.'

'You and him go back, right?'

'And that's the problem.' Loftus huffed. 'He knows how to play me. One thing about you, Simon, is you've got different angles. You're probing different aspects of my personality. And I need that. Likewise, I think you benefit from a different type of management.'

'I appreciate the offer, but...' Fenchurch gritted his teeth.

Working for Jason Bell.

'Sod it. I'll take it.'

SIMON FENCHURCH WILL RETURN

Sometime in the future!

Subscribe to the Ed James newsletter to keep on top of upcoming releases —
http://eepurl.com/pyjv9

OTHER BOOKS BY ED JAMES

AFTERWORD

Thanks for buying and reading this book, it means the world to me.

This was supposed to be a novella. Just that first part. But it felt unresolved. So it grew two book-end chapters, and the novella was basically Fenchurch's testimony. Then some little sparks ignited and, well. It grew into a full novel. I've got previous with this sort of thing: Cullen 3 was a short story, then became a novel; Cullen 6 was two short novellas that became a linked novel. But I'm really pleased with how this one has turned out, dotting a few Is and crossing a few Ts.

I'm changing the publishing model for my police procedural books, where I'm waiting until they hit a certain sales threshold. So if you want more Cullen, Hunter, or Fenchurch (sorry, but there won't be any more Dodds novels), then encourage people to buy them. Seriously, it's just so it's financially worthwhile for me to write the books. It's currently looking like Fenchurch 7 will be the next one, but subscribe to my mailing list for news on how that progresses. And I've got some ideas on how to expand out this series into something new and fresh.

Thanks again,
Ed James
Scottish Borders, February 2019

(How the hell did it become 2019?)

ACKNOWLEDGMENTS

Without the following, this book wouldn't exist:

Development Editing
Allan Guthrie

Procedural Analysis
James Mackay

Copy Editing
Eleanor Abraham

Proofing
John Rickards

As ever, infinite thanks to Kitty for putting up with me and all of my nonsense.

Printed in Great Britain
by Amazon